INTRODUCTION

Monday, September 26
Wright State University Nutter Center, Dayton, Ohio

The moment Bob Carson arrived, the atmosphere in the room changed. Harriet felt it; they all did. She'd been trying so hard to strike the right chord rehearsing for the first debate in the presidential race proper. It was easy to demean Dennis Saxon and talk down to him. But the guy was obviously doing something right; he was ahead of her in the polls. She had to be civil, even nice. Whatever, she just had to keep smiling and not lose her cool.

"Just one more time, Harriet. You're almost there." Sally Smith, her aide and closest confidante, was asking her repeatedly how she was going to make America great again.

They'd been stuck in a stuffy student center office for nearly three hours. It took Harriet most of that time to hide the irritation in her face.

Then Bob arrived. Suddenly, it was all about him. Bob looked thin and pale; he leaned over and pecked her on the cheek. "I've missed you sweetheart. I just wanted to see if I could help with any last minute tricks."

"I'm fine, darling. Honest, I am."

After so many years, how could she tell her husband she didn't need him? Harriet Carson had been struggling with that long before the start of this presidential campaign.

"We're running through what Harriet will say when Saxon talks about making America great again." Sally said.

She missed Harriet's flashing eyes. "Any thoughts, Mr. President."

"Dennis," Bob said, smiling. Three other aides in the room stopped shuffling papers and listened. "Dennis, I really appreciate you adopting the 'Make America Great Again' strategy I first used back in 1992, but you've missed the most important point. It's not America that has failed; it's certainly not the people. It's our leaders, the politicians on Capitol Hill who've been preventing the President from making the changes he was elected to make, the business executives who have taken their manufacturing abroad and the Wall Street fat cats living in their mansions while ordinary people are losing their homes... How does that sound?"

The room went silent for a second. Then one of the younger aides punched the air. "Yeah! That's awesome, Sir." The others clapped, even Sally.

Typical, Harriet thought. Wearily, she rubbed her temples. She didn't want Bob getting involved, but right now she knew she needed him. He charmed folks...he charmed her. It had pretty much gotten him everything he wanted.

Harriet suddenly felt exhausted and quite old; a woman trying to play big boy games with... well with boys. But play she must.

"You need to keep smiling," Bob told her gently. "Your mouth droops when you relax. Looks like you got a whiff of something bad."

"I did - Dennis Saxon," Harriet sniffed, the corners of her mouth drooping in fake disgust. "I still find it hard to believe this is really happening."

Her husband came around the table and she gratefully leaned into him, resigned, as he put his arm around her shoulder. "You'll do great. You're the most capable person I know. Just keep smiling."

"Let's hope America has as much faith in me as you do..."

She stood up and said she was taking a break. The parking garage was next door. She needed some air. She looked over her shoulder at a Secret Service agent and an aide trailing behind. For once I'd like to be alone, she thought.

She was on the third level, looking across a line of satellite trucks to where the debate was being held that evening. It was strangely quiet. She'd been to countless debates like this. There was usually a buzz of anticipation...but she didn't give it much further thought.

~~~~~~~~~

A pile of briefing papers about a foot thick was sitting on the coffee table in Dennis Saxon's suite at the Hilton, just outside Dayton. The man himself was on the phone and several aides were

The iCandidate
Looking for Heroes

David & Michelle Gardner

Copyright © 2017 David & Michelle Gardner
Immediate Books
ISBN: 0-9985957-0-5
ISBN-13: 978-0-9985957-0-2

Let us not seek the Republican answer or the Democratic answer, but the right answer. Let us not seek to fix the blame for the past. Let us accept our own responsibility for the future.

Change is the law of life. And those who look only to the past or the present are certain to miss the future.

John F. Kennedy

Immediate Books, California.
www.immediatebooks.com
admin@immediatebooks.com

ACKNOWLEDGMENTS

Cover design: Keith Groshans, Keith G Design

Editing: Whitney Butler

Thanks to: Jeff Ourvan of The Jennifer Lyons Literary Agency, Michelle and Richard Forsythe, NoteStream, Mickey, Jazmin & Savannah Gardner
.

slumped on sofas exhausted from trying to get their candidate to rehearse his lines. Saxon ended the conversation smiling. "That was Rupert Murdoch - he loves me."

He grabbed the stack of papers and flicked through it. "Nothing too complicated here. Seen it all before."

"But what about Harriet? This is your first time up against her. What's your line of attack going to be?" GOP staffer Steve Miles had worked on Mitt Romney's 2012 campaign and was second on the Saxon team. He was used to being ignored. Saxon was checking a text.

"Dennis? What's your best attack? I spent three days working on questions like this with Mitt before he went on TV against Obama."

Saxon ignored him and shouted across to his PA. "I'm getting messages from the Secret Service saying the traffic is jammed up between here and Wright State. Is that everyone arriving to watch the debate?"

He put the papers down, picked up an apple and took a bite. The PA already had her laptop out. "No, the gridlock's around Dayton State University. We need to go past there to get to the Nutter Center. Better leave 30 minutes or so early. The Dems are already there."

~~~~~~~~~~

Just before 7:00 p.m., the Wright University facilitator was in a panic arguing with network execs to delay for 5 minutes. Only half of the auditorium was filled and most of the students had yet to take their seats. "I can't understand why this is happening," she cried. "This has been planned for months."

"Five minutes, no longer." The executive producer was furious.

For Harriet Carson and Dennis Saxon, the delay meant a few extra minutes together at the side of the stage. They swapped pleasantries about their families and stood in awkward silence. Carson preferred the quiet, Saxon couldn't stand it.

"You know why there's a delay, don't you?" He smirked.

"No idea."

"The kids are all over at Dayton State University. Different college."

"So they're all late? She wished he'd shut up.

"No, they're not coming. They're watching the debate on that political reality show, The iCandidate."

Harriet was aghast. Saxon thought it was pretty funny.

1 GAME ON

Staring down at his feet, Desmond James felt the world slow down as he blocked out everything but the tiny ball and the hands carefully linked by the pinky of his right hand and the index finger of his left. Eye on the ball, he thought. Just keep your eyes on the ball. The back lift was strong and sure, the product of countless lessons. Desmond could see the downswing in his mind's eye. Hips shifted forwards, head resolutely down, the club slicing through the dampness of the morning.

David Mason was next. Sighing, he half closed his eyes as he silently wished for just one stroke of luck. The ugly thump as the club face cut into the turf, the spray of mud and grass and the familiar lurch of the stomach as the ball skewed off the fairway and hopped into the trees. "Godammit! I hate this game."

Leaning on their bags a few feet away, Andy Kristoff and Desmond didn't try and hide their amusement. Already on the green and waiting for her friends to catch up, Jacqueline Toscane made a great show of looking at her watch.

"How long have we been at this, Mase? We've been playing together since college and you still can't hit the stupid ball." Kristoff checked his phone for the umpteenth time. "Some of us have to get back to work sometime this week." He flashed his lazy smile, which really meant he could do whatever he pleased, as no-one at the studio would ever question him.

"Lucky for you." Mason tried to keep the bitterness out of his voice as he waded into the undergrowth. He'd just been fired from his columnist job on a newspaper that was now an online site.

"I'm in no hurry. Got nowhere to go." Mason took his time looking for his ball.

"Well you certainly need the practice," Des shot back with a grin. They all went quiet as Kristoff smoothly struck his ball onto the green and joined Mason and Desmond's fruitless search in the bushes.

"I think it went out of bounds." Desmond pointed to the fence guarding a footpath down towards the Pacific Ocean.

Mason shook his head in frustration. "It's not like we're doing the kind of work we dreamed about in school. Remember, I was gonna be a fearless globe-trotting war correspondent."

Kristoff found Mason's ball a few inches over the wrong side of the boundary. "I'm doing what I always wanted." He settled his shades back over his eyes.

"Yeah right." Mason snorted. "Posing around on a talent show with a bunch of kid acrobats and 12-year-old opera singers? Give me a break."

Kristoff was unfazed. "I think you'll find it was the most watched show on television."

"I didn't say you weren't successful," said Mason. "The amount of money you're raking in is obscene. But you were going to make documentaries about things that matter. Be the next Ken Burns if you recall." Mason dropped a ball and clouted it in the right direction for a change and headed to meet Jacqueline by the next hole at the edge of a bunker. With the sweetest of touches Desmond lofted it over the hump and within a few inches of the hole.

"Will you boys stop chatting and play? I'm getting old standing around waiting for you to catch up." In tight black pants, cream sleeveless polo shirt and giant sunglasses pushed up over her tight ponytail, Jacqueline looked like a blonde Jackie O. She stroked in her putt for a birdie. "I can't believe I'll be taking all your money again. Aren't you a little embarrassed for your gender? Three hulking men beaten again by a mere girl."

"You should be better than Tiger Woods with the amount of time you spend on a golf course," Kristoff joked. "You're never in the office."

"That's why law firms have associates and interns. To make money for the partners," Jacqueline checked her lips in her compact before delivering her signature cooler-than-the-rest-of-you-schmucks smile.

"There you go." Mason pressed his point. He was wearing a crumpled white shirt hung over an ill-fitting pair of black pants. "Jacqueline sold out too."

Kristoff just laughed. "She's one of the top attorneys in the country. Hey Des, how much is your property empire worth now?" It always amused Kristoff how easy it was to get under Mason's skin.

Des glanced at Mason. "Can't complain. Actually I heard this course was up for sale, I'm thinking of buying it. You're looking a little red in the face Mase, you should put some sunscreen on."

Kristoff gave Mason a good-natured shove. "In fact, from where I'm standing Mase, we're all doing great...except you. A touch bitter are we?"

But Mason was still on a roll. "Yeah, well maybe I am. But remember at college? All those nights Jackie would give us a hard time saying how she was going to be this hero pro bono lawyer, helping the downtrodden."

"What are you guys talking about?" Jacqueline didn't look happy.

Desmond grinned. "Mase thinks we're all big disappointments who haven't lived up to our potential."

"Oh poor, sad little David is stuck in one of his pity fests again is he?" Jacqueline joined in. "Would you like me to read you your favorite bedtime story tonight hun?"

"Shut up Jacks. I'm serious. We had dreams!" There was a wait at the next hole and an elderly man in a canary yellow sweater was looking daggers at them for talking.

"What's your next big idea Kris?" Mason whispered. "A dating show for midgets? Oh wait, that's already been done."

At some point either Desmond or Jacqueline usually had to step in and keep Mason and Kristoff apart. "Lay off, Mase. You'll get us kicked off the course," Desmond said.

Mason shrugged. "They're hardly going to ask the great Andy Kristoff to leave, are they? They don't want to end up in the tabloids."

Kristoff turned to Mason and surprised him by putting an arm around his shoulders. "Chill out my friend. Maybe I've got something different up my sleeve."

Mason shook himself free. "The last time you said something like that at college we ended up in jail for the night."

"I'm serious," said Kristoff. "You can come work for me. In fact, I'd like all of you to."

The canary sweater group was already half way down the fairway but Jacqueline, who was supposed to tee-off first, made no attempt to place her ball.

"You're not serious?"

"Deadly serious," Kristoff held her stare.

"We don't want your money, Kris. We're all doing quite nicely thank you."

Mason resisted the temptation to object. Being a journalist wasn't in the same pay grade as a lawyer. He had to pay them to write. Some extra cash would be nice.

"It's not about money." Kristoff pointed to the tee and gestured to Jacqueline to get on with it. "See what I mean? Kris loves to boss everyone around."

"Okay, okay. Well I suppose that's true but it's still not about money."

"So what is it all about then?" Mason really wanted it to be about the money.

A light seemed to turn on above Desmond and he grabbed Kristoff's arm. "Do you mean my idea I told you about?"

"Might be." Kristoff looked sheepish. "Well, the last crazy idea I worked on ended up being the most watched show in the world." With that, Kristoff hopped up to the elevated lawn as if to make an announcement to the gaggle of golfers waiting impatiently for them to play. "I'm going to give Des what he really wants. And you, Mase. And yes, even you, Jacqueline."

"And what's that?" Jacqueline wasn't impressed.

"Power." Kristoff paused like he was waiting for a commercial break.

"Will you please just tell them and stop holding everyone up." The voice came from the group behind.

"We're going to change the world," said Kristoff.

"Oh yeah! HOW?" Mason secretly crossed his fingers.

"We're gonna find the next President of the United States."

2 COUNTDOWN

Sound engineers and lighting technicians were in their places and cameramen peered from every corner of the studio as the judges walked in and took their seats at the very last minute. Compacts and brushes flew through the deft fingers of make-up artists, and the audience fidgeted in their seats, necks craning for the best view of the stage. This was the time in live TV when even an experienced veteran like Andy Kristoff felt his nerves flutter a little — he clutched his hands together to keep them steady.

Less than six months after first blurting out the political reality show idea on the sixth hole of the Pebble Beach Golf Course, he had the biggest hit of his life on his hands. He hadn't been serious about the show at first; he just wanted to stop David Mason from ranting about how they'd all sold their principles down the river. Even more incredibly, the others were all involved. Even Mase.

It all came together incredibly smoothly. TV talent shows were hardly a new concept when he came up with StarStruck; he just tweaked it to make it sexier. Why should presidential elections be so different?

It was all smoke and mirrors. It was all show business.

Desmond was the key; his quick business mind had seen the value in technology long before most of the country and his property portfolio was almost equaled by his substantial stake in Silicon Valley. If he didn't own the big tech companies it was quite possible he owned the buildings they worked from. It meant he had the people with the technical know-how; they had to come up with a foolproof online voting system to make the whole thing possible. He would oversee everything behind the scenes —the show's conscience.

Jacqueline was more difficult to convince. "How on earth are you going to find suitable candidates?" she asked a few days later, when the four friends met again in a tapas bar in Hollywood.

Kristoff shrugged. "We have auditions in cities around the US, just like I did for StarStruck. First, they have to show proof they'll be at least 35 by the time of the next election and born in the U.S. We don't want any birther controversies, even if they are based on bigotry. That would be disastrous for us. We'll do the usual background checks and interviews to help weed out the crazies.

"Next, Desmond has devised a bunch of challenges testing IQ, general knowledge and politics —hopefully we get some heated debates going. Then, of course, there's the physical obstacle course."

"Wait. Why would they need to run around a bunch of bright red cones? Jacqueline said disdainfully, sipping her chardonnay. "It would make a mockery of the whole thing."

"I don't agree," a big smile spread over Desmond's face. "We don't want a slob running the country, now do we? It's the politically correct way to say fat people need not apply."

Mason almost choked on his beer. "Wow! You're serious aren't you? So Dennis Saxon would never have made the cut in our show?"

"That's right. Harriet may not make it, either. She could do with losing a few pounds. Any other questions?"

"Yes," Jacqueline cut in. "Why are you such a sexist pig, Des?"

Mason was warming to this show idea by the minute. "If you're going to all this trouble to find a brilliant candidate with killer abs, who picks them out? Not Des, for sure. How can we be sure we're getting the best candidates?"

Desmond put his arm around Mason's shoulder. "Great question. We're going to handpick them ourselves. I know there's presidential material out there. He's just waiting to be found."

"Or she." Jacqueline said loudly.

"She what?" Desmond looked blankly at her.

"You said HE is waiting to be found. If I'm going to have anything to do with this spectacle, then we must give women an equal chance to apply."

"Of course, Jacqueline. That goes without saying." There was a slight pause. Desmond looked around the table. "So we're really doing this?"

"Hell yeah!" Mason could already see his bank balance improving. They all raised their glasses. They were on. Kristoff was the host. Of course he was. America loved him. And despite his complaining, Mason was along for the ride. He was Communications Director; he'd write all the show news in his blog, It was everything he wanted.

When the show got commissioned, Jacqueline couldn't resist the offer of a place on the judging panel, and a $10,000-a-month clothing stipend.

"I always wanted to be a judge." Jacqueline shook on the deal with a mischievous glance at Kristoff. "I'd kinda thought it would be on the Supreme Court, but this might turn out to be more powerful. Just don't expect me to agree with anything you say."

Kristoff watched now as Jacqueline took her place at the Judge's table, cool and imperious. She looked across at him and they shared a smile.

At the back of the hall he could see Mason running around in his element, ushering the press into their seats. And Kristoff could rest easy knowing that Desmond, hidden away in the tech room, was taking care of vital last minute checks.

He felt a shiver go down his spine as everything slowed. The magic was happening. He loved these moments - the preamble, full of anticipation, the organized chaos, last minute jitters, doubts mixed with heady excitement, the flushed faces, the exquisite details that determine if a show will be an almighty flop or a rip-roaring success. And then, just the sound of his own heartbeat.

He thought back to the initial auditions and how he had assumed it would be so easy to attract people. Just an ad or two and the nation would come running with the chance to shine.

How wrong he'd been.

3 WHO WANTS TO BE A POLITICIAN?

A paltry 500 people had been waiting patiently since 5:00 a.m. at the Los Angeles Sports Arena on South Figueroa Street. Dreams of political greatness were fast becoming soggy around the edges as iCandidate hopefuls stood in a steady drizzle on a Sunday morning in early November.

They knew little from the brief mentions in the media other than it was a political reality show where no singing, dancing or juggling was required. Some of the crowd had already drifted away when Rich Francombe screeched up in his Ferrari, and parked diagonally between two rows of steel barricades assembled to herd the thousands of people expected to show up.

The idle TV crew jumped into action, surrounding the legendary former quarterback.

"Rich, over here," an enthusiastic reporter shouted. "Are you one of the judges?"

"Nope. I'm just trying out." He ignored a security guard's offer to show him into the foyer and instead joined the back of the line, which suddenly came to life. "I don't need any special treatment. I'm just one of you guys today."

Tanned and ripped, he signed autographs on audition sheets as they were thrust in front of him. "But I kind of expected a few more folks."

The multi-millionaire athlete was led away with a group of strangers to begin a citizenship quiz. He wondered if it was worth the hype. He never was any good at tests.

Houston was the next stop two days later. David Mason, wearing his official iCandidate tag around his neck, counted heads as 615 people dribbled into the George R. Brown Conference Center downtown. After sending most of the temporary staff home for the day, he led what remained of the group into the cavernous hall for the general knowledge 'Pride of the States' challenge, when a portly, precisely dressed Hispanic woman tapped him on the arm.

"Excuse me, sir, is the show going to be canceled?" Dulce Ramirez asked.

"Why would you think that?" Mason answered, irritated.

"Because there's hardly anyone here. I just don't want to be wasting my time on all these tests and challenges if it isn't going anywhere." She introduced her husband and five children to Mason.

"I promise that you're not wasting your time," Mason reassured her. "We're just getting started." He was trying to convince himself as much as he was Dulce.

After the hall cleared out—much earlier than expected—Mason, still consumed with doubts, drove back to his hotel. They'd found two good finalists despite the poor turnout and camera angles would ensure the qualifying rounds would make fun TV to watch if only there were more people interested enough to take part. Perhaps they were kidding themselves. Perhaps America wasn't ready for this. Then, his phone rang. It was Desmond. "We need to talk. Catch the next flight back to LA."

When Mason arrived in Kristoff's office at the Paramount lot, Desmond was pacing up and down, demanding to know how the turnout in L.A. and Houston could have been so lousy. Jacqueline was sprawled on the couch checking emails on her iPhone.

"These things take time," Mason argued.

Desmond was pissed. "We don't have time. The auditions run for two weeks only. I thought you said the advertising would get everyone pumped up." He rubbed his face impatiently.

Mason looked to Kristoff for support. "The same budget brought in thousands for StarStruck last summer," Kristoff reasoned. "But I guess for every million Taylor Swift wannabes out there, there's only a handful of Bushes or Obamas…"

"So what can we do? If we don't fix this now the whole idea is going to fall on its face."

"I knew it was a waste of my time," Jacqueline drawled without lifting her head from her phone. Desmond took out a slim leather attaché case from his drawer and started to jot figures in the notebook. "So we had 500 in L.A. and a mere 600 in Houston…"

"Err, 615 actually," Mason interjected.

Desmond shot him a look, and Mason sank miserably into his chair. "Wait? We rented the Broncos stadium in Denver for the Friday audition? Jesus, doesn't that hold 50,000 people?"

"76,000," Kristoff grimaced.

"We're going to be a laughing stock. Saxon was on Kimmel the other night slating us and said we were a joke. Eight more cities and back to L.A. for the final audition in just 12 days. We can't do it." Desmond's expression was stony. He reached for a Tums. Failure gave him indigestion.

"We need to bring in at least 50,000 people to make this all possible." The number hung in the air like a blimp about to burst. "Are we going to have to cancel the show, Andy?" Desmond was beside himself.

"We can't give up now," Mason argued. "There must be something we can do. Hey! We got some publicity when Rich Francombe auditioned in L.A."

"Yeah, but that's sports," Jacqueline said, "not politics. It doesn't help people take it seriously. He may have been one of the greatest quarterbacks of all time, but he's not exactly Einstein. The show's a bust."

It fell silent in the room. Kristoff wondered if he should just cut his losses. "We can't force people to audition, Des. Perhaps your vision, as brilliant as it is, is just too ambitious for the American people."

Mason could feel it slipping away. "But people hate the way politics is run in this country! I know we're only talking about a TV show, but look at the two party system— either way we get a crap president."

Jacqueline walked over to Mason and ruffled his hair. "Yep, but it takes someone with really big balls to think they can change the system darling." Jacqueline was just glad she hadn't quit her law firm.

Desmond sat in the leather chair that faced Kristoff's desk, staring out the window, the Hollywood sign dominating the view, reminding him how big dreams can come and go in a fleeting moment.

"You know what, to hell with this." Kristoff was on his feet. "We've come this far, I say we saturate all of the TV networks with commercials on the hour, every hour for the next ten days. And let's stick a huge billboard over the goddamn sign out there too, that'll get people's attention!"

Des and Mason sat up, daring to get excited again. "We can do that?"

"Well, perhaps we should leave the sign alone, but we have the finances, we can do what we like. Let's shovel cash into the marketing campaign. We'll blitz everywhere today, and by the time this thing gets back to L.A. next Monday, we'll have billboards coming out of every sidewalk crack in the city. No more tiptoeing around. Let's force feed the idea of political stardom down their throats."

Desmond brightened, Mason grinned and even Jacqueline showed a spark of interest in her raised eyebrow.

"You think that'll work?" Desmond looked eagerly around the room.

Kristoff leaned back in his chair, enjoying the change of tempo. "I don't know, but let's give it a go anyway?

"Drink anyone?"

4 THE SEARCH CONTINUES

A large area of the Mile High Stadium in Denver, Colorado was cordoned off to hide the empty sections and the contestants gathered on the bleachers at one end. But the numbers were up to a little over 6,000. Part of the field was turned into an obstacle course, and those who made it through to the third round faced a real risk of elimination by humiliation. Watching in the chilly sunshine, and to the delight of many of the contestants waiting their turn, the entertainment had finally arrived: a pudgy-shaped woman was seen running down the start leg of the assault course in a purple velour pantsuit.

At closer glance, she was a he with a visibly darkening five o'clock shadow. His wig slipped as he tried to reach up and catch a zip-line, cross a pool filled with water, and land on a bank on the other side. He missed and slipped down one side, ending up in an undignified muddy heap.

From the number on his vest, he appeared to be Tom Jodes, the Mayor of Rayville, a small town in the Rockies about an hour from Denver. After lying slumped in the dirt for a few seconds, he popped his head up and said with a smile: "How did I do?" His wife and the other contestants cheered him on, as he took an elaborate bow before changing into a turquoise floral dress with matching heels. He joined his fellow contestants in the stands to wait for Round Four.

There were two paths leading from the arena to the exits. The first was the Walk of Shame, for contestants who failed to advance on. Hitching up his dress, Tom ran triumphantly down the Walk of Fame path bordered with hundreds of mini American flags that led him back into the arena and onto the next challenge.

"Do you think America is ready for a transgender president?" Tom was asked as he was leaving.

"Of course not. But it's going to be a helluva lot of fun for them watching me try!"

Salt Lake City, Utah: 8,000, Memphis, Tennessee: 9,000, Miami, Florida: 14,900.

A reinvigorated Mason boarded a flight to Washington DC for the next audition. His spirits were rising with every new city. Kristoff and Desmond joined him for the East Coast auditions with interviews booked on the local radio and TV talk shows, as well as the Today show in New York on Friday morning. Desmond watched from behind the cameras as Kristoff delivered his smooth patter; he started to relax, he knew the buzz was growing.

Washington D.C.: 16,000.

It was late afternoon at the Walter E. Washington Convention Center, across the street from the new City Museum in D.C. Advertising executive, Cameron Banks was on the brink of becoming the fourth finalist in The iCandidate. He spent his life riding a knife-edge of arrogance that brought success and trouble in equal measure. But the show was manna from heaven for the smooth-talking, dark-haired Jude Law lookalike. His wasted good looks drew plenty of attention from the women in the audience.

"We give you a negative situation and you tell us how the Washington spin masters would say it," said assistant producer Hannah Woodson. " You have thirty seconds."

"It's half done," Hannah said.

"It's essentially complete," shot back Cameron.

"They won't even talk to us," continued Hannah.

"A basic agreement has been reached," quipped Cameron.

"We're making up the numbers so they will agree with our conclusions."

"Results are being quantified."

"Nobody's even thought about it."

"Not well defined at this time."

"We hope to God!"

"We predict."

"It'll take a miracle."

"Serious but not insurmountable problems."

"Totally out of control!"

"Requires further analysis and management attention."

"We think you could be presidential material."

"I'm through to the next round!"

By the time the auditions reached New York, 22,000 wannabe politicians were standing in line outside Madison Square Garden.

The atmosphere outside the arena was very different to the one at the Los Angeles sports arena twelve days earlier. The line snaked along 34th Street with contestants standing on every available inch of sidewalk, huddling in groups to keep warm while they practiced their speeches, or danced in front of dozens of TV cameras. One man wearing a tux was singing The Star Spangled Banner at the top of his voice; another dressed in Stars and Stripes pajamas juggled while reciting the Bill of Rights. Two or three Statues of Liberty were wandering around, and the American flag was everywhere, draped into costumes or flying high in the morning sky. Two guys in 'Dennis Saxon: Make America Great' t-shirts stood apart, ignored by the crowd.

It was official. The iCandidate was a phenomenon.

Jennifer Flynt wasn't used to standing in line. The iceberg blonde suffered in silence until it was time for her to move into the Garden and away from the madness outside. No one would ever guess from her pristine appearance, but inside her nerves rattled and her feet were killing her. In an immaculate, figure-hugging black dress and stiletto heels, she stalked effortlessly through the earlier rounds before she was told to give a minute speech on a leader she most admired in the 'Do or Die' challenge.

She spoke about former British Prime Minister Margaret Thatcher, identifying with the Iron Lady's determination, her conservative views and her 'Special Relationship' with Jennifer's favorite President Ronald Reagan. She finished with a favorite Thatcher quote:

"I am extraordinarily patient, provided I get my own way in the end."

The producers weren't the only ones impressed by Jennifer's haughty sexuality. Start-up app entrepreneur Todd Greenacre, in a royal blue cashmere turtleneck, faded jeans with an ironed crease running down the front, watched her audition as he sat waiting for his turn. Heading for the bathroom, he checked his reflection in the mirror, ensuring his surfer scruffy blonde hair was carefully mussed before taking his seat again. He'd recently doubled his workouts at his East Village gym; he was in the best physical shape of his life. He looked good. He felt powerful.

His phone beeped and he opened the text.

'How are you feeling? Are you ready?'

He typed back. 'Of course I am. Never been more ready for anything in my life.'

Everything was riding on the next couple of rounds. He was almost there, the competition was dropping like flies, and the preparation was paying off. He felt it in his bones. He could do this, if only they'd hurry up and call his name.

In Chicago, the parking lot of the United Center was full, but the traffic kept coming, backing up the whole street. Police reinforcements were being shipped in to appease contestants who worried they were too late to try out. Grace Conwright stood in the ever growing, never moving line for three hours, and it was still only 9:00 a.m. Her slim frame hidden under a heavy overcoat, Grace made little attempt to talk to anyone, her detachment more shyness than anything else. Suddenly an inebriated man got in her face telling her she looked like the actress Halle Berry and she decided she'd just about had enough. She pulled a hood over her hair and turned to leave when her cell phone rang.

Seeing the name flash up on the iPhone, she answered.

"I've changed my mind. I'm going home, this is insufferable."

"It'll be worth it, I promise," the caller said.

"You'd better give me an idea how long this is going to take. I'm dying for a pee and the guy next to me thinks he's Bob Carson. He keeps serenading me with his trumpet."

"Bob plays the saxophone."

"Whatever, I can't stand here for much longer not moving."

Grace only came home from the Carolinas after being told about the audition. She forgot how cold it got. "There's thousands upon thousands of people here. When did it suddenly get so popular anyway?"

"I know, fantastic isn't it?"

"Not really, not from where I'm standing."

"Hold on, I'll call you back." A minute later, show staffer Hannah Woodson, her close friend, was back on the phone. "Okay, I want you to leave the line, and discreetly move towards the front. Look out for a man with white hair in a green jacket with a pass around his neck. His name is Nick. He's going to slip you in ahead of the crowd."

"Really? That would be great...But is that fair? I'll just stay here and wait."

Which holding area are you standing in right now, Grace?"

"It's letter M."

"Okay, my estimation is you won't be inside until about 3:00 p.m. this afternoon." Grace paused. "Green jacket you say. I'm coming."

Hannah and Grace's families were close when they were younger. That was before Grace's father, a U.S. Senator from Chicago, was killed along with his wife in a race-hate assassination at a political rally ten years earlier. There was nothing Grace could do to bring her parents back, but Hannah had persuaded her that the show would keep their memory alive.

By the end of the day, 33,000 people had filed through the United Center.

When the final audition came full circle back to Los Angeles on the third week of November, record numbers of potential presidents had lined up through the night. Hopefuls were sent home with wristbands that served as their tickets to come back during the next two days; there just wasn't time to fit all 40,000 people into one day.

Dr. Gillian Lawfull sat patiently with her 10-year-old daughter Clara, and her assistant Sadie. She felt guilty for dragging them along for such a long day.

"Mom, we've been here for hours. When is it your turn?" Clara asked, close to tears.

"Looks like now, my angel. Wish me luck and if I'm gone a long time, just blame Sadie. She's the one who talked me into this."

"Yes, but you'll be thanking me when they put you through. Good luck boss!"

Gillian put a hand through her messy hair and wondered if the touch of mascara she'd put on that morning was enough. Distracted, she forgot about the cup of green tea on the armrest and spilled it all over herself as she got up. While Sadie tried to scrub the tea stain out of Gillian's hemp skirt, Clara scraped her mom's hair back into a half ponytail, securing it with a silver barrette, and tried again to persuade her that she should at least wear some lip gloss.

"The judges will just have to like the natural look, stains and all," Gillian smiled. "Perhaps they'll appreciate my depth and intellect instead. Oh shoot! What did I do with my audition number?" Gillian started rooting through her bag.

"It's on your chest," Sadie and Clara said at the same time.

A clinical nutritionist and naturopath, Gillian wanted to change a health system she believed was both flawed and unfair; it's what she told her friends when they asked why she thought it was worth giving The iCandidate a try. In truth, her reasons were more complex. She'd moved West from her home in Brooklyn when her Marine lieutenant husband was drafted to Camp Pendleton north of San Diego and she hadn't felt able to move back following his death in Syria 18 months earlier. It's like it would be an admission that he was really gone. The weather in Seattle, where she was living now, had suited her mood. But this was an opportunity to move on, even if it was crazy.

In her high school political debate team, Gillian was known as 'the preying pussycat.' She was no pushover. Ruffling her daughter's hair, Gillian took the stage in Los Angeles to become the eighth and last iCandidate finalist.

The Huffington Post reported the next day: EIGHT FINALISTS MAKE THE CUT AFTER 150,000 AUDITION IN NINE STATES

5 THE JUDGES

The stage manager was nodding frantically at Kristoff; she held up both hands and counted down from ten. A buzz reverberated around the studio and everyone realized it was time. TEN, NINE, EIGHT...the last dab of powder...SEVEN, SIX, FIVE... everyone in their place. Kristoff moved to the center of the stage, the crowd roared and then died as a voice boomed across the loudspeaker: "Complete silence please until the introductions are made"... FOUR, THREE, TWO, ONE...

"Just six short weeks ago, the journey began," said Kristoff. "One hundred and fifty thousand of you came forward to audition in states across America. You came from farms, towns and cities. Lawyers, actresses, bankers, cowboys, post office workers, athletes, teachers, doctors, and construction workers. Black, white, Latino, Asian, you all had a common purpose, a shared dream - knowing that given the chance you could make a difference and have your life mean so much more."

It was pretty much the same speech he gave at the opening of StarStruck. "You came, you tried, and 8 of you succeeded. Now, America, it's come down to this. We have your eight finalists competing for a chance to achieve what only 43 people have done in history. We're giving the winner an opportunity to seek the most powerful position on the planet. Welcome, ladies and gentlemen, to THE iCANDIDATE!"

The screaming and applause was deafening. Cameras panned wildly around the audience as fans jumped up and down waving banners covered in names and decorated with the pictures of the nation's most talked about reality stars.

"Thank you. Thank you, everyone. I have to thank you all for being here tonight." Kristoff shouted over the noise, using his hands to try and bring the levels down. "I also want to thank everyone for watching at home. We have been told that we are officially the number one watched show this season and we are just getting to the contest proper. We're changing politics one iVote at a time."

Kristoff walked quickly across to the giant plinth facing the stage. "Before we get going, I would like for you to meet my three incredible judges." The camera crews kept trained on Kristoff.

"First, we have a man who knows a thing or two about the comings and goings at the White House, America's former Vice President, Walter Penske." Walter, a giant bear of a man, nodded his patrician head while his chest puffed out in acknowledgment of the applause. He wore a tux with white shirt and bow tie; he looked like he'd taken a wrong turn on the way to the opera.

"Our second judge is beautiful, talented, and, dare I say it on a family TV show, a little sexy? She is one of the country's top lawyers and best known as former general counsel in the Bush administration. Please welcome my friend, the lovely, Jacqueline Toscane."

The audience went crazy. With her expensively teased blonde hair and plunging necklines, Jacqueline was clearly a fan favorite, especially with the men. She responded with a smile toward the host and a wink at the camera.

"Lastly," Kristoff put on his serious face, "I am honored to introduce a man who is not shy to voice his opinions. He is actively involved in charitable organizations around the world; he's a Goodwill Ambassador for the United Nations, speaks at many rallies and meetings, sharing his political opinions with world leaders and anyone who will listen. He just happens to also be the lead singer for the multi-platinum rock band, Legacy. Please welcome, Rob Balfour!"

This time the screams drowned out any attempts to move the show along and Kristoff stepped back to enjoy the crowd's excitement. Rob looked like he'd just climbed out of bed; he pushed back on his chair and waved at the crowd. When he could finally get his voice heard, Kristoff managed to ask the question that had been stuck on his autocue for what seemed like a lifetime. "Rob, let me ask you, are you surprised how popular this show has become in such a short space of time?"

"No man, not at all. The iCandidate has captured the imagination of the people. It lets you believe that we truly do live in a democracy. Hell, the winner could go on to become the next President of the United States. Dude, That's crazy!"

"And Jacqueline. A political reality show? Why does it work?"

"You know Andy, everyone loves reality shows—I love them! But how many of them really affect our day-to-day lives? Sure it's cool to find a good singer or dancer, but to find someone who wants to change the world, someone who's in tune with the American people, and will listen to them, someone who's smart, politically astute and, of course, has millions of people behind them, now that's what really matters."

"Walter, you were Vice President back in the day," Kristoff said. "Do you think one of our eight finalists could fill your shoes, or the President's for that matter?"

Walter moved his large frame forward in his seat, one hand rubbed his chin thoughtfully.

"I don't know if anyone back there has what it takes to lead our country, I'll be honest. You have to be incredibly knowledgeable and sharp in the game of politics."

"Like you, you mean," Kristoff smiled.

"Of course!" he replied without a trace of humor.

"Are They Ready? You've watched their journey, it's been a tough battle to get where they are today. Do you think they're ready?" asked Kristoff.

"That remains to be seen," said Walter. "It'll be interesting though. I will say this to the people out there voting: America has quite a responsibility." Penske was clearly enjoying his moment. "Be very careful whom you give the power to. You don't want it in the wrong hands."

"Dramatic words indeed from our former Vice President," Kristoff quickened the pace, heeding the anxious appeal in his earpiece to wrap it up. "The contestants are going to have to show something very special to impress Walter. Thank you, judges for your thoughts. With that said, let's introduce them America...your eight finalists."

6 THE FINALISTS

The curtains at the back of the stage swung open to reveal the silhouettes of the eight finalists standing in front of a massive American Flag. The National Anthem blasted out as the eight slowly walked forward to their assigned stools, smiling and waving.

Finally the crowd calmed down and Kristoff tried not to shout.

"Congratulations all of you. Now, I have good news and bad. The good news is you made it through to the final eight. The bad news is if you thought it was hard getting to this point, you ain't seen nothing yet. Now you are really going to be tested. The challenges are going to get even tougher." Turning to face the camera, he continued:"You all know our iCandidates by now, but in case you've been living under a rock for the last few months, here they are."

Kristoff walked across to where Todd Greenacre was standing at the other end of the stage. They shook hands. The tech mogul wore a gray turtleneck and towered over Kristoff.

"Todd Greenacre is a man going somewhere, and he's only 34-years-old. Todd's hero is Bill Gates, but don't let his casual good looks confuse you, he has swept through his opponents with all the ruthless skills of a born winner." Kristoff edged a little closer. "Todd, if you were accused of stepping on people to get ahead, how would you respond to that?"

Todd paused, looking deliberately around the audience, making eye contact with a few in the front row. "I'm not afraid to tell the truth if I believe in a cause. As Winston Churchill once said, 'You have enemies? Good. That means you've stood up for something, sometime in your life."

"It seems to me that life usually works out your way, Todd," Kristoff said.

"I like to blow people away with my brilliance!" His expression didn't change and the audience didn't know how to react.

"You seem pretty intense, Todd. What do you do for fun?"

Todd seemed suddenly unnerved by the question.

"What's your favorite movie," Kristoff asked. "Your favorite song?"

Todd relaxed. "Star Wars," he laughed. "The Empire Strikes Back."

"And the song?" "Bruce Springsteen...Born to Run."

"Good choice," shouted Rob. "I like him, he's got taste."

Kristoff joined the applause and turned to the next iCandidate. Next up, from New York City, was Jennifer Flynt. A few boos were clearly heard amid the thunderous applause. The public relations powerhouse known for representing some of the biggest names in the fashion world was the contestant who'd attracted the most controversy - and the most hits on Google images. Kristoff was more than happy to move in closer.

"How's your journey been so far, Jennifer?" he asked her.

"Incredible,"she replied. With not an ounce of fat on her 37-year-old figure, Jennifer's straight blonde hair framed her perfectly made-up features.

"When I first entered this competition I truly thought I might run into some trouble keeping up with the more experienced contestants, but that hasn't been the case at all. If anything, it's exactly the opposite."

A collective murmuring of disapproval together with some appreciative oohs could be heard; Jennifer smiled and jutted her chin playfully.

"You seem to thrive on controversy," Kristoff said. "So here's a question for you; what public figure do you most despise?"

"Dennis Saxon. He's tacky. And his hair?..." She left the comment hanging in the air.

Kristoff put his hand around her waist.

"Funny, he speaks very highly of you."

She shrugged. "Well, of course he would."

"You don't seem phased by anything, Jennifer. What's your biggest fear?"

"That's where you've got me, Andy." She struck a pose. "All this takes a lot of time and effort. It would depress the hell out of me to be a Size 4. I'm sorry but it's true."

Again, the crowd's reaction was mixed. One woman shouted out: "Have a burger - put some meat on those bones."

Kristoff greeted Los Angeles native Rich Francombe like an

old friend. It was the way he liked to behave with other famous people.

"You've surprised a lot of folks, making it this far, Rich."

The 6-and-a-half-foot tall athlete turned on his megawatt smile and Kristoff watched the cogs turn as he struggled to find an answer. The 42-year-old football legend lifted his hand to his left eye, trying to disguise the familiar nervous twitch. His legendary career as a two-time Super Bowl winning quarterback had required little more reading than the coach's playbook. This show, so far, had involved way too much thinking for him.

"So, Rich, tell us a little about yourself. I know you're a great student of football, but what kind of books does a guy like you read for fun?

"Harry Potter."

"Which one is your favorite Rich?"

"There's more than one?"

Kristoff coughed and slapped the sportsman on the shoulder. "Nice one, Rich. Let's get serious for a second. Here's one of the questions our voters sent in via the NoteStream app, one of our show sponsors. If you had to make the choice, would you bomb North Korea or make peace with Putin?"

"Who's Putin?" Rich shot back. There was an awkward silence in the studio. "I'm just kidding. I'd bomb Korea, of course," said Rich, furiously rubbing at his left eye.

Grace Conwright, 45, was the only African-American contestant. She also had one of the most compelling stories. Never one to shy away from a TV "moment", Kristoff put his arm around Grace's slight shoulders.

"Everybody knows by now that you lost your parents. Your father, Steadman Conwright, was one of our best-loved Senators and a leading light in the civil rights struggle. His death, along with your mother at the Freedom March in your hometown of Chicago, shocked the world. I know how much they meant to you." He paused a second. "They would be so proud of you, Grace."

Grace was wearing a white wrap around dress and coral pumps. Her ebony hair was straight and cut to her chin, which accentuated her flawless skin and high cheekbones. The political science professor from the University of North Carolina at Chapel Hill looked young for her age and was more uncomfortable in the spotlight than her competitors.

She smiled, embarrassed. "That's kind of you, Andy, but I

don't need any sympathy."

She spoke in a soft, yet surprisingly firm voice. "I just want to carry on the work my parents gave their lives for."

Kristoff was momentarily lost for words. He found real emotions tricky to handle.

"Going back to our NoteStream questions," he said, looking down at his tablet.

"Favorite song? Favorite book?"

"I have loved Jane Eyre by Charlotte Bronte since I was a teenager at school and my all time favorite song has to be Marvin Gaye's, Let's Get It On."

There was a burst of applause.

"That's my kind of woman," said Jacqueline, clapping enthusiastically.

Gillian Lawfull was next. Her unkempt chestnut, shoulder-length hair was pulled back in a loosely tied ponytail. She was wearing a simple blue dress and had fought off the makeup artist.

"If anybody thinks our only single-mom finalist from Seattle is a push-over, they haven't been watching closely enough." Kristoff introduced a clip of an earlier debate showing Gillian the nutritionist, 47, demolishing a cocky stockbroker in a debate on health reform. "See that? He didn't stand a chance. I'm sure he went home and sobbed after that pummeling." Kristoff, back in control, feigned being afraid.

"Oh no, he was fine. We chatted afterwards, he gets dreadful migraines you know, so I gave him some complex B vitamins. Always does the trick," she said with a smile.

She's crazy, Kristoff thought to himself.

"Your turn then, Gillian. What's the trait you most deplore in others?"

"I can't abide liars. That's my pet peeve."

"Not too keen on politicians then?" said Kristoff.

"Isn't that why you came up with this show? We don't need another Bob Carson."

"Excellent answer," Kristoff was wrapping it up. "She'll go far, America."

Tom Jodes was the surprise survivor of the group. He stood on stage in a lime green dress and a short, wavy brunette wig. Kristoff still wasn't sure what to make of him.

"Ladies and Gentlemen, we found our sixth finalist at the Denver, Colorado auditions.

"Tom, do you think the fact that you, well...err, you prefer to dress as a woman will harm your chances of winning this competition?"

"Would you vote for a 61-year-old man who was pretty ugly even before he started dressing up as a woman? No, I don't suppose you would," Tom said cheerfully.

"So why did you enter The iCandidate? Did you hope to further the gay and transgender agenda?"

"That didn't cross my mind actually. I'm not gay - I have a wife I love and adore very much - but now you mention it, that would be a good thing, don't you think? No, I remember thinking one day, that I do a pretty darn good job at being Mayor in my home town of Rayville, and would like to have a go at becoming President. I think I'd probably be quite good at it. Harriet Carson may have plenty of estrogen, and Dennis Saxon certainly has balls. But I've got both!"

Gillian put her arm around him and kissed him on the cheek. "He's such a sweetheart."

Tom blushed. "Frankly, I didn't realize I could get so far purely on my looks!," he joked. "My master plan is to bring my personality into play now and wipe the floor with the rest of my rivals."

The audience cheered and Tom bobbed a curtsey.

"One last question from our online voters," said Kristoff. "What is the trait you most deplore in other people?"

"Intolerance." Tom wasn't laughing any more. He was deadly serious.

Fifty-two-year-old advertising millionaire Cameron Banks, from Washington D.C., was already a hot favorite with the women.

"Your critics are labeling you a flirt with an over-sized ego." Kristoff acted like it was a compliment. "If you get to the White House one day, will you be able to keep your libido in check?" His question was greeted with laughs and sniggers from the audience.

"I'll be totally professional, just as I am now in my working life." Cameron paused to think. "But that's not a bad chat up line is it? Hello, I am the President of the United States. Can I buy you dinner?"

"Yes please!" "LOVE you Cameron!!" Various calls from the audience had Cameron smiling and waving.

Kristoff pressed him. "So why should you be President?"

"Because I'm not just a pretty face," said Cameron. "I'm a master persuader."

Now women in the audience were whooping.

"Calm down, calm down." Kristoff pleaded. "But seriously, Cameron, who is your hero?"

"President Harry Truman. His parents couldn't even afford to send him to college and look what he did with his life? He lived the American dream."

The video of Cameron's journey included an angry behind-the-scenes argument with Todd, a rivalry the producers had done their best to exploit.

"Hey, if I agreed with everyone's opinions it wouldn't be much of a political show, now would it?" Cameron quipped as the lights came back up. "I enjoy the debates, not just with Todd, but with all the contestants. We have some real firecrackers here, I can tell you."

A ripple of laughter went through the audience. Cameron clearly meant the women in the group and caught a sultry look from Jennifer. Grace rolled her eyes, unimpressed.

Dulce Ramirez stood just over 5-feet-tall and had levered into a tight-fitting pale blue suit. She looked up fiercely when Kristoff took her hand. She'd started out with a tiny family diner close to the El Paso Texas border with Ciudad Juarez and turned it into a massive international restaurant chain. She was 59 and an outsider in the betting.

"What's your biggest fear, Dulce?" Kristoff was worried about running over time.

"Well, I have five kids and I'm a fierce Latina mother, so keeping them safe is my biggest worry. As a matter of fact, Andy, I feel like that about all children."

"Who's your hero?" Kristoff looked into Dulce's eyes.

"It's Rosa Parks. No doubt."

Kristoff checked his tablet. "Our NoteStream voters have an interesting question for you. Would you rather witness the birth of Jesus or hunt with a caveman? Not a question you'll be asked every day."

"I don't like violence; I don't like guns or spears. I'm a religious woman. I'd love to see the birth of Jesus. Wouldn't everyone?"

"Do you have a message to your supporters and people out there who may be thinking about voting for you?" Kristoff asked.

Dulce spoke with a slight accent. "I want all those other Hispanic ladies out there still cleaning rich people's houses and doing menial jobs beneath their capabilities to know that the sky really is the limit. If I can do it, so can you."

Kristoff joined in the polite applause while moving back center stage, where he was most at home. "Well you've met them folks; our finalists. Could one of these men or women be your next President? We're taking a short commercial break, don't go anywhere though. The unveiling of our iVOTING SYSTEM is happening right here. It's going to revolutionize the future and how YOU vote at the next election. BRB!!!"

7 IVOTE

Kristoff stood by himself in the spotlight; darkness blanketing out the contestants.

"Okay, America, you've met our finalists, and now we invite you to be a part of something sensational. "We are going to make history one iVote at a time. Viewers at home can cast their votes online at www.theicandidate.com or on their iCandidate smartphone app.

He pointed to the screen behind him and the names of the links flashed up in huge letters. "More on that later, but here in the studio, you have an important job to do tonight. You can change someone's life and ultimately change your own as we work together to make our political system a true democracy."

These were the moments Kristoff lived for. He felt like he was slap bang in the center of the universe. Like a TV god. The rush was intoxicating.

"Tonight, each and every one of you will be equipped with an iVote device to participate in The iCandidate's landmark poll. The initial votes will be cast right here in the studio, which provide instant results. When we come back after the break, we will have our first challenge," he paused for effect…" and then the iVoting begins!"

Emily Boomstra sat in the audience with her fingers in her ears discreetly trying to drown out the din. Next to her was a Russian student, Maria, who was on an exchange program at UCLA. Emily was helping her acclimate to the United States. It couldn't be more different from her native Novosibirsk, but Maria didn't look phased in the least.

Emily's company in the Netherlands specialized in cultural exchange visits and had been sent free tickets to a studio taping of The iCandidate. A reality show to find a president, for goodness sake! Emily hadn't wanted to go but her boss insisted it was an example of democracy in action that would be very instructive for Maria.

"Who came up with this idea? Only in America. It's bad enough that they might put Dennis Saxon in the White House." Emily was speaking to Maria but the young girl couldn't hear her in the chaos of the studio and was staring transfixed at the stage.

She turned and gave Emily the biggest smile. Emily loved working with young people; it fed her soul, even if they didn't know what was good for them. She was leaving the next day for the East Coast to see more of her students at Harvard and NYU. Perhaps she could take them to see something real, like Capitol Hill or the White House?

Emily thought back to that day just a few weeks ago when she was told she had to come back to America. She'd vowed never to return after studying in New York as a teenager. The color had drained from her face in an instant, like she'd seen a ghost...

~~~~~

"Emily, are you okay? Do you need to sit down?"

Her boss in Amsterdam, Josh Peters, had never seen her like this before. He thought she'd be pleased.

"What? No, I'm fine. Excuse me, where did you say you wanted me to go again?"

Emily's boss had worked at the European Education Cooperative in Amsterdam for more years than he cared to remember, but his favorite day of all was the day Emily had joined the firm ten years earlier. He was happily married with two kids and was far too in love with his wife to ever make a fool of himself, but he always had a special place in his heart for Emily Boomstra.

It wasn't hard. She was gorgeous, and the way she looked at him now, her sparkling blue eyes dulled by a sheen of tears, and her pale skin white under the harsh office light, it was all he could do not to walk around the desk in his office and hug her. She may be the most accomplished, independent woman he'd ever met, but he still felt overwhelmingly protective towards her.

"The United States," he repeated. "I want you to check personally on the students we just placed over there."

"That's Graham's territory," she stammered. The last place in the world she wanted to go was there.

"Look, I know you usually cover Europe and Asia but if you remember, Graham is taking a sabbatical next month and frankly Emily, I don't trust anyone else to do the job in his place."

He paused. "It's supposed to be a good thing," he added gently.

Emily stared at him, saying nothing, trying to gather herself. She wiped back a tear.

He carried on. "Look, relations can be extremely delicate between countries like Somalia, Afghanistan and Russia and the United States. There's a lot of suspicion either way. We need for their students to feel wanted and accepted. You see that don't you?"

But all Emily could think about was what happened all those years ago. She'd lost her baby and the man she loved the same day. It wasn't something you could easily forget. The pain would always be with her, and she had never spoken about it to anyone, not even her parents. She'd vowed back then when she got on the plane two days after her dead son had been taken from her that she would never go back. And she hadn't.

She remembered too, vividly, the wrath of her father when she got home to Holland on that rainy Monday. He never understood why she would want to drop out of school and so suddenly. She couldn't tell him or her mother. It would have killed them just as it had been slowly killing her. She made up something that she couldn't even remember anymore. She stopped drinking; she finished her degree in Holland and worked with children, trying to fill the hole in her heart. She had dated, of course, but never seriously. She couldn't let anyone in after what he had done to her. It was easier to hide in her loneliness.

Her boss was looking expectantly at her.

"Are you telling me that there's no-one else you can ask in this entire company?"

"I need the best," he said simply.

~~~~~~~~

And so now here she was, sitting in the front row of the audience on an American reality show, wishing with every ounce of her body that she could get on a plane and fly back to Holland. At least she was leaving for Boston in the morning. Halfway home should make her feel a little better, but it was a whole lot nearer to New York.

She felt the familiar ache in her heart and that same flat dullness spread behind her eyes. She swallowed and tried to push the memories back down.

Kristoff was back from the break, his face flushed. He took a moment to look around. His eyes rested on a blonde woman looking down at her phone and a young, bright-faced, dark haired girl. Mother and daughter, he wondered? The blonde glanced up and for a second their eyes locked. She looked so sad, so wistful...he shook his head and focused on the prompt.

"Get ready America, change is coming. We'll be back after these messages."

8 SHAKING THINGS UP

Back from commercials, the contestants looked up at an over-sized electronic screen with the words BILL-BOARD plastered across the top in flashing lights. Underneath were listed some of the more bizarre earmarks that had been added to legislation over the years by congressional lawmakers. Kristoff was explaining how the so-called 'pork barrel' cash was tacked onto other bills by politicians, who promised their support for the legislation as long as extra money was allocated, in the small print, for specific projects in their districts. Most of the time, the other senators and representatives voting through the measures didn't even realize they contained these extras that amount to hundreds of millions of dollars.

The earmarks listed on the board included a $150 million indoor rain forest in Iowa, a $5 million grizzly bear tracking project in Montana, and $13.5 million for a World Toilet Summit in Ireland.

"Is this the way to conduct business in Washington?" Kristoff asked the audience. "Tonight, our iCandidates are going to be given the details of a series of bills passed over the last ten years and decide whether Congress was misled."

Rich's eyes had already glassed over. He didn't have a clue what Kristoff was talking about. When he felt the first jolt, he thought it was members of the audience stomping their feet in appreciation like they used to do at his games.

Then the stage moved sideways, knocking all of them off their stools, and an earsplitting siren suddenly filled the air. The contestants looked around, wondering what to do. There were screams coming from the bleachers as the crowd fell over one another to reach the exits. There was a loud crack as the corner of the stage gantry toppled over, fortunately in an area where no one stood.

One side of the floor slipped, making it almost impossible for any of the finalists to keep their footing. All of them had their hands clapped over their ears trying to keep out the deafening noise. The crew looked just as shocked, and all but the cameramen were panicking and screaming.

"Earthquake! Earthquake!"

Todd felt his phone vibrate. He looked down at the text:

'Be a hero!'

The alarm stopped and a loud voice boomed over the sirens.

"This is security. Please do not panic. Make your way in an orderly fashion to the exits at the back of the studio and my officers will direct you to safety. I repeat, please do not panic. Everything is under control."

Rich helped Jen and Grace to their feet and led them down to where the public pushed to get out. Jen cursed, picking up one of her shoes. She looked distraught.

"My heels came off. Does anyone have any superglue?"

The others followed behind.

"It's okay girls. This is California. We're used to earthquakes out here." Rich tried his best to sound unconcerned. "It's probably nothing, just a little hiccup." As he spoke, another section of the stage where they'd all just been sitting collapsed and several of the larger Klieg lights crashed to the floor. The ground started shaking more violently. Dulce held on to Gillian and started to pray. Rich's stomach churned. There was no sign of the judges.

Kristoff appeared in front of them, his eyes wild and his white shirt ripped and covered in dirt. "Over here," he shouted above the din. "All of you come over here." He led them away from the seats where the audience scrambled for the doors and towards a dark area backstage. "It's safe back here. There's a bunker where we can ride this thing out. It's just this way, hurry!"

"My daughter! My daughter was in the audience," Gillian Lawfull cried out. "I can't leave without my daughter." She was already running over to where the families had been sitting, but there was no one there.

"Clara! Clara! Where are you?" Gillian screamed hysterically. "I can't go without her. I can't," she sobbed as Kristoff ran over and tried to steer her back to the others.

"I have her safe," he told her." All the family members are safe. I guarantee it."

"I don't care. I'm not leaving this room until I know where she is." Red-faced, Gillian refused to budge. Her mouth set in a firm line, she stared him down.

Kristoff sighed. "Okay, wait up a minute." He held his walkie-talkie to his mouth, trying his best to be understood in the melee. "Hannah, do you read me? Do you read me? Please bring Clara Lawfull back into Studio B. Use the fire door and be quick. Her mother insists on it. Over."

"Will do," came the crackly voice.

Moments later, the frightened face of the 9 year-old tousle-haired girl appeared to the right of the broken stage and ran into the grateful arms of her relieved mother.

"You okay, then?" Kristoff asked, impatient to move on.

"Yes," Gillian replied, her smile back. "Thank you, Andy."

"Not at all. I'd do the same."

"Look over there, that woman's hurt," Grace broke away from the group.

"Come back! I'll get someone to take care of her. There's nothing you guys can do. It's my responsibility to ensure your safety." Kristoff was still trying to herd them to the exit.

"Maybe now isn't the time for heroics, sweetheart," Cameron held back.

Ignoring him, Gillian followed Grace, who turned to shout over her shoulder. "Don't be so condescending, Cameron. Really, are you always such an ass?"

Cameron put his hands up in mock surrender as the clouds of dust began to clear and the shape of an injured woman emerged. She was propped up against a wall and moaning. Grace was there in a heartbeat.

"Oh, to hell with it," Cameron ran over to where another sobbing woman lay on the ground clutching her ankle. He swooped her up into a fireman's carry and ran back to where the others were waiting. "Everybody else looks okay. Let's go."

Kristoff shepherded the iCandidates through a door, and the siren immediately receded, but they were running back into a cloud of thick smoke.

"I can't see a thing!" Todd pushed ahead, calling out orders for the others to help.

Firemen emerged from the darkness and more people lay on the ground, groaning. Kristoff had disappeared again.

Jen picked her way through the debris in bare feet, and knelt down by a victim who moaned incoherently, "Someone, help over here."

Tom was instantly at her side. "We need something to stem the bleeding."

Tom took off his jacket, pulled off his t-shirt and handed it to Jennifer, who tore it into strips. Glancing at Tom, she did a double take. "Put your jacket on, Tom."

"Oh, yes, that would be best," he replied, hurriedly putting his jacket on and zipping it up over his pink bra and ample, naked stomach.

Gillian stopped a fireman and asked what she could to help. He told her they needed to evacuate the area, as it was still unsafe. Grace raced to her side and they worked together checking people for injuries and comforting them. Todd ran, stooping from patient to patient, lifting them to clear ground. He checked to see what aid they needed before running back for another. He spoke loudly and purposefully, asserting himself as the leader.

Dulce wiped her brow, it was hot and dusty; she was incredibly thirsty. No time to stop, she thought, while tending to another victim. A young blonde woman had fallen in the mayhem and cut her leg. Dulce needed some gauze to stem the bleeding. "I'll be right back. What's your name? Caroline? Don't worry, Caroline, I'm just going for supplies, I'll be two minutes." She turned the corner and an elderly Hispanic lady reached out and grabbed her by the jacket.

"Please, don't leave me," she cried out in Spanish. "I can't walk and my chest is hurting. I think I'm having a heart attack." There was nobody else around so Dulce had no choice. She stopped to try and comfort the sobbing woman.

Kristoff was back, angrily extolling all of the iCandidates to follow him and to leave the emergency services to do their job. "We need to get out of this area," he shouted. "The whole area is being evacuated in case the buildings collapse. Everyone must GET OUT NOW!"

A fire chief stood with Kristoff, beckoning them all to follow him when Grace stopped.

"I can't see Rich or Tom. They were here a few minutes ago but they've gone."

She pushed past a cameraman and started running back in the direction they had just come from, but Todd grabbed her arm. "You can't go back in there. It's too dangerous. I'll go look."

"No need, we're fine," Tom said, emerging out of the shadows.

"Rich and I just got a little lost trying to help some people out, didn't we, my friend?"

"We did," Rich looked pale and shaken, quite unlike his usual confident self. "Took a wrong turn."

"Don't worry," Kristoff said. "As long as we're together. I want you to all follow the chief to the bunker. Then we'll regroup and decide what to do next. I've got my staff working with the authorities to find out the full extent of the damage, and the number of casualties. Hold on. Where's Dulce?"

"Is she the Latino lady?" An injured woman looked up from receiving treatment from a paramedic. Kristoff nodded and she added: "She kind of abandoned me. She went off to get some bandages and she never came back."

They all walked back into the smoke to find Dulce sitting on a folding chair drinking a bottle of water and talking to an old lady in Spanish.

"Let's go. We've already wasted too much time," Kristoff was impatient to get back and didn't wait to hear Dulce's explanation.

They were led through two long corridors at the back of the lot. The shaking stopped and this area looked remarkably untouched by the events of the past thirty minutes. The fire chief led them down a set of stairs before opening a big double door and telling them to run through to the stage area. As soon as he pulled open the door, the silence of the dark corridor was replaced by a crescendo of lights and noise. It took several seconds for most of the finalists to register that the noise was applause, and the flashing lights came from The iCandidate stage, which was an exact replica of the one they had all just escaped.

9 EARTHQUAKE DAMAGE

Todd was first to recover, sprinting down the aisle, waving and grinning at the crowd. The others walked in a dazed shambles to the front of the stage, where Kristoff and the three judges were waiting to welcome them.

"Ladies and gentlemen, here they are, your iCandidate finalists!" Kristoff milked the moment. "We told you, when this show started, that anything could happen. Now do you see what we mean?" He stuck his microphone in Gillian's face.

"You mean that was all fake?" She couldn't believe it. "None of those people were really hurt?"

"Actors and stunt people, my dear. A little more dramatic than the Bob-BOARD idea, don't you think?"

"I was intrigued by the indoor rainforest, actually," Grace looked disappointed.

"Sorry about that, Grace. But we like to keep you on your toes."

Turning to the audience, Kristoff was in his element again. "Let's hear it for the cast, and for the wonderful job done by the extras in our audience. Thanks to everybody for going along with our little secret. I almost believed it myself."

"You know, you terrified my daughter, and scared the life out of all of us." Gillian quivered from rage or delayed shock, she wasn't sure. "All that expense to prove what exactly?"

"To see what you're made of," interjected Jacqueline. "Becoming The iCandidate isn't all about how clever you are, or how well you can spout facts on healthcare and the economy. It's about what's in here," she pointed to her heart.

Rich looked devastated. "You mean, you saw everything? Everybody saw everything?"

"We did, indeed." Kristoff was loving it. "While you were dealing with the disaster, the audience in here – and all our viewers at home – watched the whole thing courtesy of our hidden cameras. Compelling viewing, I must say…

Give them another round of applause, please! I think they deserve it."

Kristoff pointed out a woman in the audience to Cameron.

"Recognize her do you?" The woman he thought was seriously hurt and carried from the other studio was now standing and waving with a guilty smile.

"But I saw your ankle, it was badly bruised, you couldn't stand on it." Cameron was puzzled.

"You'll have to talk to the makeup department about that, they are very good at fake bruises," she said.

"Wow. I feel violated." He winked at the young woman, who giggled.

Kristoff moved into the audience. "Stand up if you received treatment for your fake injuries today from one of our first aid crew."

Fifty people slowly stood and waved at their rescuers.

"Dulce, I think Caroline wants a word," Kristoff said.

"Thanks for forgetting me, Dulce," said the pouting blonde. "But you don't have to worry. Look, no blood!" she laughed.

"This is so surreal," Todd pointed out a couple in the fourth row. "Those two over there were unconscious. I carried them out of the smoke!"

"Thank you for that," called out the woman. "You have strong arms!"

An elderly lady jumped up. "He carried me too."

"And it was my pleasure." Todd was gracious. "I hope all of this didn't cause you to much stress?"

"I'm just fine. You're a true gentleman," the lady beamed.

"How do you think they did?" Kristoff asked Walter. "Would you have handled it differently?"

"They were adequate without proving the kind of leadership qualities I would like to see. Other than Todd, I'm not sure if we saw enough urgency out there, if you want my honest opinion.

"How about you, Rob? How'd they do in the eye of the storm?"

"They were fantastic, really hard core. Todd's a rock star, lifting bodies like feather pillows. Well done, man! Jen, Grace, Gillian, even Cameron, you were all totally on it. But I'm not so sure about Rich…or Dulce. You both seemed pretty shaken back there."

Kristoff looked squarely into the camera. "By the time we reach our grand finale this summer, there will be only two iCandidates on the brink of a historic political campaign for the White House.

"They said we'd never get this far, but The iCandidate is already well on the road to D.C. Who's to say that one of these impressive individuals standing before you won't become the next President of the United States of America?"

10 THE CUTTING ROOM

Back in the editing room, Kristoff sat with Mason and Desmond going through the earthquake footage. They were trying to decide what to run in the Results Show.

"I think we should definitely lead with this piece." He clicked a link on the giant computer monitor. At first all you could see was a cloud of smoke, then it slowly cleared to reveal Rich sitting alone on the floor, angrily wiping away his tears. Tom appeared in the frame and tried at first to help the quarterback to his feet, but stopped when it became clear Rich had been crying.

Tom sat down next to him and Rich, his voice raw with emotion, explained how his younger brother had died in the 1994 Northridge earthquake. How he'd never really come to terms with it. The earthquake challenge had forced him to face the grief he'd buried away.

"What was his name?" Tom asked.

"Joe. We were really close...I still think about him every single day."

Kristoff paced the floor. "Great TV! The viewers are going to love it: Rich, this big, super-successful jock that women love and men want to hang out with, showing his vulnerability. What do you reckon Mase?"

Mason was in charge of media and publicizing the show, but since it had become a ratings phenomenon, his role became more concerned with controlling the message.

"It'll probably win Rich a bunch of iVotes. At the moment people think he lost his nerve during the quake."

"But if we show it all, that will give him an unfair advantage and I'm hands down against that," Desmond butted in.

"This is a TV show Des, not an election debate. It's entertaining seeing a tough guy cry."

Kristoff looked at Mase, waiting for his agreement. Desmond

was brilliant at what he did, but he needed to let Kristoff do what he was good at.

"I'm okay with it." Mason had his feet up on the editing desk. "You know best...

But what I'm not okay with is you slobbering all over Jen every time you talk to her on air. You don't want the public to think you've got a thing for her."

Kristoff couldn't believe his ears. "I don't know what you're talking about. I've been the perfect professional."

"You're practically raping her with your eyes in front of the entire world."

"You're such a jerk, Mase. You've been lusting after her ever since she showed up at the New York audition." Kristoff walked away from the console to stand across from Mason.

Desmond had heard enough. "Will you two just give it a rest? Nobody should be lusting after any of the contestants. The media will have a field day if they think there's a conflict of interest. You know she's married, don't you?"

That stopped the arguing. "What do you mean, she's married?" Mason looked crushed.

"She says she's single. It's on all her forms."

"Well she's not. Simple as that."

"We should kick her off." Kristoff was furious. "She can't lie like that and get away with it. We're supposed to be choosing the next potential president and we can't even vet a candidate to see if they're married?"

Desmond shrugged. "We'll just have to hope she doesn't win." The other two went quiet. "Besides, we have a more pressing matter. I don't think we should use the film of Rich crying."

"Why?" Kristoff and Mason turned on him now.

Desmond looked up to see the scene playing again on the monitor. "I think it's a private moment for Rich. If he's okay with it then fine. Otherwise we should spike it."

"But this is a reality show and Rich knows full well what he signed up for." Kristoff was not happy. "The public eats up this stuff."

"Andy, this isn't like all your other reality shows." Desmond was standing up in the cramped control room. "It's supposed to stand for something better than that, no offense."

"Man, you're crazy, it's the reason we do these shows, for these candid moments! What do you think Mase?"

"As much as I hate agreeing with him, I can't really see what the problem is, Des. The guy was genuinely upset and he had good reason to be. Why shouldn't we show it?"

Right from the outset, the others had agreed Desmond would be the conscience of the show and this was the first time they'd really come to blows over it.

"I don't believe we should edit to show any of the candidates in a better or worse light. We should just show what happens in front of the cameras. This was obviously a private conversation and Rich had no idea it was being taped."

"He's on a reality show!" Kristoff slammed his hand on the desk.

"But it's a reality show in the truest sense of the word." Desmond was not backing down. "It has to be fair and it has to be 100% ethical."

Mason shrugged at Kristoff. "We did say that we'd all have to agree on stuff."

"So let's check with Rich," said Desmond. "And if he doesn't want to be seen blubbering on national television, we respect his wishes."

Kristoff glowered at Desmond. "I don't agree, but whatever." His mouth was set in a grim line.

"You'll thank me later," Desmond tried to make light of it.

"I doubt that," Kristoff put his headphones on and stared at the monitor, signalling that the conversation was over.

11 IVOTE

Kristoff was back center stage, all business. "So, are we READY studio audience? It's Super Tuesday. Time to show those Dems and Republicans out there how to iVote in the 21st century. Are you watching America? You'd better be watching because this is the future."

The audience roared.

"Let me explain the iVoting system. On your armrest, you will notice a leather flap. Please flip it over. You will see your iVote device embedded in the arm. Press that big release button; you can hold it in your hand, that's right. It's like one of those entertainment remotes on an airliner. Now the screen is asking you to register with your thumbprint. Place your thumb in the highlighted box in the center of your screen and hold until you hear a beep. That's all you need to do and you're in! A new screen will appear. You should see the names of the eight contestants. Click on the names of the three iCandidates who you would like to stay in this competition. A VOTE button will appear to confirm. Hit that and you are done!

"Ready everyone in the audience?... iVOTE NOW!" Kristoff looked straight into the nearest camera lens. "Everyone at home, hopefully you've downloaded your iCandidate app by now from the iTunes store or wherever you get your favorite apps. So listen up, make sure you've registered with your thumbprint. Just follow the instructions on the app. It truly gives credibility and meaning to the whole idea of one person one vote. No room for error this way! Okay, now once you're thumbprint verified, you'll see a button appear labeled "Cast My iVote!" Click that, and you'll see a rundown of the eight iCandidates right there on the app. I want you to go ahead and click on your top 3 favorites. A check will show next to your selections. Then hit iVOTE. It's that simple."

Kristoff walked back to where the eight iCandidates were waiting.

They looked a little uncertain what to do next. He stopped behind them one by one, an old trick he'd used to great effect on his talent shows. "Who are you going to save, America? Who is your choice as a candidate for the next President of the United States?" Kristoff squeezed Todd's shoulder, hugged Gillian, pausing just a second or two beside each iCandidate before moving on to the next.

Watching from the wings, Mason winced as the TV host planted a kiss on Jennifer's cheek. But he had to give it to Kristoff; the guy knew how to work an audience.

"Get your partner and your kids to download our app. Your grandparents, friends, aunts and uncles - anyone you know. If you want your iCandidate to move into the next round it's super important to iVote." Kristoff hesitated theatrically to listen to a voice in his earphone. "The results are already in from the studio audience and, believe me, it's not what you'd expect. More of that on the Results Show, but it's the viewers votes that really counts. You have until next Monday.. There's no time to waste - iVOTE NOW!"

12 THE WHITE HOUSE

Walking in from the chill of the Rose Garden, the President felt the telltale buzz in his pocket, his phone alerting him to a new message. He sent a grammatically perfect text to his wife, telling her he was downstairs, and then turned on the TV. He slumped behind his Resolute desk, piled high with official-looking letters and wondered how nice it would be to have just a few minutes to himself. At least it was warm. The fire in the elliptical-shaped room seemed to magically light every evening, even if it was warm outside.

He'd never expected it to be easy, and it hadn't been. He was tired now; he was nearing the end of his second term and looking forward to a time he could play a round of golf without interruptions or grief from the press. It would be nice to relive some of the initial fervor of his early days in office. But right now, he'd have settled for a nap in front of the TV.

"Mr. President. Mr. President?" He awoke with a start.

"I'm sorry, man. I never have been able to sleep on planes, not even on Air Force One. It was a long flight back this afternoon."

"Don't worry boss." White House Chief-of-Staff David Platt was standing over him. "I know how you feel. I won't keep you long, but there's something we should talk about."

"Not the VP, surely. He hasn't gone and put his foot in it again, has he?"

"Not this time, Mr. President. He's been on his best behavior since that episode when he was caught on a hot mic trash talking the Secretary of State."

"What is it, then? Or can it wait until tomorrow's briefing?"

"Afraid not. Mind if I change the channel?"

"Be my guest. Haven't you got a pile of papers for me to plow through?"

"I have, actually, but I figured you'd want to see this." The television set erupted in a blaze of noise and flashing lights. "Ladies and gentlemen," a familiar celebrity's voice filled the room. "It is my great privilege to introduce you to your finalists in The iCandidate."

"Are we really going to take this seriously? It's a game show, for goodness sake."

"Well, half the country is watching it and these guys are polling more votes a week than some of your would be successors are pulling in. So, I guess somebody had better start paying attention."

"I'm just glad it's not me." The President stretched. "Never thought we'd be taking on the winner of American Idol."

"It's The iCandidate, sir."

"Whatever. That's what worries me about Harriet's obstinacy about fighting this election. She's going to have her hands full with Dennis Saxon if he manages to bully his way to the Republican nomination."

"Oh I'm sure she'll beat him," Platt said confidently.

"Don't be so certain. We desperately need a new face, not another Carson. Now voters are going to want The Bachelor, Amazing Race and Survivor all rolled into one.

"Just as long as Harriet doesn't have to sing."

"She might just have to… to beat one of these," he nodded at the television.

"I'd pay money to see that."

Both men sat down in front of the flat screen television and watched in silence as the finalists were introduced to the public once more. The smiles evaporated. This was no laughing matter.

13 JUDGED

There was panic in the control room moments before the first Results Show went to air.

"What do you mean, you can't find Penske?" Kristoff was furious. "He must be in the bathroom again. Knock on the door and tell him he's on." In fact, Walter Penske was fast asleep in the Green Room, defying all attempts by his assistant to wake him.

Under no illusions why her boss was so hard to wake, she tried with all her might to move his buffalo frame to push him on stage. As she lifted his head, he belched into her face and she recoiled in disgust.

"Dunk his head under water, blast him with smelling salts – give him a tumbler of Grey Goose – I don't care, just get him into the studio in exactly thirty seconds," Kristoff roared.

"He's got vodka in his water glass. He's sozzled," the assistant explained. "The trouble is the less he has to do, the more he drinks."

"Twenty seconds, Shirley. Or you're fired."

"Okay, okay." She grabbed two burly security guards. "Each of you, take an arm and drag him in. He'll come to when he sees the cameras and the lights."

With literally a second to spare, Penske slumped in his seat, only perking up and smiling through raw, red eyes when Kristoff acknowledged the judges and teased viewers with the news: the results were in. Penske gave a presidential wave, took a big slurp from his water glass and closed his eyes as soon as the lights went out for the next set of commercials.

14 AND THEN THERE WERE SEVEN

Kristoff was back after the break to announce that a record number of iVotes had come in on The iCandidate app following the earthquake challenge. The three contestants with the highest votes would be safe and go on to the next round - The iPrimaries.

"So, America, we've decided we can't wait to get into the Oval Office proper - we've built our own." Kristoff stepped aside and the curtains pulled back.

Revealed behind him was a beautifully decorated room fitted with cream couches, blue and gold Regency-style chairs, all set on a pale blue and gold oval rug with an inlaid presidential seal. In front of the three narrow windows was an ornate wooden desk.

Ooohs rang out from the audience.

"Please close the curtains." The curtains automatically closed and Kristoff waited for quiet. "America, you have delivered your verdict."

He used the same line he'd made famous on 'StarStruck.'

"Here are your three favorite iCandidates…"

The curtains drew back, and this time Todd, Gillian and Grace were relaxing in the mock Oval Office, both women smiling happily on the couch facing the stage, while Todd perched on one of the chairs, looking rather presidential.

The sight was met with thunderous applause and Gillian couldn't seem to help herself; she blew a kiss at the audience.

"Walter Penske, how do you like our Oval Office?" Kristoff asked.

"Fitting, very fitting. Not bad at all. Well done."

"Now it's time to learn who else has made it into our final seven." Kristoff walked stage left where the other five iCandidates were standing in a small group facing the audience.

Desmond had insisted the results should not be prolonged for effect, a trademark of 'StarStruck' and Kristoff's other talent shows that traded on the discomfort of the contestants.

Kristoff had protested. He loved knowing who was going out and withholding the information until the very last moment; it was like playing God.

But Desmond wanted the losing iCandidates to have a dignified exit. "This has to be different. It may be entertaining, but this is not entertainment. The likes of Saxon and company are already trying to turn the presidential selection process into a mockery." He slammed his hand down on Kristoff's desk. "We MUST be held to a higher standard. We may be a reality show, but we have a real purpose."

His argument was so impassioned and sincere that even Kristoff backed down. They agreed to make the departures as simple, and as dignified as humanly possible.

"The iCandidates who will be joining Grace, Todd and Gillian in our Oval Office are...

"Jennifer... Rich... Cameron"... At the calling of each name, a huge roar rang out from the studio audience and the surviving iCandidates walked across the stage to sit down on the couches in the Oval Office.

Only Tom and Dulce were left standing. Kristoff positioned himself between them. He was a showman; he couldn't help himself. Looking towards the judges table he knew who to put on the spot. "Rob, which contestant deserves to survive another round?"

Rob leaned back in his chair, put his hands behind his head and studied the contestants.

"This is hard, Andy. I think they both have such big hearts, and the Earthquake Challenge wasn't easy." He stopped for a moment, and looked intently from one contestant to the other. "I'd like to see them both go through and get another chance."

"Oh, for goodness sake, Rob, don't be so diplomatic!" Jacqueline Toscane cut in. "Just make the call!"

Rob put his hands up in mock surrender. "Hey, if you're such an expert, Jacqueline, it's all yours."

Jacqueline rolled her eyes at Rob before looking at Kristoff. "Tom should stay. I think the vote will go against Dulce because folks were confused about what went on during the earthquake. Dulce is obviously a very compassionate and caring person but, for whatever reason, she said she was going to help somebody and then never went back. Politics is about perception, and to me, that didn't look good." Jacqueline slowly tucked a lock of hair back behind her ear with a manicured hand. Her eyes softened as she looked at Dulce. "And I think the vote will reflect that."

The camera zipped back to Kristoff, who looked down at his tablet as if he'd forgotten who got the lowest number of votes.

Desmond barked in his earpiece: "Get on with it!"

"Tom… the voters agreed with Jacqueline, you're safe."

The crowd's reaction was mixed. Some of the public was clearly still unsure what to make of Tom and a big section in the studio had come from Texas to support Dulce.

Tom, in a slightly overstretched, pale-blue twin set, reached out a hand to Dulce, and then awkwardly engulfed her in a bear hug. The mic picked up his whispered comments in her ear. "Dulce, so sorry. I'm so sorry."

Then Tom walked slowly across the stage to join the others, who were overjoyed that he'd made it through. Grace, Gillian and Cameron all jumped up to give him a hug.

Kristoff put his arm around Dulce. "We're sorry to lose you Dulce. What would you like to say to everyone who voted for you?" Kristoff handed her the microphone.

"Thank you everyone for getting me this far. I really am grateful for this opportunity and I promise you, I didn't forget the injured lady. It's just that there were other hurt people there as well… at least I thought there were." She shrugged with a sad smile. "But I won't give up fighting for you," she added bravely.

"I have a feeling we haven't seen the last of Dulce," Kristoff announced. "She's not a lady to ride off quietly into the sunset."

There were no cheesy reality show farewells. An assistant ushered Dulce off stage right as the seven finalists were led back onstage where they received a standing ovation.

"Next week's challenge is going to really test our remaining iCandidates. We have a big surprise in store for them with some incredible guests!" Kristoff was back where he liked it in the spotlight. "Whatever you do, don't miss it! Be ready to see two political worlds collide! Don't forget, we're changing the world…"

"…One iVote at a time," the audience shouted back in unison.

"On behalf of our fabulous contestants and our judges, Walter Penske, Jacqueline Toscane and Rob Balfour, this is Andy Kristoff signing out from The iCandidate! Goodnight America !"

15 SLIPPING AWAY

When the final lights went down on the Results Show, Chrissie kept her eyes locked on Jennifer. Sitting way behind the section where the other family members and friends were, gathered close to the front of the stage, it was difficult to see the expression on her face. Chrissie didn't want to be seen; she'd promised Jen faithfully that she wouldn't come. She found it hard to believe that after two years of marriage, she was kept hidden away like some guilty secret.

To keep her one step ahead of her opponents, Jennifer had four junior members of her PR firm working around the clock to help her prepare for The iCandidate. That's how she tried to explain it to Chrissie, as her excuse for pretending to be single. Jennifer had enough to worry about trying to become America's first woman president, let alone America's first bisexual president. Chrissie had to stay away.

The researchers told Jen that was her best bet – to use her sexuality to win over the men, and to not confuse them. Chrissie first met Jen at the gym. Back then, she was crazy for her, but now she wasn't so sure, not while she didn't exist. The lights went down and Chrissie joined the line crowding out of the exit. She turned one last time to see Jennifer laughing and hugging one of the men on the show. She looked very much at home.

As Chrissie headed back to her hotel alone, Jennifer and the other would-be Presidents were ferried in a fleet of limos to the whitewashed, coastal mansion in Malibu, the producers had named 'The White House.' Chrissie couldn't help feel the further her wife went in the competition the further she slipped away.

16 SEXTING

Jen headed to the bathroom as soon as the show finished. Grace was already there washing her hands. She tried to make conversation.

"So Jennifer, good first challenge, don't you think?"

"Yep." Jen studied her lips intently as she applied a red lipstick.

"Did you want to ride back to The White House together? Maybe you, Gillian and I could have a drink and hang out. You know, just us girls?"

Jen ignored the question as she pulled out her phone. She had a new text.

'My room? Champagne?'

She smiled before replying. 'Sure, give me a few minutes'...

'I'll be waiting'...

Jen walked out of the bathroom and as an afterthought looked back at Grace. "Sorry, I have plans." There was no smile, no warmth, as she looked back down at her phone.

"Nice chatting with you!" Grace called out breezily to the closed door. Grace went straight into the green room to collect her things. She almost u-turned straight out again.

Cameron was alone, leaning against the wall and texting, with that lopsided smile on his face. She had a pretty good idea who he was talking to. She slipped her simple navy jacket over a cream Nicole Miller dress and picked up her bag.

Grace liked to mix designer with cheap, cheerful accessories she found in vintage stores and street market stalls. Cameron glanced up and she decided to make the effort. He would probably be a real ass, but maybe not. "I thought you did good in the challenge Cameron, really good."

"You sound surprised."

"Well, I am surprised. I didn't know you cared about anyone but yourself." Oops. Her efforts were short-lived she realized.

"There are a few things I'm actually pretty passionate about," he smiled, glancing back at his phone. "Other than myself."

"Well, I'm not interested in your other passions. You did a good job during the earthquake, that's all I wanted to say." She walked across the room, almost dropping her things in a hurry.

"What's your problem?" he asked. Grace pulled the door shut behind her. Cameron shrugged off Grace's reaction. He'd expected to go out. Thank God for women voters, he thought, looking happily back down to a new text.

17 MADAM MAYOR

Tom was in no hurry to leave the studios. He had lots of friends in his hometown, Rayville, Colorado. They liked him enough to vote him Mayor. But in Los Angeles he felt more like a freak outsider. Gillian came over and gave him a hug. "Congratulations, Tom. You stand up there in some old, silly outfit, looking like a dumpy, brunette Meryl Streep with a five o'clock shadow, and then you have this way of making better people of us all. I just don't know how you do it," she told him.

"Estrogen capsules and a pair of melons," he joked playfully.

"No, I'm serious. You know I love you, but every ounce of logic tells me you should be laughed out of there. And yet, here you are. "

"It's my legs, you know. They're sensational!"

Gillian frowned. "What I want to say...what I'm trying to say, Tom, is that I am honored to be your friend. You are a wonderful man and I genuinely believe you would make a first class President." Tom was genuinely touched. He relied on jokes for protection, but Gillian was a pure, genuine sweetheart and he allowed his guard to slip down for a moment.

"That's a huge compliment coming from you." He kept his head bowed to hide his tear-filled eyes.

18 SEVEN DEGREES CELSIUS

Jen felt bad about Chrissie, but she really was willing to do anything necessary to become The iCandidate. Instead of going back to her room at The White House she crossed to the other side of the building and slipped into a dimly lit room. She locked the door behind her. On a table next to the bed, two glasses of Veuve Clicquot were still bubbling; the bottle had been placed back in a silver ice bucket by the window. Stepping out of her dress, she crossed the room in stiletto heels and tasted the champagne. It was heavenly.

"Seven degrees Celsius, the perfect temperature." He wrapped his arms around her.

"Is that a fact?" she started to turn around.

"Stay still." He rested his hands lightly on her waist as he kissed her neck and shoulders. "You didn't waste time getting here." His voice was low and soft.

"More to the point, will this be worth missing my beauty sleep?" she responded, turning slowly.

"You should already know the answer to that, Jennifer."

"Ah, well, you should never assume."

"I'm finding that impossible to do with you." She downed her glass of champagne. "Do you want more?" he asked huskily.

Jen pushed him on the bed.

"I guess that's a no," he smiled.

19 THE TODAY SHOW

Matt Lauer thought he'd seen everything in nearly 20 years of hosting 'The Today Show.'

He'd interviewed presidents and princes, argued with Tom Cruise, and been handcuffed to Sacha Baron Cohen. But the more he thought about the next segment, the more he worried. The makeup girl rushed over to dab some powder on his face. That almost never happened. He was sweating.

The commercials were over and the light flashed. He was on.

"In the studio this morning we are hosting an impromptu debate that is, well, something of a departure for this presidential campaign season." Matt went to straighten his tie and remembered he wasn't wearing one. "But the people on our debate panel aren't the usual suspects you've been watching over the past couple of months in the nomination process. In fact, they're not running for office at all - they're trying to win a reality show."

Matt stood and led the cameras through to the familiar Studio 1A. His appearance led to a huge cheer from the early morning crowd huddling up to the barrier outside. They weren't holding the usual "Hello Mom" and "Good Morning, Ohio" banners. Once the roar of recognition died away they were replaced by a cacophony of chants that sounded like football fans trapped in an elevator.

"Go Grace!"

"Cameron rocks."

"Jen, Jen."

"Start-Me-Up, Todd!"

"I love you, Gillian."

"Tom Terrific."

"Rich for President."

Matt walked across to where the seven remaining iCandidates were standing, each behind individual lecterns, as if they were taking part in a televised Democrat or GOP debate. The producers had gone to the trouble of getting the furniture out of storage from the last CNBC debate in Boulder, Colorado and hauling it across the country.

"As many viewers will know, The iCandidate political reality show has been pulling in huge ratings, bigger even than the debates in this strangest of presidential campaigns."

Matt was settling back into his rhythm now, as he always did. The producers had been pushing this segment for days. He'd worried about political impartiality. Now he'd just have to go with it. "An op-ed in the 'New York Times' even went so far as to suggest that The iCandidate offered better and more qualified people to be president than the politicians fighting it out in our primaries and caucuses." Matt moved back towards the window and smiled at a familiar face hidden from view of the public outside. "This man needs no introduction - my old friend Andy Kristoff, host of The iCandidate. Andy, tell us what this is all about?"

"Well Matt, we're really pleased to be here. We shook things up in the competition last week with our Earthquake Challenge and I'm afraid the lovely Dulce Ramirez was the one to leave us after our viewers' iVote. Now we're trying something a little different, thanks to you and our friends on 'The Today Show.'"

Kristoff pointed across to where judges Jacqueline Toscane, Walter Penske and Rob Balfour were sitting at the desk where Matt usually presented the show alongside Samantha Guthrie, Al Roker, and Carson Daly.

"We've brought our judges…and now we want to put our iCandidates to their second test."

"But Andy, don't you have a surprise for them?" Matt interjected. The two men had worked together on WNEW-TV in New York City during the 1980s and remained in touch.

"Thanks Matt. We do, indeed. We wanted our moderator for this unique, 'Today Show' debate to be someone who knows all about this political process - and who understands a thing or two about perception and reality. We wanted someone who knows about holding an audience and motivating that person who's never cared enough to vote, that's key.

We invited all the nominees from both the GOP and the Democrats to come and put our iCandidates to the test. We received just one reply." Kristoff looked at Matt and took a half-step back. The 'Today Show' presenter paused a moment. "Ladies and Gentlemen, please welcome…Dennis Saxon!"

Saxon wore an unbuttoned, navy, pinstriped Brioni suit with a red Hermes tie. He marched on to the sounds of the Star Spangled Banner playing and shook hands with Matt and Kristoff before walking down the line of iCandidates.

He sat in a chair facing them. An assistant handed him a sheaf of papers and a white trucker cap with the words, 'Make America Great - Vote Saxon.'

He put both of them down on the desk in front of him.

Outside the glass, the audience was going wild. Nobody had warned the iCandidates they'd be seeing Dennis Saxon when they arrived at the crack of dawn. The atmosphere had suddenly become static in the studio; sparks were going to fly.

"Right, let's get to it then," Kristoff had promised the producers he'd keep the segment under 20 minutes. "Mr. Saxon, Dennis… they're all yours."

Saxon cleared his throat. He was already loving this. "Todd, you seem like a sensible kind of guy." Saxon leaned back, stretching. "The media has been causing trouble by twisting my words over this Muslim thing. They're acting like I'm against all Muslims, when I have very good friends who are Muslim and they agree with me."

Up until this point, Todd was looking his usual calm, unflappable self. Suddenly the studio lights seemed to have turned up ten degrees. Sweat prickled his armpits. "Of course, I don't mean all 1.6 billion Muslims around the world hate America," Saxon continued. "That wouldn't be right…but I do mean a lot of them. There's some tremendous hatred out there. A tremendous amount." Saxon looked up at Todd. "What I want to ask you, Todd, is whether you agree with me that all Muslims who have this hatred of the United States should be stopped from coming into the country. Common sense, right?"

Todd was a deer in headlights. "I don't…well, I know what you're saying but…" He felt like he was about to be fired. He took a deep breath and started again. He'd practiced over and over for such a situation. He couldn't allow the surprise appearance to throw him. "Of course I don't believe we should allow Muslim extremists into the U.S., and I do happen to believe, Mr. Saxon, that you've been misrepresented by the liberal media. I, too, have Muslim friends and they are every bit as much concerned as we are about the Islamic State and al Qaeda terrorists. They are distorting

Islam in the eyes of the rest of the world." Saxon was nodding his approval. "Where our opinions diverge, however, is that I don't believe there should be a temporary ban on Muslims entering the country; too many good people with genuine business and other interests will get caught in that net."

Saxon stopped nodding.

"I do believe, nevertheless, that the Watch List compiled by the security services should be widened to include anyone with even the slightest question mark over them. If more funds are needed for the intelligence services to make this possible, then so be it. I understand when you say, Mr. Saxon, that a lot of Muslims hate us, and that may well be true in some Islamic countries, but much of that is achieved through brainwashing by antagonistic governments or plain ignorance. We must try to change that, not just block them out."

Saxon was nodding again. He even joined the applause from the crowd outside. "And here I was thinking you're a Saxon guy," he smiled.

"I am, sir. But I'm also my own man. I like to go my own way…like you." Todd may have been sweating under his jacket, but it didn't show. He smiled back and the spotlight moved across to Tom.

Saxon was still grinning. "We're the guys around here that get all the grief about our hair. Oh, I'm sorry, Tom, is it okay if I call you a guy?"

"You can me whatever you like, Dennis, just as long as you don't insult my wigmaker, Joan. She gives me a terrific discount."

"She'll be giving you a cut of the business after that plug!" Saxon was smiling. "Tom, I didn't want to ask you the obvious question, but I can't help it. I'm very much in favor of traditional marriage and I've taken some flak from the liberals for questioning gay unions. Where do you stand on the issue?"

Tom wasn't in the least phased. "Dennis, I'll tell you what I tell the people of Rayville, when they come to see me, the Mayor, and expect me to tell them how they're supposed to behave. The Rayville Middle School principal, Mrs. Collins - who can be rather quick to judge at times; I'm sure she wouldn't mind me telling you that - she wanted me to recommend the trustees suspend a young fella who was wearing an NRA t-shirt to class. I asked her, 'Mrs Collins, does the shirt say anything offensive?' 'Just NRA,' she said. 'But it's not appropriate.'

"So I said to her, 'Mrs Collins, is there a dress code at the Middle School?'"

"Well no, but…"

"'Well Mrs Collins,' I said to her, 'If there's no dress code and the shirt doesn't say anything offensive then I can't see why he shouldn't wear it. It's a free country, after all. It's what makes us great. It's why people with hair like us can be here on 'The Today Show, Dennis."

Saxon joined in with the applause again, but stopped short. "I took you for more of a traditionalist, Tom."

Tom waited a beat. "Dennis, you've given the traditional marriage route a try three times. Perhaps it's not working so well and members of the gay and transgender community may suggest it's time to allow people to try the untraditional route. What would you say to them?"

Saxon put up his hands. "I'd probably say they have a good point." Clearly uncomfortable with the setup, Saxon moved on to the next question.

"Before I decided to run for President, most of you know I was the host on my own reality show, 'The Intern,' which was hugely successful and made many millions for this network. If you were given the opportunity to create a reality show of your own, what would it be about?"

Matt winced at mention of the conflict of interest but Saxon didn't care. He studied the iCandidate faces, his eyes screwed up in concentration. He settled on Jennifer. "This question is for you, Jen."

"Well hello, Dennis," her voice was low and smooth. "That's an easy question actually. I would devise a show to find the next Editor-in-Chief of 'Vogue' magazine, the next Anna Wintour."

"Why am I not surprised, coming from a lady of such obvious taste and class?"

Saxon didn't try and hide his interest. "And how would your contestants prove they have what it takes to run 'Vogue'?"

"They would be expected to achieve the impossible, of course, and under the most ridiculously intense circumstances. The challenges would involve tasks that have to be completed in 24 hours straight with no sleep, maybe having to write an article to deadline with no resources, or to get an interview with a celebrity when no one else can."

"Okay, but what will make your show fresh? What will you

bring to the table that hasn't been done before, Ms. Flynt?

"Sex appeal." She left it hanging in the air for a second before adding: "Just kidding, I'm actually friends with Anna, Dennis. I think she'd love to be one of the judges. As you know, she doesn't suffer fools gladly, neither do I. That's why we're friends."

She tilted her head slightly and smiled at him. Saxon's wife, Sasha, was looking daggers from the side of the studio. Dennis smiled, raising his eyebrows in obvious approval. Matt quickly moved in. "Well, Jen, thank you. It seems like you answered the question satisfactorily. Do you agree, Mr. Saxon?"

Saxon pursed his mouth. "Well if she doesn't make the finale of The iCandidate, maybe I'll choose her for VP." He gave her a hungry look.

Grace and Gillian exchanged a glance. Jennifer was clearly going to be playing by her own rules. Saxon peered across at his wife nervously, shuffled his papers and moved along.

"Okay, so everyone knows what I think of the Affordable Care Act. It's gotta go! Do you guys agree with me on that?"

"I'd like to take that question if I may," Gillian perked up. "I actually think that the Affordable Care Act is a great program. Lots of people that have been able to navigate the website successfully and now have health insurance they can afford and provides them with the coverage they need."

"You have to be kidding," Saxon went on the attack. "You must surely agree that we should leave the health system to the experts. That's the only way America can be great!"

Gillian was wary. She knew she could bury herself now if she said the wrong thing. But this was close to her heart. "Mr. Saxon, with all due respect, you have been quoted as saying that you hate our current health system, but when asked what you would replace it with, you have sometimes said you like the single payer system adopted in Scotland and Canada, and other times, you've bowed to the private companies. I still have no idea what your position is…"

Dennis snorted. "The Affordable Care Act is a joke. Everyone knows it doesn't work. But I'm supposed to be the one asking you questions young lady."

"Well here's what I think, health insurance here is ten times more expensive than in any other country in the world. Prices are inflated and a three-day stay in a hospital or an operation should not deplete a family's savings account that they have spent years building. In a civilized nation such as ours, we should not be afraid to go to the doctor because we cannot afford the bills."

"Yeah well I think you may find this is your last week on The iCandidate Gillian. I'll tell you now, America does not agree with you."

The camera picked up reactions from the other iCandidates. Jen raised an eyebrow, a slight smirk on her porcelain features. Tom looked nervously at Gillian whose expression was stony. Grace squeezed her friend's hand and shook her head. Rich was sitting stock still on his stool and hadn't joined in with the laughter. He was trying so hard to think about what he knew about Saxon, he was hardly listening to what the others were saying. He knew the guy owned a bunch of casinos, and that he might end up being the president, but he had been so busy with The iCandidate, he hadn't paid him too much attention.

Saxon turned to him and he almost winced. "Rich, how you doing? It's been a while."

In the dim recess of Rich's mind a light switched on. He thought he remembered Saxon from somewhere. For now it was safest to smile and nod. "Good. Very good."

"Remember when we hung out after the Super Bowl. Great times." Saxon was the one who came off star struck.

"Good to see you again." Rich vaguely recalled meeting Dennis Saxon, but there had been so many famous faces after the Super Bowls. He mostly remembered actresses and models. Saxon pursed his lips again, and lobbed Rich an easy catch. "You must be a big fan of my campaign to make America great again. Hell Rich, you're the kind of guy we should be holding up as a symbol of greatness. Two Super Bowl rings. Man, you're terrific. What do you like best about my campaign?"

The only thing Rich knew for sure was that Saxon had a hot wife. He was pretty sure she was standing behind the camera. Then he remembered. "You were with those Miss Universe finalists, a blonde and a brunette. Both perfect 10s." It was out before he thought about it. "Don't you own that show?"

"I was and I did," smirked Saxon.

"You actually went home with the blonde. Miss Sweden, if I recall." Rich smiled at the memory. "I have to say, Mr. Saxon, that the work you do with that show, bringing the world together to discuss peace, allowing guys from all walks of life and nationalities to check out gorgeous women, well, it's inspiring to me. That's what makes America great."

Grace's jaw dropped and Gillian let out a loud snort. Only Jen's expression was unchanged. Saxon looked happy enough with the compliment. But Rich hadn't finished. "I'm not saying we have the best looking women in the world; obviously there's beautiful babes from all over. But you, well, you put them on TV and, to be honest with you, Miss America always looks like a winner to me!"

"Thanks Rich. I really appreciate that. America certainly is the greatest country in the world and I think there's a danger that people might forget how great we are."

"Not me," beamed Rich, relieved his spot was over.

Kristoff looked at Matt Lauer in shock and the anchor shook his head in amazement.

Saxon turned to Cameron. What do you think of the Chinese?"

"The food?"

"No Cameron. Not the noodles, I'm talking about trade and the ways the Chinese stack the odds so they can come over to America, steal all our business and then make their own tariffs so meteorically high that American businesses can't get a foothold into China's markets. Do you think that's fair?"

"I've actually been to China a bunch of times. My view is that yes, we do have to seek parity over tariffs with China, but if you start a trade war it is the American consumer that is going to be hurt. Let's not threaten another super power; that's not how the world is going to work in the future." Cameron was usually so flip, his serious frown surprised even his fellow contestants. He continued. "Let's initiate trade talks and see if we can work something out. The problem is that China has a huge, cheap workforce and we simply can't compete with their costs."

"The U.S. has to be strong, correct?" Saxon was insistent.

"Yes, but flexible. It's the only way."

Saxon was looking down at his notes. He no longer looked like he was enjoying himself. He'd been avoiding Grace. He had his own campaign to think about and had achieved too much and come too far to allow Grace to derail him. But he'd come to the last iCandidate. He couldn't avoid her any longer.

"Grace, how nice to meet to you. I've been very impressed by your work so far. Can I rely on your vote in November?" He hadn't meant to say the last bit. Something about the nonchalant way she was looking at him made him confrontational. It was the dealmaker in him; always deal from a position of strength. But it didn't work.

She held her ground.

"I'm afraid not, Mr. Saxon. Can I rely on yours tonight?"

"I'm afraid not yet, Miss Conwright. But you have a chance to change my mind. Grace, do you agree with me that a wall along the United States border with Mexico is urgently needed? The bigger and longer the better?" Saxon was trying to stare Grace down.

"No, I certainly do not." Grace stared back. "I think it's a terrible idea. I don't think it would be appropriate to turn a nation founded and settled by immigrants into a fortress."

Saxon had been down this road plenty of times before in the past few months. "Do you think it's okay for people to come illegally into our country and steal our jobs then?"

"To me, a wall covered in barbed wire is the kind of idea the Nazis would have come up with. We are a rich and diverse culture and we should continue to cultivate such a mix. Mexico isn't going to pay for a wall, and there isn't even a need for one. If you do your research you'll see illegal immigration hasn't been a major problem for years. Surely you can think of better ways to spend the country's money, Dennis?"

Saxon's complexion turned a pinker shade of orange, and for the first time, he looked angry, so much so that Grace instantly regretted the Nazi comparison. He was about to answer when Kristoff came from side stage and put out his hand.

"Thank you so much, Dennis, for being an amazingly good sport. We're going to have to wrap it up now or Matt is going to kill me. The news is coming up in a couple minutes but we have to go to commercials first.Thank you, Dennis and thank you, Matt and 'The Today Show.'"

He shook hands with the anchor and with Samantha Guthrie, who was also standing there, and turned back to the camera. "Thank you so much for watching this morning and I'll take this opportunity to invite everybody to tune into our next iVote show tomorrow night...

We'll round up tonight's Saxon Debate and get the verdicts from the man himself on each of our iCandidates; we'll get the judges' views and perhaps hear from a couple more special guests. Then it'll be time to iVote again." Kristoff let out a deep breath.

"Thanks Andy and that's it for us. From 'The Today Show,' here at the Rockefeller Center. This is Matt Lauer and all the team wishing you a great rest of your day."

20 BERT'S BACKING

A familiar face loomed on the large TV screen. "I am happy to give my endorsement to....The iCandidate." Bert Skyler smiled and the lens pulled back to show the Democrat presidential candidate standing on the reality show stage with Andy Kristoff. Behind them were the seven remaining contestants sitting in the brightly lit, mock Oval Office.

"We're delighted to have Bert Skyler in the studio. He's kindly taken time out of his busy schedule to pay us a visit." Kristoff put his arm around the older man's shoulders. "It's great to have you here, Senator."

"Delighted to take you up on your offer, Andy." His grueling campaign against Harriet Carson for the party nomination didn't seem to have taken a toll. He was upbeat and enthusiastic. "I have my own reasons for coming on this show."

He stepped forward and the camera once again framed his face. "We need a political revolution in this country. I've been say-ing this right from the start in my campaign and I believe it with all my heart. The young people know it; everybody outside Washing-ton knows it. It's the reason I am standing for the presidency. There's no time to waste." Skyler was giving the iCandidates a mas-ter class in politics. But he was deadly serious.

"I haven't had the time to grow my campaign the way I wanted to. At this point, it may well be that Secretary of State Carson wins the nomination, and that's fine, too. "But," he paused dramatically, "I believe that where I failed, The iCandidate may succeed. This show has the potential to shake up the tired election system in the United States. I'm not alone in thinking this; the President feels much the same. The iCandidate is not just a reality show. It may well have found the best way to elect all our politicians in the fu-ture, including the President!"

The audience had listened in rapt attention, not quite sure

whether this was a TV gimmick. But then, Kristoff stepped forward to join Skyler again, and the crowd erupted.

Everyone was on their feet, including the iCandidates, the judges, even the crew. They were starting to believe.

Skyler turned and entered the studio's 'Oval Office' to shake hands with the contestants while Kristoff calmed the audience.

"As you know, tonight is our second results show following last night's 'Saxon Debate' challenge. You can say what you like about 'The Dennis' but he's certainly a great sport. He put our iCandidates on the spot and now it's up to you, America, to decide how they did. You know the score; the finalist with the lowest number of votes in our unique online iVote will be on their way home tonight."

Kristoff walked over to the judges' panel. "Jacqueline, how do you think they did?"

"Good, really good. I like the way Todd stood his ground against Dennis, and Tom was just darling, as usual. But I'm not really sure what Rich was thinking...if anything. I mean if Dennis Saxon's best contribution to this country is providing good looking babes for guys to look at, then God help us all! Now if it were the other way around..."

"Kudos to Grace, too," chimed in Rob. "She wasn't intimidated in the least. That was the point of the challenge - to see how our iCandidates perform under pressure."

"Nonsense!" said Walter Penske. "The girl's a fool and she's turned off every Conservative in the nation."

"Isn't the whole point that our guys are apolitical? They don't have to be pigeonholed." Rob was sitting next to Penske, and they couldn't look more different. The rail-thin rocker with an untidy, shoulder-length mop, and the robin-breasted politician with a shock of white hair.

"Before you iVote, America," he said, "take a look at this video and see how Dennis rated our ICandidates."

The lights dimmed and this time it was Dennis Saxon's face that filled the screen.

"I think I did great tonight," he said. "But I've been asked by Andy Kristoff to rate how the iCandidates did answering my questions, so I can help America make up its mind in the vote. So here goes...Todd. I'm right here and you're wrong. A lot of Muslims hate the United States and that's why we need to keep them out until there's a more stable situation. But hey, you're a young guy, you'll learn and I like you, I really do. You have some good ideas. I'd certainly keep you around. I have to say, I'm surprised by how well Tom has done on this show. It's the truth. It's what I do. But he seems like a terrific gal and I'm pulling for him. I'm friends with all my ex-wives; marriage is a tough thing to get right even when you're doing it the traditional way. It may surprise you but I'm wishing Tom all the best. I'd give Jen a job tomorrow in the Saxon organization. I don't think I can speak more highly of her than that. As for Gillian, well she's delusional if she thinks she has what it takes to be president. This President has devastated the health system in this great country and she is trying to persuade us that he did us all a favor. No! It's just wrong and America agrees with me. In my humble opinion, Gillian should go. Rich Francombe is a legend. Period. I don't know how you folks managed to get him to run in this contest but you guys must be geniuses, too. Two Super Bowl rings. Legend. He's got my vote.

Cameron came across a little weedy to me. You have to be strong with a country like China. Let them know who's boss. Is Cameron tough enough? It's your call really. I say no. And so we come to the lovely Grace Conwright. I didn't know her late parents, but I do know that they were good people and my sympathies go to this young woman. She seems like a tough cookie and I can appreciate that. We don't necessarily see eye-to-eye but she's someone who has strong opinions and so do I. Perhaps she could think next time before she compares someone to a Nazi though… Good luck everyone—and by the way—the winner is invited to come visit me in the White House next January."

Back on stage, Kristoff was now surrounded by the iCandidates. Tension showed in all their faces.

"I'd like to thank Bert and Dennis. But now we have some more important business to handle. "It's time to iVote America. As Bert said earlier, we are spearheading a political revolution here, one iVote at a time." Kristoff moved out of the bright lights on the stage and moved into the audience, putting his hand on the shoulder of a viewer. "Open your app and cast your iVotes for your three top iCandidates this week. The one with the least iVotes will be going home. You have just one week to make your iVote count, so do it NOW!"

~~~~~~~

The lights went out, the closing credits rolled and Kristoff breathed a sigh of relief. It had gone well, he thought. He'd spent an entire day arguing with Desmond, Mase and Jacqueline over whether they should cross that fourth wall dividing their reality show with the real presidential campaign. Desmond and Jacqueline were against it; he and Mase were, for once, in agreement, and in the end Kristoff had insisted on the casting vote.

Desmond was heading his way now. His face was always hard to read. He was right next to Kristoff when his face cracked into an enormous smile and he wrapped him in a bear hug.

"You did it! You were right - that was fantastic! Now it's going to really be tough for the American people to separate fact from fiction. I hate to say it Andy, but you are exceptional at this...I've got a feeling we are going to break all the records with this next iVote."

21 THEN THERE WERE SIX

It all happened very quickly. Kristoff walked briskly onto the stage and after introducing the judges and all the contestants, he asked for the lights to be dimmed. "America, we may be a young country but our history is stamped across our landscape and we are so proud of what we have achieved in our relatively young life." He'd worked with the writers on this little speech; he was rather proud of it. "We've faced tragedies, and we have mourned. We have celebrated countless triumphs; we are not ashamed to idolize our heroes. And no-one knows how to throw a party quite like America!" The crowd clapped, whooped and cheered their approval. "This is why tonight is so interesting."

The lights turned even lower, leaving just one tight light on Kristoff's face. "We have taken a serious topic - politics - put it in a reality show setting, and asked you, America, to take your job seriously. We are asking you to pioneer a revolution that may stand alongside some of the great leaps that have made this nation what it is today. Pick your heroes, yes, but do it with careful thought. Be entertained, yes, but listen to your moral conscience. It's time for us to show those people across the country in D.C. how things should be done. We love our heroes, we cheer them on, and we want them to succeed! We love our traditions, we love entertainment, movies, music, and we love sports. Baseball, hockey and football, of course…yes, we love our legends…Richard Francombe is one them and we love him." There was no sound in the studio as the lights went on again. "Rich, please join me."

Rich stood slowly to his feet from one of the ornate couches in the studio's Oval Office, set up at the back of the stage. He got to Kristoff in three giant strides, and then the two men shared an embrace. The quarterback's face relaxed a little; he allowed himself a smile.

"As you all know," said Kristoff, "in the last challenge, Dennis

Saxon put our contestants the spot, covering topics like the health-care system, immigration, and trade with China.

Rich and Dennis discussed the Miss Universe pageant. It was light, it was entertaining, and it spoke volumes."

Rich looked uneasy again. His agent had given him hell after the show for talking about hot women, but Rich figured presidents could appreciate beauty, particularly if she were single.

"America has cast their iVote, Rich, and they love you..."

The sportsman turned to embrace Kristoff again but the presenter was still talking to the camera. "The American people have made it clear they're taking this competition very seriously," he continued. "We love our legends, yes we do! We want a leader who inspires us, yes we do! And we want a leader who is in tune with our beliefs, our dreams. The public's voice sounded as one when they voted, and it was extremely clear...

"The people love you, Rich, but on the football field, not in the White House. "Rich, I'm afraid you're leaving us tonight."

22: HOMESICK

By the time Emily arrived in Cambridge, Massachusetts, she was beginning to relax. Her trip to the west coast - whistle stop visits to see students in Stanford, Berkeley and UCLA - was over now, the home stretch in sight. Harvard was the second to last stop on her itinerary of schools where the non-profit organization that Emily worked for placed students on one-year exchange programs. It hadn't been as bad as Emily feared being back in the U.S. The kids were bright, clever, and most seemed to be thriving in their privileged surroundings.

Emily made sure she focused all her energies on making them feel as comfortable as possible, and suppressed any unhappy memories that stirred inside her. The small things hurt most; couples holding hands, moms pushing strollers. But that pain was no different than what she felt back home in the Netherlands. Emily had two students at Harvard, one from Russia, the other from Somalia. She would check on them before flying to New York, her last stop, and then home. As much as she was dreading being back there, a part of her hoped it would be cathartic; she would face the memories that still haunted her. Perhaps she could finally lay them to rest.

Walking towards the Widener Library for her meeting, she took a deep breath, immersing her senses in the history of her surroundings.

A student in a Harvard sweatshirt gave her the once over as he walked past. Emily picked up her credentials at reception and was escorted to a small seminar room on the top floor; the students were waiting to meet her. She settled into a chair by a bay window where two small, sad-looking girls sat silently on a sofa. Unlike the other students she'd seen, they didn't look happy at all.

"I'd love to hear how you are settling into Harvard, and about some of your experiences so far at the school." Emily smiled at the girls, trying to put them at ease. It was hard work getting them to speak, but one of the girls, Alma, said she was settling in and had begun to make new friends.

"It's just been me and Alina up to now," Alma said in a soft, indiscernible voice. "But now Alina wants to go home, so I figure I need to make some new friends."

Alina kept staring out of the window, across to the South Gate.

"Is that right, Alina? You want to go home."

"Yes."

"But you've been here less than a month. Wouldn't you like to give it a little longer?

"No."

"I have something for you." Emily rifled through her bag. "I was just at UCLA where your friend Maria is studying. She asked me to say hi and give you this." Emily handed Alina a white button emblazoned with the words "iVoted The iCandidate" and a program of the show. "Maria thought you'd like the button. She said you were interested in politics and she took notes about all the contestants in the TV show."

Alina said nothing. She didn't turn from the window. Emily tried again, keeping her voice light and casual. "She's settling in really well…"

"Thank you," Alina said flatly.

Try as she might, Emily couldn't get more than one word answers from the sad girl. Her eyes remained locked on the garden below. Emily had dealt with homesickness cases before. Sometimes a student just wasn't ready to be so far from home.

"I'll make some enquiries and let you know later today how soon we can fly you home to Moscow. Is that okay?"

Alina barely registered what Emily was saying but nodded her assent.

Emily's own flight to New York was in a couple of days. Now it looked like she would have to stay until Alina's arrangements were sorted out. She couldn't leave her here like this.

"Can we talk some more, Alina? I can come by your dorm this afternoon."

Alina's mind was far away. She was back in the garment factory in Moscow, sewing with her mom and her sisters. Perhaps that was all she was good for.

23 WORLDS APART

Moscow, Russia: (Two months earlier)

Alina sat perched on a steel chair opposite her mother. The clattering of the giant sewing machines made any conversation almost impossible. As she grew older, Alina's fingers grew nimbler; she was faster now than she was as a child. She was first wrestled from her sleep before dawn to start work at the sewing factory in Moscow's West Biryulyovo neighborhood when she was just 12. Even now she could recall the choking pollution.

Everyday before school, Alina would sew shirts until her fingers were raw. Only when she went to college was she forgiven the chore, and only because her baby sister was old enough to take her place and help towards the meager family finances. In her three years at Lomonosov Moscow State University, Alina had come home every night to help her mother cook and clean the house and look after her younger siblings. She was the first woman in her neighborhood to graduate high school, the first to go to university. At 25, Alina knew her mother hoped her eldest daughter would get married and stay home for good when her studies were done.

Now Alina sat across from her mother in the half-light wondering how to tell her she wanted a different life. Every time she tried to talk about the future her mother made some excuse. Here, at least in the familiar gloom of the concrete, windowless room in the gloomy factory, there was no escape.

"It's not that I'm not grateful," she said, leaning forwards to make herself heard above the noisy machines. "But there's this amazing opportunity I have to tell you about."

The older woman, her graying hair tied tightly back off her deeply lined face didn't look up as Alina stumbled on. "I've got a scholarship to study in America. At Harvard."

The only sign that her mother had heard her, was a momentary pause before she reached for another shirt. "It's for a year, just one year, for my Masters." Alina kept talking, desperately trying to fill the silence. "Everything would be paid for by this non-profit; it's like an exchange program. I get to go to the United States to study and an American kid comes here."

Still nothing from the old woman.

"Harvard is one of the world's top universities. It's Ivy League."

Her mother couldn't even read the bus number. The only way she knew which one to take was because the driver was her brother. She wouldn't know anything about Ivy League.

"I have to go. Mom, I have to."

Alina's voice fell away and she put her hands up to her face, drowning her senses with her childhood. Her lips quivered and hot tears streamed down her cheeks; and still, her mother said nothing, toiling away over her sewing.

"I have to go." Alina meant she couldn't sit there any longer and got up. But she meant what she said. She was leaving whatever. "I'll get a job there too and send money back, I promise," she said, looking back over her shoulder as she slowly walked away.

24 - FIELD TRIP

The only thing The iCandidate contestants were told when they boarded the plane was that they were being taken to a military air base. The location was top secret, but the hours spent on the plane gave them the impression they were no longer in the United States. Kristoff made them leave their watches and cellphones behind to add to their sense of disorientation.

They landed in a bleak landscape with desert as far as the eye could see. There was a cluster of tents and outbuildings around two or three big hangars and a control tower. Three officers came up and saluted without introducing themselves.

"Each team will go with one of the Army officers," Desmond announced.

"Can I ask where we are?" Cameron turned to the soldiers. "It doesn't look like the Caribbean."

"You are in Kurdish-controlled Northern Syria," one of the soldiers said. "On behalf of the 101st Airborne Division, I am happy to welcome the iCandidates to Qamishli."

"Jesus," Grace said. "I guess this is getting serious. How safe is it here? Just asking..."

"It should be perfectly safe, particularly as the gate guard has been doubled tonight for our important guests."

"Who are they?" Cameron asked.

"You are, my friend. All of you," said Desmond, "which is all the more reason for us to be careful. Just keep your heads down."

Gillian lagged behind and Grace fell back, she could tell something wasn't right.

"You okay?"

"I will be in a second. Just looking for something."

Gillian had her head in her bag, obviously fighting back tears.

"Here, have a drink."

She took a sip of water and handed the bottle back to Grace.

"I don't know if I can do this." Her hands were shaking.

"You can do this, Gillian. But you're going to have to give me a clue here so I can help."

Desmond was looking back wondering what was going on as he waited to brief them all for the challenge. Grace held up a hand to gesture they would just be a second.

"What is it, Gillian?" Grace tried again. "It's just a bit of a shock – being at a military camp over here."

"Why?" Grace's voice was gentle.

"Because, Neil, Clara's dad, was deployed in Syria and… well…he never made it home. He was my husband, my best friend, the love of my life."

"Oh, Gillian, I am so sorry." Grace moved to hug her but Gillian shook her head.

"No, not here. I need to hold it together. I'm okay, really. Thank you, Grace."

Before they could say anything else, Desmond put them in teams and sent them off with their guides.

"You'll be told what to do," he said.

They had to almost run to keep up with the soldiers and were led to three separate tents in a corner of the camp that was surprisingly quiet considering the number of troops.

25 HURTING

A sharp wind blew across campus as Emily headed towards Alina's dorm building. The student's mood had rubbed off on her and she found herself thinking about the misery of those last few days in New York, a lifetime ago. All she had wanted to do then was get home, and she recognized the same look now in Alina's dull eyes. She was about to open the door to the residence hall when she spotted Alina across the quad, sitting on a bench by the South Gate. If anything, she looked smaller and more broken than she had that morning.

"Well, hello. Do you mind if I join you?" It wasn't until Emily was sitting down that she noticed Alina was crying. She instinctively put her arms around the sobbing girl and pulled her in. "I know it's hard being so far from your family," she said. "But you're safe here. You really are. I'm here for you."

Alina sobbed into Emily's chest. "I'm so sorry," she said, gasping. "I don't know what's happened to me." It was the first time Emily had heard her speak and she was surprised by how good Alina's English was. "Something happened and it really hurt me. I haven't been able to hold it together since. I don't understand why."

"Did someone hurt you?" Emily was shocked. This would explain everything.

"Nothing like that. But there is a boy. Well, a man…"

26 HARVARD

Back home, Alina had defied the hard looks she got from women who criticized her for wanting to get away and make a better life for herself. She considered herself a good daughter, but she refused to accept she would be trapped for the rest of her life on the circle of poverty that had worn down her mother.

Yet everything was so alien here: from the snow, piled high on the Cambridge sidewalk, to the gurgling warmth of her centrally-heated dorm room, to the lovers idling together in the quad.

She'd been roomed with an equally timid girl from Somalia named Alma, who had won a similar scholarship. Neither left their room the first week, other than for class or food. But an invite to an alumni reception, welcoming them to Harvard, appeared to demand their attendance at Loeb House on Quincy. They decided to go together, but when it came time to go, Alma wouldn't get out of bed, and Alina had to go alone. She figured she would show her face and her gratitude, then bolt back to her room.

Alina was already regretting her decision when she walked in and received a sticky nameplate on her sweater and a plate of canapés shoved in her face. Feeling invisible, she slowly weaved through the noisy crowd, and headed to the open window at the back of the room. Dappled twilight played through an oak tree outside, it helped calm her and she opened the window wider to get some more air. That's when she noticed him. He was tall with a kind face, and looked vaguely familiar as he listened patiently to a small group of students. She thought he was one of the younger lecturers. He scribbled something on a book and handed it back to one of the young men. She saw his eyes drawn to the same window.

He wants to escape too, she thought.

Looking away, she went back to battling with the canapé. When she tried to break off a piece of the dry pastry it exploded all over her clothes and onto the floor.

"Oh, no!" Alina glanced across to see the man grinning at her. "Having trouble?"

"We don't have food like this back home." She blushed.

"Probably because your country is much smarter than ours." Roman wasn't sure which country the girl was from. All he could see were her eyes. She spoke perfect English. "Here, let me help." He gently took the soggy remains from her hand. He picked up a napkin and took her wrist, discreetly wiping a blob of prawn sauce from her finger.

"Thank you, for helping," she stammered. His brown eyes were close to hers, much closer than she was comfortable with. She could smell a hint of lemon. It reminded her of home.

"You have the most beautiful eyes." He was still holding her hand.

Someone coughed politely beside them. "How are you doing, Alina Dzorovetski?" An older man with thick swept-back black hair was holding out his hand. She wondered how he knew her name. The busy room came rushing back, an assault of loud voices and laughter surrounded her once more. She realized he was reading her name tag.

"Err, I'm fine, thank you," she managed.

"You must be one of our wonderful scholarship students."

Vladimir was looking at her expectantly. He'd backed her into a lamp in the corner of the room. "Where are you from? Moscow? St Petersburg? Omsk perhaps" He moved even closer.

"Moscow."

Panicking, she looked in vain for his name badge. "I'm sorry I don't know your name."

"Is he bothering you?" Roman cut in. He was wearing a suit; his short, blonde hair was ruffled and unkempt. "I can call security."

Alina wasn't sure if he was joking. He didn't have a badge either.

Vladimir just smiled. "I was just asking where Alina was from."

"And what did she tell you?" asked Roman, smiling.

"I'm from Moscow." Alina looked nervously from one man to the other. People in America didn't usually know what to say when she said she came from Russia. Every introduction felt like a TSA inspection.

Alina noticed that other guests were trying to catch the attention of the younger man.

"Why are they all staring at you?" Alina asked.

"You're wrong," he whispered in her ear. "They're looking at you."

"Most of the alumni at this reception help fund the international scholarships to bring disadvantaged students to Harvard," Vladimir, the older man, said. "We both went to college here, he was an undergrad, I did my Masters."

"That is truly wonderful. I am so grateful for this opportunity."

"It's the one event we try and turn up to. It's our way of giving back. My foundation helped bring two boys over from Russia. They're from the Moscow area, as well. Their names are Ivan and Boris. Good boys. I'm sure you must have seen them around the college."

Alina had seen them. They were on the same flights over from Russia, but she hadn't talked to them.

"Welcome to Harvard, Alina." Vladimir excused himself and was now talking to the two Russian boys from her flight. They looked pretty awkward and out of place, too.

Alina stood by the window and felt more at ease than she had since arriving at Boston's Logan International airport, just a week earlier.

Roman left her to give a speech. She sensed the two men were Harvard celebrities, but nobody ever mentioned why. He came back afterwards and wished her well. "If there is anything I can do for you while you're here, please call me any time."

They had to go, he told her. Roman wrote his name and number on a restaurant check he fished from the pocket of his jacket and handed Alina the paper. "If you need anything - even if you just want to be rescued from the madness here - give me a call."

Alina took the paper and thanked him. Having finally found her voice she asked Roman,

"And who's going to rescue you?"

"Whatever makes you think I need rescuing?" He couldn't tell what she was thinking behind her blue eyes. As beautiful as they were, they gave little away.

"Just a feeling... I saw you looking out of the window."

Someone touched Roman's shoulder. They had to go, they were late, said an assistant.

"Call me please," he said as he was pulled away. Then he looked back over his shoulder smiling: "I need you to rescue me.

27 TORURE

After the iCandidates were split into groups of two, a gruff sergeant ordered Jen and Todd to follow him. He marched ahead towards a huddle of four Army tents, barking at them to hurry. Almost running to keep up, they were shown into the first tent and found Walter Penske sitting behind a desk.

"Well, what a surprise," Jen tried to sound excited at seeing the old man.

Todd rushed forward and shook Walter's hand enthusiastically. "What an honor. I was just telling Jennifer how great it would be to get the opportunity to talk to you some more and benefit from your amazing experience."

Walter brightened a little. "Well, thank you, Todd. We can absolutely do that later, but it's my job right now to introduce you to the person who's going to explain your next challenge, Lieutenant Kyle Kelly." The officer entered through a flap in the back of the tent and behind him were three soldiers dragging a bearded man, who was tied at the hands and feet.

"We have a dilemma. We are absolutely convinced that this man knows the precise whereabouts of the Islamic State leadership in Syria." Lt. Kelly pointed at the downcast man now sitting on a chair in the middle of the tent. "The problem is that he won't tell us anything. We've been trying for two days and during that time we haven't allowed him to sleep. He's still not cooperating. We're running out of time. The terrorists know we have one of their top men. We need to get this man to talk. Do you give us permission to use harsh interrogation methods?"

"How harsh exactly?" Jen asked.

"Legitimate interrogation methods have failed. We want to waterboard him," the Lieutenant said.

"But isn't that illegal? It's been banned by the Geneva Convention."

"Lives are at stake."

"So is America's reputation." Jen was worried about the prisoner. He looked terrified.

"It's only as illegal as the President wants it to be. It depends on your priorities, I guess."

"And what priorities are they?" Todd asked.

"Well you can keep the liberals in Washington happy by using feather dusters to tickle the information out of ISIS, or al Qaeda, or whoever you're fighting. Or you can give us a very real chance to kill off these terror groups once and for all. It's your choice."

Todd's phone vibrated and he discreetly checked the message. "I don't see that there is a choice at all," Todd said. "This could save thousands, or even millions of American lives.."

"Shouldn't we discuss it first? We're supposed to be a team," Jen was insistent. "There's international law to consider."

"I am considering it – but we have to keep Americans safe. I have no doubts."

"I need a majority vote," Lt. Kelly said.

"But there are only two of us." Todd didn't want to waste any more time.

"Mr. Penske, he has a vote, too. And one more thing, if you give us the go ahead, we're going to do the waterboarding right here in front of you. Perhaps you should bear that in mind when you vote," the officer said stiffly.

"Let's do it." Todd was certain the old man would be in agreement. "If Jennifer doesn't have the stomach for it, perhaps she can leave the room. Mr. Penske, what do you think?"

"My feeling is the same as it was when I was Vice President and the CIA had some people in Cairo they wanted to extract information from by force. I told them that it was wrong and that they couldn't do it. That was my advice to the President then and it's the same to you now."

Todd looked stunned. "But..."

"I also made it known to the Station Chief over there that he made an error in asking permission from the White House. Of course we had to say no because we would be crucified if it came out that a Democratic administration was effectively torturing prisoners. But if we didn't know about it, there wouldn't really have been a problem, now would there?"

"But that hardly helps us now, does it?" Todd said curtly. "Jennifer, I guess it's down to you."

She shook her head. "I can't agree to it. I'm sorry."

"Look, I don't necessarily agree with much Dennis Saxon says, but he's right on waterboarding." Todd was getting desperate.

"Oh! Saxon says it's okay, so we're fine."

"He's winning the GOP nomination at this point. The American people like what they're hearing. He says ISIS are going around chopping off people's heads and doing mass drownings in cages and we're saying we can't waterboard. Look, we're not killing anybody. It's just water. This is ridiculous - I'm pretty sure we will be voted off if we don't step up." Todd sounded really worried.

"You don't know that. Americans believe in fair treatment."

"We also believe in making tough decisions when we have to. Evil won on 9/11 – we can't let that happen again. I'm begging you, Jennifer."

Jen looked from Todd to the prisoner. She hated to be rushed.

"I'm going to have to ask you for a decision ma'am," the officer said.

"Dammit! Okay, but do we have to see it?"

"I am afraid that's part of the deal," Lt. Kelly told them.

The prisoner, who had been staring balefully at the ground until then, suddenly looked up. "I am just a local merchant," he said in broken English. "I have nothing to do with terrorism. There has been a terrible mistake. I came across from Tunisia to bring food and grain. I have children, a wife. Please don't hurt me!"

Any further appeals were silenced as one of the soldiers cuffed the prisoner across the head. Jen looked rattled.

"I think you should start," Todd gave the order.

"If you're sure?" Lt. Kelly looked at Jen.

"She's sure," said Todd.

The soldiers picked up the prisoner and put him on the desk, which wasn't a desk at all, but a reclining board. The guards tied the man down using three straps and draped a towel over his face before setting the bed so that his feet were raised. One guard leaned down to pick up a hose and turned on the tap.

As the water started pouring onto his head, the man began convulsing and spluttering. Jen couldn't bear it any longer. "Stop. This isn't right."

"They can't stop now," Todd sounded frustrated.

"We must," Lt. Kelly said. "If anyone of you asks us to stop at any time then that's what we must do. Are you sure?"

Jen nodded. "I'm sorry Todd, but this is torture."

The board with the man still bound on it was wheeled right out of the tent and the soldiers departed.

Todd turned to Jen. "Why did you stop it? America doesn't want to see weak, easily spooked leaders. They wants us to show strength and they wants results. I can't believe that just happened."

"It didn't feel right to me. We don't even know if that guy knew anything."

"I guess we're never going to find out now." Todd looked furious.

Jennifer exited the tent, relieved to leave the confined space and all its horrors. Taking a deep breath of fresh air she found a place to sit down, and a few soldiers sauntered over to talk. She started to feel better.

28 FIRST DATE

Roman hadn't expected Alina to call and was surprised at how nervous he felt as he walked through Harvard Square. He had a couple of days off so he'd booked a cross-country flight just to see her – not that he'd tell her that.

Alina was waiting in the relative calm inside the campus gates looking out like a caged bird. She was having second thoughts. Whatever possessed her to call this man? He was a complete stranger. Her mother would have a heart attack if she knew her daughter had behaved so brazenly.

Standing up from the bench, she was about to flee back to the safety of her dorm when she saw him walking towards her. He was dressed in a blue Nike jacket and jeans, and it struck her again how he looked a little like some of the younger professors she saw around campus, only he really was much better looking!

He walked like he hadn't a care in the world. Roman stopped in front of the wrought iron gates, looking at her through the black bars. He'd seen her start to walk away.

"So, I just posted bail; we won't need to break you out of here after all." His lips were turned up in the beginnings of a smile. "You're free to leave," he said more gently.

And then she smiled, too. He didn't look dangerous. Her mother still wouldn't have approved. Now she remembered; he had a kind face. Taking a deep breath she stepped outside the gates and onto the pavement beyond. "Hello," she said shyly.

She was just as intriguing as he remembered. She had a way of holding her head forward and looking up at him, seeking his eyes in a way few American girls ever would.

For a moment, neither knew what to say. In the end, it was Roman who broke the silence.

"So where are the hotspots in this little town of yours?"

She looked blankly at him. Perhaps he hadn't really seen her at all. "Favorite restaurant or cafe?"

"I don't have one," she answered quietly.

"Okay, well where do you go when…" And then it dawned on him. "Have you been out in Boston since you've been here? She shook her head. "Have you been out in Cambridge?"

Another small shake of the head. "I'm quite happy in there," she said, looking back at the campus.

He was about to make another joke but stopped himself. This was a big deal for her. "Alright then, well, as it happens, I have a favorite place from my days at school here. How about a walk first?"

"Okay," she nodded, relieved.

They walked through the leafy streets, passing restaurants and boutiques, making small talk, before rounding a corner into a cobbled courtyard. Alina stayed close to the buildings. She seemed to glide, he noticed, her posture so straight and perfect. Yet she kept her arms folded in front of her, guarded; she was protecting herself.

"Do you like hot chocolate?"

"Not really. I tried it for the first time from the vending machine on campus the other day." She grimaced.

"That doesn't count. Come on, in here." He opened the door to the rich aroma of melting chocolate. "I used to live in this place when I studied here. They have the best hand made truffles, but my favorite is their hot chocolate. You have to try one."

Roman led Alina to a small table in a pretty alcove at the back of the shop. She chose the corner seat and gratefully slid into it, pushing her chair even further back, as if to melt into the wall. "I'll be right back. Don't disappear on me now."

She watched as he walked to the bar and ordered their drinks. He joked easily with the cashier who laughed and fluttered her eyelashes at him, yet he seemed oblivious to her flirting. Alina liked that. With his back to her, she noticed his hair curled at the nape of his neck. Then he turned around and smiled at her from across the shop. That's when she felt something move deep inside.

"Try it, tell me what you think," he said, placing a white bowl in front of her filled with thick dark chocolate, a heart carved into the swirly cream on top. "Is it too hot?"

She blew carefully onto her cup and took her first sip. Her eyes widened. "It's good," she whispered. "Very good."

They spoke of their families and growing up, her in Russia and him in America. "I would not have guessed you were Russian, you look like you're from California," she said.

"Well my mother was European, and my father is from St. Petersburg."

"But you were born here? Went to school here?"

"Yep. I pledged my allegiance to the United States of America every day in school."

"You really are all American," she smiled.

He noticed she sat very still in her seat, her eyes occasionally flitting around the cafe, taking in the boisterous exchanges between friends and families as they slouched happily on couches, leaning across tables to grab sugar, or a crumpled magazine.

She began to feel more comfortable, and for the first time, almost at home in her new surroundings.

"I wouldn't say all American. I may not have grown up in Russia, but my father and grandmother never let me forget who I am and where I come from." Roman wanted Alina to understand that he was, first and foremost, a Russian.

"My father's very involved in improving relations with Russia and America. That's why he's involved in sponsoring students, like those two boys. That's my father's dream, his life's work. A story for another time though." Roman paused. He didn't want to bore her. "Tell me why you came here."

"I didn't want to work in a factory for the rest of my life."

"It's hard for me to imagine you ever working in a place like that." He reached across the table for her hand..

"Why are you staring?"

"Oh, I'm sorry." He looked taken aback. "I didn't realize I was."

She glanced down, her long lashes grazing her cheeks.

"Would you like another hot chocolate, Alina?" he asked gently.

"If it's not too much trouble, I would like that," she smiled.

Much later, alone in his hotel room, and after walking her back to campus, Roman stood by the window. He could see the tower at Harvard, and the tip of the west building. He knew she was somewhere inside one of those rooms, and he tried to imagine what she was doing.

29 BOUNDARIES

In another Army tent, a similar scenario played out in front of two more iCandidates.

But Jacqueline Toscane told Gillian and Tom that she didn't harbor any doubts. "These people are avowed enemies of the United States. Do you think they'd be worried about political correctness if the roles were reversed? Waterboard him, deprive him of sleep, force him to listen to rap music for 24-hours...do what you need to do to get the terrorist to tell us where the ISIS butchers are hiding. We catch them and we could end all the bloodshed. To decide anything else, in my opinion, could be fatal for your hopes in this contest."

Gillian, still feeling shaky, had no doubts either. "Thank you, Jacqueline, but there's no way I'm going to agree to this kind of barbaric behavior. We aren't terrorists, we're Americans. If there are no boundaries then we're all down there in the jungle, fighting it out. I lost my husband over here and the thought of him being tortured is abhorrent to me. If I say yes, then that's just the same as endorsing the Taliban to do the same to my husband. So my answer is a very definite no." Gillian sounded strong, but she was struggling to hold it together.

Tom squeezed her hand and nodded his agreement. "I cry like a baby when I get my back waxed; I wouldn't stand two seconds of water torture. I'd be giving up any hiding place faster than you can say Aleppo, whether I knew it or not. I totally understand what Jacqueline said and I get that a leader must sometimes make tough decisions for the greater good. If I could be sure this gentleman wouldn't be somehow scarred by what you want to do to him I would think it worth giving it a go."

Tom looked across at the humble Tunisian, head bowed and dressed in the traditional white Jebba with Sirouel pants and a silk sash around his waist. He lowered his voice: "I once had to ban the city treasurer from Rayville's candy store because he kept trying to pretend his gangrenous leg had nothing to do with his diabetes, so I know what it's like to be unpopular in power. But I can't help wondering what would happen if this man really doesn't have a clue about Islamic State's leadership. Do you just keep waterboarding him until he drowns?" Tom's mind was made up. "For that reason, although I am a little conflicted, I'm going to agree with Gillian and say no."

The soldiers withdrew and Jacqueline, disappointed that her advice was ignored, snipped: "Good luck with the results show. I won't be holding my breath."

30 GOING FOR IT

In the third Army tent, Grace was busy surprising Cameron. He considered his politics neither left nor right, but practical. Until the previous presidential election he hadn't even bothered to vote. But as soon as the challenge was explained to them he expected trouble, because in his eyes Grace was a trendy lefty in every sense. Peace and love and big government and to hell with the budget deficit. He prepared himself for a head on collision that would leave both their chances mortally wounded. Then she started talking.

"What kind of assurances do we have that this man knows where our targets are?" she asked the officer, a Lieutenant Colin Ellis.

"We have three different sources saying that he just came from there. He was almost certainly with the terrorists two days ago."

"He says he's married and a local merchant. Is that true?"

"If he has a wife and children, he hasn't seen them for years. Our information says he has been recruiting al Qaeda fighters and shipping them over to fight in Syria with ISIS."

"In that case, I say we should go ahead with the water boarding," Grace declared.

"Go ahead with it?" Cameron looked at Grace in disbelief. "Did I hear right?"

"That's what I said, didn't I?"

"Yes, but..."

"But what?"

"But I thought you were going to say no."

"Why would you think that?"

"Because you're a bleeding heart socialist. Or at least that's what I thought."

The prisoner stared at the floor, occasionally looking up at Grace and Cameron with mournful eyes."

"You thought wrong. I try my best to make the right decision. Not right or left, just right."

"Good. I think you've made the correct decision here.. We have to try everything possible."

"Well, Hallelujah! So glad I have your approval."

Cameron could not understand this woman at all. "Perhaps we should stick you on the waterboard table. See how long it takes for you to shake off that attitude."

Grace ignored him. "What about you, Rob?" Grace asked Rob Balfour, the assigned judge to their team. "It looks like we're doing it anyway."

"I am your bleeding heart liberal, guys. I'm 100 percent against invading anyone's personal freedoms using torture, whatever the reason...you start saying this is okay and where does it end? Do you start putting people on the rack? Chopping off their fingers? Putting electrodes on their packages? No, man. It's not cool with me, but it's your call. I guess I'm outnumbered."

The soldiers went ahead with the drowning procedure, but when Grace and Cameron's resolve showed no sign of breaking after several minutes, they allowed the prisoner to sit up and show them the breathing tube he had in his mouth to avoid the full effect of the treatment.

"Oh, thank God," Grace finally took a breath, glancing at Cameron.

Cameron felt the relief wash over him too. Although he had been pretty sure it was just a test, in those last seconds, he was beginning to wonder. "You're badass, Conwright."

31 TWENTY-NINE PALMS

Cameron and Grace were led into another larger tent where they joined the other four contestants and the Army officers. As it turned out, none of them were soldiers. "We all work on stunts at Warner Brothers," said the man who introduced himself as Lt. Ellis. "It's just Colin Ellis, actually. Perhaps we can start up a sideline in water boarding. We could do it on the politicians to make sure they tell us the truth."

"Great idea," Tom said. "Which reminds me of a joke. Why do politicians envy ventriloquists?

"Because they can lie without moving their lips."

The actors and soldiers laughed simultaneously; then the group walked out of the tent to find the whole area besieged with real servicemen and women. Word got out quickly that The iCandidate contestants were at the base even though the visit had been shrouded in secrecy. They signed autographs in a sea of camouflage fatigues as hundreds of servicemen and women joined the fray, taking photographs and asking the iCandidates to scribble their names on every conceivable surface.

"It's pretty warm but I really thought it would be hotter than this," Grace remarked to one of the Marines. He started to laugh. "What's so funny," she asked.

"You do realize that you're not actually overseas, don't you?"

Grace just looked at him quizzically, wondering why on earth this man would say something so ridiculous.

"You're at Twenty-Nine Palms Marine base in the middle of the Mojave Desert, about 130 miles from L.A."

Grace was stunned. Had the Marine suffered a breakdown? "No, you see, that's not possible," she smiled. "We were in the air forever. How long would you say, Tom? Eleven hours?"

"At least." Tom answered.

"Well ma'am, I'm afraid you were duped. Most of your flight

time was simulated to get you disorientated, and make you believe we were over there."

Gillian couldn't believe her ears.

Cameron laughed. "There's no way that happened. Where are we, really?"

The Marine just shrugged and walked away.

With his secret out, Desmond explained: "We needed you to believe in the authenticity of the challenge. Water boarding in Palm Springs doesn't quite have the same ring, does it now?"

32 OUT FOR BLOOD

It still took a while for Desmond to convince the iCandidates they weren't in a war zone before they were whisked back to L.A. in limos. In the end, he showed them an app on his iPhone that pinpointed the nearest coffee shop. It was a Starbucks.

Safely away from the others, back at the White House, Gillian started to cry; Grace hugged her before gently wiping away the tears. "The producers know my husband died over there Grace, how could they do this?"

"Gillian, I'm sure they didn't even think when they set up the challenge. But even if they did, you have to show them what you're made of; that you can do anything, even put your grief aside. They are expecting us to be more weak and vulnerable than the men. But we're strong. You're a leader, and don't you forget it."

Gillian thought for a moment. "You're right. Annoying as hell, but right."

Grace smiled. "That's my girl. Why don't we head down to the bar so you and I can go and do what any normal man would do after a day like today…"

"Have a beer?"

"Don't be such a wimp. We'll have ourselves some whiskey!"

****

Back in her room, Jen was grateful to be alone. Just for once she'd started something she couldn't control. The texts were flashing up every couple of minutes. It was insane. First things first, she had to nix the affair.

She lit a candle, ran a bubble bath and was just lowering herself in when there was a knock on her door. She ignored it. Five minutes later her phone beeped.

'I'm outside, let me in???'

'I'm in the bath.'

'I'll join you?'

'Not tonight'

'Why?'

'I need to save my energy for the competition.'

Later that evening, as Jen was getting into bed, the texts resumed:

'Let me come over? ...Please Jennifer, I want you so bad! ! Don't play hard to get ...Why aren't you answering? ...That's it, I'm coming over.'

Exasperated, Jen jabbed at the buttons.

'Please understand that NO actually means NO!'

There was no response. "Thank God," she said out loud, turning her bedside light out.

She awoke with the bright sunlight streaming through her windows and another slew of ever more aggressive texts.

'You know that we're great together.'

She had breakfast in her room but still her phone flashed over and over again.

'Tonight. Let's talk...Jennifer?'

Hadn't she made it crystal clear? She texted back. 'No thx...it's over by the way.'

But it wasn't. The texts continued all evening and the next day, each threatening to expose her racy behavior or intimate details from her professional life: client names, people she worked with, restaurants and bars she frequented. He knew where she shopped, where she had her hair styled.

Where was he getting all this information? Then it hit her. He was stalking her, obsessively digging up every little thing about her until she got the text she knew was going to come.

'We have 2 talk otherwise'... He was playing with her. She opened the text with dread:

'I'll tell them your little secret...u r married' She knew what was next... 'to a girl!'

With a sickening jolt, she realized she had picked the wrong man to mess with.

He was out for blood.

33 BAD TIMING

Vladimir studied Roman as he walked towards him across the parking lot at Los Angeles International Airport. For the millionth time Vladimir thought it incredible how much his son looked like his mother. It wasn't so much a physical resemblance, although the similarities were there. Roman had her casual smile; the same full lips and cheekbones. What always struck Vladimir was the way Roman moved, his body loose and fluid; so different from his own stiff and formal gait.

"Hello, my son, you look well." Vladimir reached out for a handshake. They were traveling in different directions but Vladimir wanted to see Roman, even if it was just a few stolen hours between flights. They were both so busy with their careers they rarely had time to talk these days.

"I always worry about you, growing up in this country, that you will forget what is important."

Vladimir didn't want to waste precious time with small talk. "Everything is good?"

There hadn't been a single conversation with his father that Roman could remember when he hadn't been reminded of what was expected of him. "Have I ever given you any reason to doubt me father? Everything is going to plan."

As happy as Roman was to check in with Vladimir, he had a plane to catch. He had a date with Alina and he didn't want to be late.

"No, of course not, Roman, but there are things we must discuss." Roman's heart sank.

Vladimir had rearranged his schedule so they would have a little longer together. "I've spoken to your assistant and put you on a later flight. I have a room booked for the evening for us at the Marriott, just a couple of minutes away. My car is waiting."

Roman couldn't tell Vladimir about Alina. Not yet. All he could think about as his father talked and the minutes ticked away was that he had no way of contacting Alina to let her know he wouldn't be there. She had no phone and there was no answer at the residential hall number.

After so many years devoted to his work and his father, Roman finally had something for himself. Now she was probably lost to him.

34 JILTED

It was very different this time. Alina sat on the same bench by the same black gates, looking in the same direction down the street, and suddenly everything on the outside seemed full of possibilities; Harvard's campus paled in comparison. She hadn't dared to go out alone since her date with Roman; she was comforted now only because she knew she would soon see him. They would drink hot chocolate and walk along the river. They may even hold hands. There were those butterflies again.

She chose a simple black t-shirt with new jeans and took special care with her make-up. Her mother certainly wouldn't approve of that, any more than she'd approve of Alina going out with a boy unaccompanied. But Roman was a man, wasn't he? A Russian man.

She was there 30 minutes early. What was the point waiting in her room on such a wonderful evening?

Thirty minutes after the time they agreed to meet, Alina had a very different feeling in the pit of her stomach. She felt sick. She'd somehow believed this stranger would care enough to return to her, but of course she was foolish. He was playing with her. Why would a man like that be interested in a ghetto girl from Moscow?

She tried to leave the bench but kept waiting and hoping, her eyes locked on the corner she'd seen Roman confidently striding from, just a couple of weeks earlier. The Russian boys walked past at one point and she flinched from their glares.

It was like they knew. She felt ashamed. After two hours, Alina stood up, and told herself what she should have done the first time – go back to her room and count the days before she could go home.

35 ICANDIMANIA

Cameras panned across the gates outside Studio 4 revealing a mass of people filling every inch of the road. The police struggled to find enough room for cars to pass through. Fans were climbing on top of each other, desperate to catch a glimpse of their favorite iCandidate.

Inside the gates, David Mason shepherded a jostling mob of TV crews and photographers.

"This is politics on steroids. It's Political Idol - who would have thought it? iCandidate fever has swept the nation." The silver-haired CNN anchor shouted over the crowds welcoming the contestants who arrived back on the set for the next round. "It's like Beatlemania here. We're not seeing the kind of violence that has sullied some of the Saxon rallies recently. There is a sense that this is going to change the voting system as we know it in America," he continued. "The producers are being extremely tight-lipped about the last challenge. The only fact we have confirmed is that they finished taping the new challenge yesterday."

The anchor was almost knocked over in the surge as Todd led the small group from the first limo. A squad of burly bodyguards prevented them from being overrun.

"As you can see behind me," he said recovering, "the contestants have arrived...Some people are estimating that this week's results show will surpass 60 million iVotes. In the studio we have Tim Western from the Washington Electoral Institute to discuss the ramifications of the show on..."

"Turn it up would you?"

White House Chief-of-Staff David Platt picked up the remote gingerly from the table in the President's private living room. He'd been advising the President since his days in the Illinois Senate and they were more friends than colleagues.

"Honestly, iCandidate fever? Has the country gone mad?" The

President pretended to look shocked. "Harriet must be pulling her hair out."

"Do you want to form an action committee to report back on how this is going to affect the next election? At the very least, the party could use some of their ideas," Platt told his boss.

"Nah, let Harriet worry about it - it'll probably fizzle out. None of these people have the sort of experience to become President."

"That's what they used to say about you Sir," Platt reminded him.

"To be honest, much of what they're saying makes a lot of sense to me. These aren't Tea Party nuts. They're the voice of America. Most people just want to see the government get things done. They don't want to see us arguing about every little detail."

"That may be true, sir, but if the iCandidate show really does become a presidential campaign, then they will be looking to tear down the very fabric of Washington. It'll be the end of the two-party system."

"Not such a bad thing, but it'll annoy the heck out of everyone on Capitol Hill."

"So, not all bad then." The President's equanimity never ceased to amaze Platt. "It would, of course, be impossible for the winner to raise the kind of money needed for a realistic challenge."

The Chief-of-Staff was paid to cover all the angles. "Not in such a short time, so Harriet probably doesn't need to panic this time around, but the party had better be ready for the future. What does the First Lady make of the show?"

"Never misses it. I think she'd pick Grace and Gillian over me if she could. I'm just happy the girls are too young to vote."

"Why's that?"

"Because they'd vote for Cameron, for sure."

36 THE ICE QUEEN IS MELTING

One of the biggest movies of the spring was premiering at Mann's Chinese Theater, but there was only a sprinkling of fans on Hollywood Boulevard and the leading lady called to say she was running late. Like everybody else, she wanted to see who was going out in The iCandidate.

"Ladies and gentleman," Kristoff was back in the spotlight. "You've watched the footage from the war zone and the extraordinary events that took place there. But now we've reached the moment you've all been waiting for. As much as it grieves me, we will be saying goodbye to another contestant. What do you think, Rob?"

"Andy, I'm telling you, we are changing politics one iVote at a time, just as we said we would. It's mind blowing, dude."

"Okay, is everyone ready?" Kristoff walked in front of the contestants, ratcheting up the tension by pausing dramatically next to each one. "Who are you going to choose, America?" his face filled the screen. "Who will your votes be sending home, I wonder? Will it be this man? This woman? It may be okay on other reality shows to get it wrong. After all, they were just choosing a singer, a dancer, or a chef...Walter, who do you think deserves to stay, or go?"

"When the going gets tough, the weakest links show themselves. In my opinion, right now, up to this moment anyway, Todd is the strongest."

Todd smiled and waved at the cheering audience.

"Big words coming from the man who rarely showers praise. Here on The iCandidate," Kristoff continued, "you the viewers, the voters, have been given a responsibility that is so immense it can reshape politics and change the system forever."

He stopped between Grace and Cameron. "Are you sending either of these two home, America?" The lights on the stage were dim, with just a tiny spotlight hovering over Kristoff's face and now Grace. "How are you feeling Grace?"

"I'm a little nervous. But all in all, I'm feeling good," she smiled.

"And what about you, Cameron?"

"Excellent as always, Andy." His trademark lopsided grin was met with screams from the women in the audience.

Jen's phone vibrated in her pocket as Kristoff walked towards her. She couldn't believe she forgot to turn it off. She was trying to find the silent button in her jacket pocket. A second or two passed before she realized Kristoff had asked her a question.

"Sorry, what was that?" Her cool exterior evaporated.

Gillian and Grace glanced at each other, puzzled.

"I asked you if you feel confident that you've made it into the iPrimaries, Jennifer? You are without doubt our most controversial and confident contestant, after all."

Jen's phone quietly buzzed again.

"I em, I er... I just don't know how it will go, Andy. I –I-I'm sure," she stammered, "America will get it right. It's anyone's game I think."

Turning to the judges, Kristoff asked: "Any thoughts, Rob?"

"Hey, okay so, Jen lacked decisiveness in the last challenge. She's tumbling but we all take a fall now and then, let's give her a round of applause for making it this far. She looks like she needs some encouragement right now."

Jennifer hardly noticed.

"Jacqueline," asked Kristoff, "who got it wrong?"

"I think the decision not to go ahead with the waterboarding made by Gillian and Tom is going to hurt them. America's not prepared to take chances when it comes to national security."

"Rob, what do you think?"

"I think they were 100% right to stand firm and refuse to agree to torture a civilian."

"Split opinions from our judges, which makes for an interesting vote," Kristoff rubbed his hands together, the adrenaline running once again. "Okay folks, It's that time again. We all know that Todd and Cameron and Grace agree with Dennis Saxon that waterboarding is an effective and justifiable means to an end. But do you at home agree with them? Or do think Gillian, Tom and Jen got it right? Do you agree with the Geneva Conventions that waterboarding is tantamount to torture? Everyone in the studio can place their votes now. For you at home, go to your app and tell us your Top 3 iCandidates. It couldn't be simpler. Just your Top 3." Switching his focus dramatically to another camera Kristoff wrapped it up. "For now, that's it from The iCandidate. For one of these fine people behind me, our next show will be their last. Good night everybody and iVOTE NOW!"

The cameras flashed back across the stage to show the finalists huddled around Jen, who appeared to have collapsed. The studio quickly went black, but not before a voice was heard calling for a paramedic.

A small light from a camera to the right of the stage came on and a heavily made up woman reporter stepped in front of the lens with a Fox11 microphone.

"Stay tuned for the latest drama from The iCandidate. The Ice Queen is melting. Much more on the news at 11."

37 AND THEN THERE WERE FIVE

After the show, Jen left out the back. She'd fainted, but regained consciousness almost immediately and shooed away the paramedics. She just needed to get out of there.

Avoiding the limos lined up to take the iCandidates to the Malibu White House, she tapped open the Uber app in her phone. A car was two minutes away. She was soon in the back of a Prius, on her way to The Mondrian on Sunset Boulevard. Chrissie had called her from there a week ago. Jen hadn't called back.

She could see that the driver recognized her and she kept her head hunched over the iPhone, challenging him to say something. She tried calling Chrissie again - for the 23rd time that day - but it went straight to voicemail. No ringing. She tried texting, prayed for a reply, however terse.

Jen told the Uber driver to wait outside and rushed over to the front desk. She noticed actor Ben Affleck checking in across the foyer, yet all eyes were on The iCandidate. A middle-aged woman edged next to her and asked if she could take a selfie with her. Begrudgingly, Jen posed; she didn't trust herself to say anything.

"I'm afraid she checked out several days ago," said a tight-faced young woman. Jen held it together long enough to get back in the car. A ring alerted her to a text and she grabbed at her phone inside her purse. If she could just talk to Chrissie and try to explain...

It was a short text. . It wasn't from Chrissie.

'You're toast'

She'd been stupid, thinking the affair would somehow help her chances in The iCandidate. Instead, it had ruined them. Jen booked a room. She couldn't face going back to the White House where he could be waiting for her, eager to gloat and flaunt his power over her.

When she arrived at the studios the next evening, a host of TV pundits had already written her off. "Jen's Breakdown" dominated the news headlines and entertainment shows with so-called experts explaining how the pressure had driven the "Ice Queen" to the edge of madness. A former employee told CNN how she had fired him by text. "She wouldn't meet me face-to-face; she was too much of a coward. Now she's getting some of her own medicine," he said on live TV.

Tom was the first to spot her. "Are you alright, love? You look terrible." He smiled and ruffled her hair gently. "Might be a good idea to get down to hair and make-up. Andy's on the warpath - he didn't think you were going to show up," he spoke in low tones, giving her a hug.

Grace and Gillian approached gently, asking if she was okay. Jen didn't want to talk; she just wanted to go home.

"So you've decided to grace us with your presence." Desmond and Mase had warned Kristoff to be understanding if Jen arrived, but he couldn't help himself. "Better get yourself cleaned up." It wasn't warm and fuzzy but it was the best that he could do. "They're already running the tapes." Most of the show was to be taken up with clips from the challenge. Kristoff walked out to a noisy ovation.

"We did rather mislead our contestants. They weren't actually in the Middle East at all….they were in Twenty-Nine Palms, California, not so far away from Palm Springs." There were gasps from the studio audience. "I think you'll agree they all did extremely well." Kristoff paused for the applause. "Perhaps we should consider your choices right now, America. The last man standing in the Republican nomination race is Dennis Saxon. Over on the Democrat side it looks like Harriet Carson's a sure bet for the nomination. The way things stand, one of these two will be your President by this time next year."

Boos rang out across the studio.

"Or, perhaps you should consider the alternative. Standing in the wings we have six men and women who are proving their mettle on this very show. You judge them every week; you're getting to know them better than any other prospective politicians in history. We will lose another one this evening, I'm sad to say. Then another, then another. And we will eventually end up with The iCandidate. Truly the choice of the people. I'm going to ask you America, what's the better choice?"

With that, the curtain closed on Kristoff and reopened a second later to swirling red, white, and blue lights, and the six remaining iCandidates seated on stools across the stage.

Kristoff had decided to do away with the Oval Office for now. He walked back on. "We are delighted to report we had a huge response - the biggest yet. You told us your three remaining favorites. And after our nationwide iVote, the iCandidate who will be going home is…" Kristoff was distracted by Jen getting off her stool and walking towards him. She pulled his arm holding the microphone towards her, sparking static with her head mic that reverberated around the studio.

"It's me," she said softly. "It should be me."

"I'm afraid that yes, it is Jen." Kristoff put his free arm around her, unsure whether this was a mini-disaster or an iconic TV moment. "Jen will be going home tonight."

"I'm sorry, Chrissie," Jen said into the mic. "I love you."

38 MAKING AMENDS

When Vladimir told Roman he had delayed his flight from LAX, Roman assumed it would set back his trip to see Alina for a couple of hours, not a couple of weeks. But Roman missed the last flight east that night and there was no way he could travel so far with his busy schedule until at least the end of the month. He'd called the Harvard dorm countless times and even left messages with the Dean, but Alina never called back.

Roman couldn't blame her; he had stood her up.

He threw himself into his job, trying to get his mind off Alina by working even longer hours. It didn't work. She was the first girl from Russia he had ever gone out with. There had been a handful of girls before but he'd never felt like this about someone he hardly knew. As much as he wanted to please his father, even now, Roman had never quite understood why Vladimir was so devoted to Russia when most of his life was spent in the United States. In Alina, he felt he may have found the answer to that particular puzzle. Just thinking about her left a hole in his heart that would take a country to fill.

He settled back into his seat in the front of the plane and wished the hours away. It was a five-hour flight to Boston, and a 20-minute taxi ride to Harvard. Then he would beg her to forgive him. As he closed his eyes and tried to imagine their reunion, Roman's head finally told him what his heart already knew; he was in love.

39 PASSING SHIPS

Roman ran up the dorm stairs two at a time. He had a bouquet of flowers and a pay-as-you-go cellphone as gifts. He just wanted to explain what had happened. Perhaps then she'd agree to take a walk with him and get that hot chocolate he'd promised her. But there was nobody in Alina's room. None of the students he asked in the study room knew anything about her. The only thing Roman could think to do was wait for her on the bench where they met on their first date.

He'd been sitting there for a while, peering at the Cambridge streets through the iron gates when he saw one of the Russian boys his father's foundation was sponsoring. Roman jumped up and ran after the boy, startling him.

"Hello, Boris," he said, out of breath and still clutching the flowers. "Have you seen Alina?"

The boy, about 18 or 19, frowned at Roman and answered him in Russian.

"I'm sorry, I don't understand, " Roman replied.

Boris tried again. His English was good. "She's gone."

"Where?" Roman felt panicked.

"Moscow."

"But she's supposed to be here for the year! She…"

"She left today. She hates America." The surly teen carried on walking and Roman ran after him, grabbing his arm. "When did she go? Did you see her?"

"She doesn't talk to me. I saw her with bags leaving with the blonde woman. Maybe two hours ago."

40 NUCLEAR CHALLENGE

At 3:00 a.m. the phone rang next to Todd's bed. He was already dressed in pants and shirt, sitting at his computer.

Gillian woke with a jolt, thinking the only reason anyone would call at that time would be because something had happened to her daughter.

Cameron, fast asleep took a few seconds to wake up, then shot up in bed, all business.

Grace struggled out from a deep sleep to answer the call. She'd popped an Ambien the night before.

Tom was lying wide awake, as he often was in the quiet hours of morning when he argued most with his body.

None of them noticed in the darkness that the oversized, old-fashioned red phones had been put in their room overnight. Nor did they see the hidden cameras recording their every move. What they could not help notice was the military officer, sitting straight-backed in a chair next to the phone. By his feet on the floor, attached by a thin metal chain to his wrist, was a black leather briefcase with a small antenna sticking out near the handle. On the table next to the phone was what looked to be a credit card with the name of each candidate, and a number code, along with a small cellphone decorated with stars and stripes.

Todd answered the ringing red phone before he realized he wasn't alone. There was no small talk from the other end of the line.

"This is a nuclear emergency. We have accurate Intel that North Korea has developed a nuclear weapon and is planning to deploy it in exactly two hours from now. The target is Washington." It was a man's voice, dispassionate and devoid of any emotion. "In your room is a Marine with the nuclear football, a case including a computer enabling you to authorize a nuclear strike. He should also have the biscuit – a plastic card with your distinctive ID code on it

– and an encrypted phone you can use as you see fit during the emergency. If you choose to order a strike, you will need to be positively identified using the biscuit. From now on, the football and the biscuit should be with you at all times."

"Okay so what's first?" Todd was totally calm.

"The first choice is where do you want to operate from: the White House, Camp David, or do you want to get aboard Air Force One and head for the military bunker at a classified underground location?"

"I don't want to be seen as running away when my country's in trouble," Todd said firmly. "I'll stay at the White House."

"Affirmative. Follow the Marine and he will take you there immediately."

Todd put down the phone and turned to the Marine. "Can you give me a moment?"

"I'll be right outside, sir," he said. "Cameras are deactivated."

Todd wanted to look his best while saving the world. He put on a tie, and checked his reflection in the mirror before following the Marine down the corridor, half-running to keep up. They took an elevator down two floors and the Marine opened an oak door to reveal a room decorated to look exactly like the Oval Office. The only obvious difference was that there was a giant TV monitor facing the presidential desk.

"Take a seat." Kristoff's face popped up on the screen. "You have some very important decisions to make."

"Can I ask you a question first? What's all this about footballs and biscuits? Is this for real?"

"Very real," Kristoff explained. "The contents of the black briefcase, or the 'football' as it's known in the White House, function as a mobile hub in the strategic defense system of the United States. In other words, it enables you to press the button and launch a nuclear strike from anywhere at any time. There are preset strike options in the computerized box that is linked directly to the National Military Command Center. The one thing you will need before ordering a launch is the code on the card, or 'biscuit', that you have been given. It is an ID number that confirms you as the Commander-in-Chief. Although you and only you can order the strike, your Defense Secretary must confirm it. Is that clear?"

"Crystal!" Todd felt his adrenalin kicking into action.

41 HARD CHOICES

At first, Gillian was more shocked that the Marine managed to get into her room than about the impending nuclear strike. *I need to talk to the North Koreans,* was her first thought.

"First you must choose your base of operations."

"Can I stay here?" she asked, eager not to waste any time.

"The Oval Office is just down the hall," said the blank voice.

"Then show me the way," she threw a shirt over her sweats. Once in the mock Oval Office, Kristoff appeared on screen to offer her four choices.

"You can contact your military chiefs, speak to your Cabinet, gauge the opinions of other world leaders, or speak directly to the North Korean leader who is threatening to attack America," he said.

Gillian knew instinctively what she should do. "I want to speak to the North Koreans."

"Do you have any intention of ordering a US strike?" Kristoff asked.

"I certainly haven't ruled it out. Can you hook this up?"

"We can indeed," Kristoff answered. "Stand by."

42 AIR FORCE ONE

Grace was just happy she put a t-shirt on when she went to bed, otherwise she would have answered the phone naked. She forced herself out of the Ambien-induced fog to hear a booming voice telling her she had to deal with a nuclear emergency. There was something nagging at her as she heard the choices; the Oval Office, Air Force One or Camp David.

"Where will the plane take me?" she asked.

"We have a central command base underground at one of our air bases. I would rather not give exact details over the phone, even though this is supposed to be encrypted."

"But I can make calls from Air Force One and decide what I am going to do from there?"

"Yes," the voice said.

"Okay, that's what I'll do. I'm not going to be much good to anybody dead, am I? Make sure the cameras are off and close your eyes a second will you darling," she told the Marine, before whipping off her t-shirt and slipping on her underwear and a blue skirt and matching jacket. She washed her face, and then realized what had been bugging her. Running back into the bedroom she picked the phone up: "We need to evacuate Washington. We've got to get the people out of here."

"We'll get right on it," the voice replied. Grace was led down an extra floor to the back of the hotel and taken across the parking lot to a plane fuselage painted to look like Air Force One. A stewardess greeted her at the top of some stairs and showed her into a spacious cabin set up with a big desk facing a giant TV screen.

"Please, make yourself comfortable," the stewardess said as Kristoff greeted her from the monitor. She chose to speak first to the military chiefs. Three older men in military uniforms immediately appeared on the screen.

"I am your Chairman of the Joint Chiefs of Staff," the man in the center said. My two colleagues are in charge of U.S. operations in North Korea. How can we help you ma'am?"

"Yes, thank you," Grace greeted them individually. "Firstly, can you tell me whether the evacuation is underway?"

"It is. Washington is in the process of being cleared, but obviously it is a huge process."

"I understand. Would you please keep me appraised? Now, how real is this threat and how long do we have?"

"Time is of the essence, ma'am. We do believe they are serious. North Korea has been enriching its own uranium for nuclear fuel for years and we know they have had help from both Russia and China in the technical area. They have the know-how, and we believe they are capable of launching the missile."

"But is it capable of reaching Washington?"

"We believe the warhead is on a plane or a sea-bound vessel."

"A boat?" Grace was surprised a nuclear-armed boat could get close enough. "Do we know where that might be?"

"We are checking coordinates right now and should know within the hour," the four-star general to the chairman's right answered. "It is our suggestion that we prepare to launch a retaliatory strike."

"Against the boat, the plane, or Pyongyang?"

"The boat or the plane by conventional missile if we get the coordinates in time, a nuclear bomb on the North Korean capital if we don't," the general said.

"And what if they're bluffing? How can we know?"

"There isn't time to know for sure, but it's your job, and our job, to protect the American public. That is the number one priority irrespective of foreign casualties," the chairman pointed out.

"I want to speak to the North Korean leader," Grace said. "And can you please put all possible FEMA and military resources into evacuating this city. Just get them as far away as possible."

43 CROSS STRESSING

Tom rarely slept more than a few hours a night. He'd seen the Marine enter his room and the Marine saw that he saw. His mind played havoc in the early hours; Tom thought that perhaps the soldier was coming for him, that maybe a man dressed up as a woman wasn't somebody the higher-up's wanted as President of the United States. The Marine put his finger to his lips and smiled. For some reason that made Tom feel better. When people got killed on TV, the assassin was usually more businesslike about it.

The intruder pushed his hands down to signal Tom to remain calm. It appeared important to remain quiet. Tom figured there wasn't much he could do about if the guy wanted to kill him, so he lay back on the pillow and went back to hoping he wasn't embarrassing his family by crossdressing on network television. He must have nodded off because when the red phone went off he jerked up so abruptly he almost fell out of bed. Answering the phone, he looked up at the Marine. He was still smiling. Not unkindly.

"I'll stay here in DC," Tom said.

"But everybody else has to go, including my fellow iCandidates."

"What do you mean by everybody?" asked the disembodied voice.

"I mean a full evacuation, including the emergency services. They can organize it, and then pull out of DC themselves. I want the National Guard taking charge of the city."

"You seem very sure." The voice wasn't questioning. It was a statement of fact. "The serviceman will show you to the Oval Office."

"I am sure." Tom threw a jacket over his unisex pajamas. "My predecessor in Colorado waited too long to order evacuations after getting a tornado warning and three people died. It sounds like the price for a delay here might be much worse. "It's important for the

President to show people he's not running scared. If it ends badly, so be it. It's not like other people couldn't do the job. Four of my fellow iCandidates would do just fine."

44 FLASH IN THE PAN

When Cameron answered the phone his voice sounded firm and his thoughts were clear. Logic suggested he should take Air Force One to a safer place and orchestrate the response from there. As he talked to the stranger on the red phone, doubts that had been gnawing inside him for days dominated. *Am I all talk with nothing to really back it up, all flash and no substance?* In his career, and in his life, it had all been about flash. It was his calling card. If people wanted flash, they'd call Cameron Banks.

Watching Dennis Saxon in the presidential nomination race had frightened Cameron; he saw too much of himself in the opportunistic real estate mogul. The thought didn't make him feel better; it depressed the hell out of him. Cameron told the caller crisply that he would be heading straight over to Air Force One.

"It should be fully fueled," he added. Pulling on his suit, and ignoring the Marine in the room, Cameron took a few extra seconds ruffling in some hair product and carefully combing it into place. *Millions of lives are at risk and I'm making sure I look good to save the world.* The confidence he'd relied on his whole life was slowly replaced by self-loathing. When he looked at people like Grace, Todd, and Gillian, even Tom, he felt himself lacking. Cameron was climbing into the mock presidential jet when he realized he had forgotten to order any kind of nuclear evacuation. The only person he was saving was himself.

45 A HELPING HAND

Todd chose to speak first to his Cabinet and got straight to the point. He knew they were all actors, but that didn't mean he was going to act like this didn't matter. "So are you all up to speed?" he asked them.

"Not really," said a balding man who claimed to be the Secretary of State.

"What's the ETA on the missile?"

"I'll need to check with the generals, sir. As I understand it, we are not certain where the missile is being launched from."

"Why not?" thundered Todd, realizing he should have gone straight to the generals. "Do you have any guidance? Any of you?"

The members of the Cabinet shook their heads; Todd was about to dismiss them when his phone buzzed in his pocket. He discreetly looked down to see a one-word text: He quickly hit delete, just as he had with his earlier text that morning. "One last thing gentlemen, since you do not feel comfortable offering me advice, can you please make certain that the greater DC area is completely evacuated within the hour? Thank you. Can I now please speak to the military chiefs?"

Todd was beginning to think that maybe he'd made the wrong decision by staying at the White House. If there was a bomb it wasn't supposed to blow up the president. But to cut and run to Air Force One now would look like cowardice. He made a snap decision. To hell with it, I'll bomb them first. Todd was quickly connected to the generals. "If you had to put a percentage on the intel's accuracy, what would it be?"

"Ninety to one-hundred percent," the chairman replied confidently. "If you want to go ahead on a first strike basis, we would urge you to use a tactical weapon rather than a strategic one. There would be far fewer casualties, but the message would be the same."

The general to the chairman's right asked: "Did you intend to speak to the Korean leader first? I am told he is making himself available."

"No, I do not believe in negotiating with terrorists and enemy regimes."

"Yes, sir," the chairman replied and Todd imagined he saw a new glint of respect in the veteran soldier's eyes before the screen went blank again. Todd pulled the biscuit codes out of his wallet and stood up. "I want to know exactly how I do this. Run it through for me one more time, would you?" he said to the waiting Marine, who had the nuclear football sitting on his lap.

46 OH GOD!

Gillian was struggling to get her point across through an interpreter after a man was introduced to her as North Korean President Kim Jong Un.

"Our nuclear plant is purely for energy. We have no interest in manufacturing weapons," he told her through an unseen woman translator.

"We must talk further. You cannot even think of doing such a terrible thing without at least understanding my position," she said.

"But we do not launch atomic bomb to America. You are misinformed."

"We have incontrovertible proof that you have, or you are about to, fire a nuclear weapon. I don't see how you can argue that." Gillian was becoming increasingly frustrated by his denials.

"That is not the case. Your intelligence is misplaced. We request of the United States that you end the sanctions punishing our people. Then perhaps we do not send weapon if there is one."

"But you said you haven't launched a warhead."

"Exactly. And we are demanding an end to all sanctions. We want peace and good energy for the people, we don't want war."

"Look, my friend," Gillian tried again. "If you are threatening the United States, as I think perhaps you are, and if you are sending a WMD in our direction, then you will force us to take precautionary action. In plain English, we will destroy your country. But I don't want to do that. I don't want innocent people to die, so what can you tell me to help you?"

"The North Korean people believe in their supreme leader to make the right decisions. Perhaps you will trust the lives of your people to your God."

"Let's leave God out of this shall we?" Gillian responded curtly.

In the studio, Desmond was pulling the strings. This challenge was his baby. Sitting next to the South Korean actor playing the North Korean leader, he held up a piece of paper on which he'd scribbled: Does she believe in God?

"Well…are you going to put YOUR trust in God?" The actor did what he was told.

"I trust in myself to make the right decision here. Not your God or any other God for that matter."

"So you don't believe in any God."

"I don't believe any God is going to help us now if you drop an atomic bomb." The moment she said it she knew she'd made a massive mistake. What president would ever admit to not believing in God? It was suicide. Gillian tried to hold it together and push on. "I need you to tell me you will not attack the United States. Then maybe we can talk."

"It's not for America to draw line. With or without a God."

Gillian was doing her best to follow what she thought was the correct protocol. If she was going to break a lifetime's worth of principles, and order the deployment of an atomic bomb, she was going to make damn sure she'd covered all her bases. She was by no means convinced that the threat was genuine. Had she missed something? Was there a question she could have asked that would have made everything suddenly clear? She doubted it. "I need to know exactly how sure you are that a nuclear weapon is trained on DC." She'd put the North Korean president on hold to talk to the Pentagon.

"We have some unimpeachable intelligence," the Joint Chief's chairman said.

"So, can you tell me more - as in, from who and where?"

"I am afraid we don't know, ma'am."

She tried the Cabinet. Time was running out. "I need to know from the Defense Minister, do you have any information that I may have missed that gives us any kind of validation for the information that a nuclear strike will destroy part of Washington in about 25 minutes?"

"I think you're aware of all the relevant information," he said with a dry cough. "As I think the military has explained to you, we have verifiable intel, but no confirmation."

"So you are not absolutely certain."

"No, not 100%."

47 TICK

Grace wasn't having much more luck. "I will launch a nuclear strike against your capital if you don't give me your absolute undertaking that you have not – or are not planning – to attack Washington," she said, her patience wearing desperately thin.

"We are peaceful nation," the North Korean President responded. "You the aggressor."

She'd been on the videoconference for 5 minutes and hadn't gotten anywhere. "I am assured by the general in my country that you are firing a nuclear warhead at Washington. Unless I hear anything to the contrary in the next 45 minutes, I am going to unleash hell on Pyongyang. Do you understand? I don't know about you, but I am definitely not bluffing. This is your last chance."

"This is your last chance," the actor playing Kim Jong Un smiled inanely.

"Please get me the Cabinet." Grace switched off the screen. "More specifically, I want the Defense Secretary. I'm not going to play games with American lives."

48 TICK-TOCK

For the first time since the contest started, Tom was lost for words. He'd asked to speak to Kim Jong Un, but the North Korean leader had unclipped his mic and walked out moments after they'd been linked up via video.

"I won't speak to this man who is dressed like woman."

Kristoff's voice could be heard in the background beseeching the actor return to his seat.

"It is not respectful," an accented voice replied. "I cannot continue."

Tom wasn't sure if the guy was playing his part method-style, getting deep into his character, or if he was genuinely offended. Either way, he wasn't coming back.

Perched on a steel chair by the mock Resolute desk in the fake Oval Office in a salmon blouse and floral skirt, his hair hastily arranged, Tom was all too aware that his next moves would likely determine whether he was to be viewed as a realistic alternative or a joke. "I want the Joint Chiefs of Staff and then the Cabinet and I want them both ready to go." This was a different Tom to the self-deprecating, comic character America was growing to love. The slow smile was gone, replaced by a clipped determination. This is a serious job, he thought, so I must be taken seriously. There was a delay and Kristoff's voice apologized:

"I'm sorry, Mr. President...err Madam President. We have located the generals and they will be with you momentarily."

"That's simply not good enough, sir." Tom's frustration boiled over. "A great many lives may be in jeopardy. I need to speak to someone who will tell me what I need to know and I need to speak to him or her NOW!"

Two men and a woman in military uniforms rushed into camera shot and sat down behind a table covered in white cloth and a phalanx of microphones.

"What do you need to know?" asked the man in the middle.

"The exact nature of the threat and the likelihood of a nuclear attack," said Tom. "Give it to me from one to ten with one being the least likely."

"I'd give it a nine." The woman soldier didn't introduce herself but her uniform was heavy with medals.

"And the nature of the threat?" Tom didn't flinch.

"We have measurable intelligence that a North Korean terrorist cell, here in DC, has a dirty bomb; we're told it's a nuclear device and that they have the means to detonate it," said the soldier in the center, who Tom assumed to be the most senior.

"Is that even possible?" Tom felt his hackles rising again. "How would they even carry it?"

"A suitcase, even a backpack," said the woman officer. "We have them and so do the Russians. I assume that's where the North Koreans would have gotten theirs, although we can't be sure."

"And the damage they could do?"

"Well they would be the equivalent of about 6 kilotons of TNT."

"That means nothing to me."

"Let me put it this way; the bombs dropped on Nagasaki and Hiroshima at the end of World War 2 were 16 to 21 kilotons each, which adds up to about 75 million sticks of dynamite."

"And how do you know these people are about to strike?"

"We have good intel on almost everything….but we can't find them in time to stop it."

49 TRUTH OR DARE

Cameron was taking a more direct approach. He didn't want to talk to North Korea or to the military chiefs. He requested time instead with the Secretary of Defense. "Is this the real thing?" he asked the balding guy in a suit, who appeared on the screen in the Air Force One studio. "If you tell me that a single American is in danger of nuclear attack, I'm going to press that button."

"We are in imminent danger, sir."

"I'll need a little more than that before I start World War 3, if you don't mind."

"They have missiles in Pyongyang trained on Washington. We're told Kim Jong Un has given the order to launch."

Cameron breathed out. "And what kind of warheads are these?"

"We're calling them Fat Man 2 and Little Boy 2."

"After the bombs the U.S. dropped in August 1945?"

"There are similarities, yes sir." The Defense Secretary suddenly looked uneasy.

"If what you are telling me is the truth, the North Koreans couldn't even get this kind of 10,000 lb. missile on a plane let alone fire it half way across the world." Cameron's entire demeanor had changed.

"I can assure you that our intelligence is verified."

Cameron was determined to be proactive and he had been quite prepared to nuke the North Koreans. Now he'd made his mind up. "That's ridiculous. I'm sorry but you must think I'm an idiot if you really think I'm going to believe that story. If that's the best you've got I'm going back to bed and I'd suggest you do the same."

50 NUKED

Gillian could hear the crowd before she saw them. The lights from the stage blinded her at first, and she blinked owl-like at the huge audience. On stage were the three judges with Todd, Grace, Tom and Cameron, all standing just in front of their stiff-backed Marines.

"...and here comes Gillian, our fifth and final remaining iCandidate finalist," Kristoff hugged her warmly. She almost felt like he meant it. "In just a few moments, we will all discover how your iCandidates decided to handle the most critical decision any American president would ever have to face. Then we will hear how you, the American public, want to deal with that 3:00 a.m. telephone call. Only after all the Internet votes are counted will we reveal what happened in the nuclear scenarios devised by our international panel of scientists and military experts." Kristoff looked at the contestants. "Would you step forward please, Grace? Have you come to a decision?"

"I have."

"Then I will ask your Marine to open his case." The Marine leaned over and took a large box out of the briefcase. On it were two big buttons, one red and one black. "

"Which one are you going to press, Grace? Red to launch America's first atomic warhead since World War Two, black to stand down. The choice is yours. What's it to be?"

Grace turned around very deliberately and took a stride to where the Marine was holding up the box.

She pressed a button. The red button.

What sounded like an immense lightning strike filled the studio and a mushroom-shaped cloud erupted behind them, filling the studio with a sweet-smelling gas.

"Don't worry. It's harmless," Kristoff said. "Now Todd. What's your decision?"

Todd didn't waste a moment. The box was barely out of the

bag and he'd pressed the red button and the stage was filled again with noise and smoke.

Gillian kicked herself for not ordering an evacuation. But she had made up her mind and nothing she heard or saw was going to change it. She pressed the black button.

"So there you have it. Two reds and a black with two more iCandidates to make the toughest choice of all - to nuke or not to nuke - that's the question," said Kristoff. He beckoned for Tom to come over. "What about you, Mr. Mayor? Have you reached a decision?"

"I have, Andy." He stood waiting.

"What is it then, Tom."

"I've wrestled with this, I don't mind telling you. But here's my answer," he continued, leaning across to press the black button. "I don't believe the threat was great enough to wipe an entire country from the face of the earth. I evacuated DC and I would contact the Russians and the Chinese to put pressure on Kim Jong Un."

"But what if a nuclear bomb went off killing thousands of Americans?"

Tom sucked in his stomach, standing straight. "I honestly don't think it was ever a real threat. I believe this is the appropriate action."

"Right, so be it." Kristoff moved across stage to where Cameron was standing. "Any surprises for us, Cam?"

"I don't think so, Andy." Cameron pushed the black button. "In my opinion, the entire story was a hoax. It's the kind of dilemma a president may well have to face, but I can go back to bed and sleep soundly knowing I've done the right thing."

Kristoff was hearing chatter in his ear. It was time for a commercial break. He ignored his producer. "Time for a vote? Let's do it. There's no time like the present. Are you ready? Everyone in the audience open up your iVote device, please decide now."

It took only a few moments for the Los Angeles audience to deliver their verdict. The bar charts on screen fluctuated wildly for the first few seconds as the instant votes were counted.

Tom trailed in last with 9%, Todd and Grace finished neck and neck with 12% each and Cameron polled 27%. To her amazement, Gillian saw that she had polled 40%, a clear winner in the studio audience poll.

51 JUDGMENT DAY

"Before we go to the rest of the country, what is the view of our judges?" Kristoff asked, while holding Gillian's hand. "Walter?"

"A big mistake. Gillian put hundreds of thousands of American lives at risk and the audience somehow thinks it was the right decision. If I had known she was an atheist I would have advised America to make her the first one voted off. Cameron and Tom; big mistake. They blew it, in my view. Grace did well. She got everyone out of Washington, but she should have stayed at the White House. Todd is my President."

"What about you, Jacqueline. Do you agree with Walter or the studio audience?"

"Look Kris, Gillian's a woman. She doesn't just storm in there, strike a macho pose and kill everything that moves. For me, her faith is her choice. It's a private matter. Todd made up his mind to fire the nuke when he was admiring himself in the mirror before even leaving his bathroom."

"Thanks, Jacqueline. What about you, Rob?"

"I'm all for the diplomatic approach Andy. But there are times when you have to act and I think Gillian dithered too much. I don't think she knew right up to the end what she intended to do. Added to that, she clearly wasn't able to draw on her faith because she doesn't appear to have one. Having said that, I applaud her decision not to press the button and I'm pleased that Tom came to the right decision in the end. But Cameron was the rock star here. He knew his own mind and he made the best decision."

"So there you have it, differing pearls of wisdom from our esteemed judges." Kristoff puffed his cheeks. "You know what to do, America. Choose your favorite three from the list of the remaining iCandidates. Don't forget, we are changing lives, not just theirs, but yours…

Whose iVote counts America?"

"MyiVote!" roared the audience.

"That's right!"

We NEED your iVOTE folks."

The commercials were running even before Kristoff could finish the autocue, but he soldiered on regardless. "For the first time, according to our polls, Tom, and even Grace and Todd could be in trouble. It's up to you at home to decide who'll have to give up their dream of becoming The iCandidate and who you want answering that 3:00 a.m. phone call. Would you prefer Dennis Saxon? Harriet Carson? No? I didn't think so! It's time to start thinking seriously about The iCandidate as your president. Our future could depend on it. So let's take this job seriously...and please cast your votes NOW!" Kristoff felt the shift; the air was quietly electric. He knew this challenge had resonated with the whole country and will have gained them a new respect through Washington. The iCandidate had proved itself as a serious contender...

"Goodnight America!"

52 FIRST LADY FAN

After launching a new anti-obesity campaign with his wife at a Richmond, Virginia community center, the President opened the press conference up for questions.

"Did you see The iCandidate challenge on TV last night, sir?" he was asked.

"Yes, I did. Great television. I may even try out myself next season," he answered with a broad smile.

"But sir," the questioner pressed on, "Do you realize this means that five contestants from a game show now have more experience with a nuclear threat than their own President. Do you feel that the show has undermined your leadership?"

He ignored the question. "I am all for a show that gets people talking about the issues that affect their lives. Let's just hope that none of us have to deal with the kind of real-life nuclear crisis depicted for the television audience last night." The President, looking for his next question, picked a reporter from a local news station. "Go ahead."

"Who do you think is going home tonight on The iCandidate?"

"If anyone has any questions about the anti-obesity campaign, the First Lady or myself would be happy to answer them..."

In the town car taking them back to Air Force One an hour later, the President admitted defeat. "I can't believe that's all everyone is talking about. There is more to life than the iCandidate, surely!"

The First Lady smiled. "Yes, but please tell the driver to hurry, I want to get back in time to see the results." Her face was deadpan before she burst out laughing. "I'm just kidding."

The President grinned.

But his wife hadn't finished. "I can watch them on my phone. My money's on Grace by the way."

The President shook his head - "Unbelievable! Unbelievable."

53 AND THEN THERE WERE FOUR

It was almost time for the results, the theater was filled to capacity, and the applause went on for so long when the five remaining finalists walked out that Kristoff almost missed his cue. "This is amazing, even Walter Penske seems excited tonight! As you now know, our panel of military experts, led by members of the Senate Armed Services Committee and including former military generals and State Department negotiators, drew up the entire scenario. They were unanimous in their findings that the North Koreans were bluffing and neither had a nuclear weapon to use nor had any intention of doing anything other than saber rattling. It would seem that Gillian, Cameron, Tom and the studio audience were correct and Todd and Grace were wrong."

The lights dimmed. "Now for your results. So America, did you vote on what you believe our contestants should have done? Were Todd and Grace right to press the button even though our experts say the US was never in any real danger? Or could Gillian, Tom and Cameron have left us fatally exposed by her decision to give the enemy the benefit of the doubt?" The camera closed in slowly for a full close up of Grace, a smile masking her nerves. Apparently unconcerned, Todd waved to the audience and Gillian appeared distracted, absentmindedly playing with her necklace. Tom looked unusually tense; the stakes were getting higher with every challenge. Even Cameron seemed nervous, pulling at his collar.

Kristoff dragged out the agony through a commercial break, but didn't have the heart to keep them waiting any longer. "We received an unprecedented number of emails and messages after the challenge and they were almost all about one thing – the revelation of one of our final three that she did not believe in God." Kristoff looked across at Gillian, who had her head bowed. "I'm afraid to say those messages were overwhelmingly negative. And they are reflected in our vote tonight. The person leaving us tonight, ladies and gentlemen is...Gillian."

It turned out that America didn't care if Gillian got it right. She was out. Todd had the winning tally by a small margin, Grace was second, Tom and Cameron a close run third and fourth and Gillian tailed way behind.

"How can that be right?" Grace asked Kristoff as soon as the cameras were off. "Gillian was on the right lines all along. She was right and we were all wrong and yet she's the one going home? I don't get it."

"I understand what you are saying, but she lost a huge percentage of the vote the moment she said she didn't believe in God," Kristoff explained. "What counts in this show is what the public wants, and that their perception is left intact. In that respect, Gillian got it wrong. The people want an uncompromising leader to make a tough decision without any pussyfooting around. They also want a Christian."

Gillian's daughter Clara joined her on stage and together, they waved goodbye to America.

And then there were four...

54 THE GOOD SAMARITAN

Grace left the building long after everyone else, her shoes crunching on the gravel. She noticed there were very few cars left in the parking lot and glanced at her watch. It was late.

As she approached her car, she thought she saw a shadow move. Hesitating, she opened her bag and fished around for her cell phone and keys. She touched the sensor button, the car unlocked with a loud whoop, and she quickly slid gratefully into the driver's seat. But before she could close the door the shadow materialized from the darkness, bursting forward and grabbing her by the arm. A man, his face covered by a black ski mask, smashed her head against the steering wheel, and she screamed out in pain.

"Shut up you black bitch!" he snarled. He threw her across the passenger seat, hitting her in the face with one hand and tearing at her clothes with the other. She tried to push him off, but his full weight was on her as he yanked violently at her skirt. His breath smelt of whiskey and cigarettes and he ranted in her ear.

"Black whore, who do you think you are - we don't need one more jig trying to run this country. I'm gonna teach you a lesson, then you better run back home to the gutter where you belong."

He had her skirt around her waist and was pulling at her underwear, sweating and grunting. All Grace could think was there was no way was this going to happen, not here, not now. He had her arms pinned behind her head and as he released his grip to loosen his pants, she managed to maneuver her knee and with all her strength, she crashed it into his groin.

He cried out and curled up in pain. She pushed to release the glove compartment door and grabbed the flashlight she kept there.

He lunged at her and she whacked him hard across the head before reaching back and pulling open the passenger door, falling backwards out of her car. He launched himself across the seat and she slammed the door, catching his fingers and he yelled in agony.

Grace started to run in her stocking feet, her shoes lost in the fight. He chased after her. She turned the corner of the parking lot, desperately hoping to see someone, anyone. But there was no one and no escape. He grabbed her by the hair and dragged her to the floor. "Give in nigger. Face it, it's just not your day." His face was inches from hers but all she could see were his eyes staring hatred back at her.

Again, he ripped at her clothes and body like a maniac. She clawed his eyes; he just laughed, banging her head against the ground. She could taste blood in her mouth as everything started to fade, the faces of her parents on that fateful day flooding her mind.

That's when the rage filled her very core. She was not going to let this punk do this to her, and with all her strength she somehow pulled her arm free and punched him hard, watching in fascination as his nose gave way under the mask. He lay sprawled out on the floor. "Stay the hell away from me you piece of shit," she screamed, crawling away.

Somehow, he grabbed her ankles and pulled her over, pushing her face down and smothering her body with his. This time she knew it was over.

Suddenly the crushing weight lifted and she heard a crack as a body part was smashed against the gravel. Opening one eye, she saw someone punching the living daylights out of her attacker. Finally, the man's masked face met the floor with a dull thud and Todd ran over to Grace, scooping her in his arms. "Grace! Grace! Are you okay?"

"Where did you come from?" she moaned.

"Shhh… shush now, you're safe." He carried her back into the building and lay her down on the couch in one of the offices before going off to get a glass of water and some ice.

"I called security, but I think he's gone. Why were you here so late, Grace?" He held the ice against her cheek.

"Just reading. We've got the big money round coming up. I need to be ready. What about you, why were you here?"

"I just came back for my bag. I left it behind."

"Todd, you saved my life, I don't even know how to thank you. He just kept coming at me," she said, trying to hold it together.

"Well, you put up one hell of a fight, Grace. I thought you were a tough candidate, now I know for sure."

"Not quite tough enough this time, though." She looked at

him, swallowing hard. "Thank you Todd."

"You're welcome," he squeezed her hand and she winced.

"Sorry!"

Grace decided against filing a police report and refused medical attention. She knew if she went to the hospital the news would get out and she couldn't face all the fuss. Nobody was to know, she told Todd. She didn't want the show to get that kind of attention or herself to receive sympathy votes.

Todd drove her home and as they pulled up at the White House, Grace turned to him. "So it's our secret, Todd?"

"My lips are sealed. I promise you that. But are you sure you don't want me to take you to the hospital? You were pretty beat up back there."

"Yes, quite sure. Thanks again Todd. For everything."

55 PATCHED UP

Back in her room, Grace could finally let it out. She took off her clothes and stepped in

the shower. Her attacker's hooded face flashed in her mind and her hands trembled as she opened the shampoo bottle, mechanically washing and rinsing. She stood for a long time, her sobs masked by the sound of the water. Wrapping herself in a towel, she heard a soft knocking on her door. She didn't answer, but Gillian let herself in anyway and found Grace sitting on the edge of the bed, the cut on her forehead still dripping blood.

"Oh my God! What happened to you?" she gasped.

"Can you just patch me up, doc?"

Gillian ran back to her room, returning seconds letter with a bag filled with ointments, homeopathic remedies and first aid supplies. As Gillian worked, Grace told her briefly about the attack, emphasizing what she told Todd: no one could know.

"Okay, okay, we can hide this one with your hair, and I have a wonderful concealer to cover the bruise on your face." Gillian also worked on the deep grazes on Grace's ribs and sternum. "Grace, you should tell the police, what if…"

"NO!"

Gillian noticed the slightest tremor in Grace's lip, and knew better than to pursue this. She worked in silence for a few moments. "So, Todd the hero? That's a new one. I always figured he was only out for himself. Bet he'd like to see that in the headlines."

"No, he promised. I trust him totally," Grace said. They looked at each other for a long moment, and finally Gillian nodded and said "Ok."

"I don't want you to leave the show, Gillian." Grace's voice cracked.

"Well, don't you worry, the producers have some ideas for us rejects!" Gillian smiled as Grace looked puzzled.

"What do you mean?"

"Never you mind, you just concentrate on winning this show and then I'll let you in on a little secret." Gillian smiled as she packed up her bag, and put Grace to bed. Gillian climbed into the bed next to her. "I'm not leaving you alone tonight."

Grace said nothing, but her body relaxed with a grateful sigh and she fell instantly asleep.

56 BETWEEN TWO WORLDS

Alina was glad to have Emily with her. The thought of leaving America with nobody to mark the fact that she'd been there at all would have been even more depressing. She'd said an awkward goodbye to Alma and ignored the two boys as she walked out with her bags, sad to be leaving the serenity of her campus for the last time. She'd heard the boys saying some things in Russian that made her feel uncomfortable. She got the impression they hated being there more than she did.

Emily had taken care of everything; the college, the tickets, and she'd even arranged for a messenger to tell Alina's parents she was on her way home. She'd tried to persuade her to stay, of course, but she empathized with Alina, and understood it was time to go.

"You must think me terribly shallow." Alina felt guilty for all the trouble she'd put Emily to; but the chaperone had insisted on going with her to the airport. Alina checked her bag, and as she watched her suitcase land with a thump on the assembly line and glide off towards her plane back to Moscow, it hit her that she had allowed all her hopes and dreams to disappear. And for what? A man - a man she barely knew.

Emily saw the color drain from her face, and she gently guided her over to a small cafe between the check-in desks and the departure gates. She sat the shocked girl down in a booth and ordered them both a sandwich and some iced tea. "It's okay, we're early for your flight. You need to eat."

Alina said nothing, but smiled weakly. Emily held her hand, waiting. Finally Alina turned to look at Emily. "I'm throwing everything away that I have worked so hard for," she said quietly. "I did it all for nothing. I just don't have the strength or the courage to stay and I don't understand why."

"You fell in love. Love makes us do crazy things," Emily squeezed her hand.

"Yes, but he doesn't care about me. Why have I been such a fool? I had this wonderful opportunity and look what I did. I didn't think I was the type of girl who falls apart after one date. One stupid date."

Alina started to cry and Emily wanted to take that pain from her; make her see that she wasn't alone. "Alina, listen to me. I understand, more than you know." Emily handed her a tissue, and the young girl looked up at her with sorrowful eyes. "You are sensitive and trusting, and you got hurt. You just need time to heal, to regain your confidence, that's all."

"I'm sure you never gave everything up for a boy, you're too smart for that," Alina said wiping her eyes. "I'm such an idiot."

Emily sat back in her chair and took a deep breath.

"That's where you're wrong.I was probably the furthest from smart on the smart spectrum that anyone can ever get, believe me." Emily placed her hands over her flushed face, her fingers cool on her eyes.

Alina looked puzzled while Emily tried to speak. A lump rose in her throat and the words just wouldn't form. This time, Alina took her hand and stroked Emily's hair. Suddenly, Emily was back in her dorm, a college kid again, madly in love with not a care in the world. Emily couldn't stop the memories, as they came flooding back.....

57 FLASHBACK

EMILY - Manhattan - 1980

My arm was draped across Vladimir's bony chest in our closet apartment in the East Village. My dry mouth tasted stale from cigarettes, and my head pounded from the cheap vodka I drank the previous night. I felt his hand stroking my bare stomach and looked up to see him staring at me. Vladimir leaned up on one elbow to check the alarm clock just as it exploded with Blondie's 'Call Me.' He squinted at the digital display, lost without his glasses. The time was 11:30 a.m. The date blinked: October 24, 1980. I saw that he couldn't believe it - he had missed his 8:00 a.m. class.

Jolted awake, I drifted into the bathroom holding my head. "I made the alarm for later," I said, leaving the door open. "You need to chill out."

He scrabbled around for his clothes and was dressed by the time I climbed back into bed. "You've missed class now. You might as well get back in here." I was wearing the unbuttoned dress shirt he'd worn the previous night and pouted up at him, hoping he would stay.

"I'm going to see the T.A.," he mumbled. "Try and get a make-up assignment."

We attended the same Stern Business School at NYU, but he knew I didn't care about missing classes. I missed more than I attended.

I called after Vladimir, but I used a different name for him, his American name; the one all his friends used. "Pick me up some aspirin would you? It must be something I ate last night. My head is killing me."

Vladimir shot out of our tiny three-room walk-up without answering me. We'd made love in a drunken frenzy, but I don't remember much about it.

I'm from the Netherlands. I'd only been in the city a few months, and hadn't made many friends yet.

Vladimir was the last person I ever thought I would hook up with; he was way too straight-laced for being so gorgeous. He pursued me relentlessly, and in the end, I thought, why not? He'd relaxed somewhat in the time we'd been together, and I still found it endearing that Vladimir was adamant about keep-

ing up his grades and going to class.

The news that changed our lives came about five weeks later, the morning after Vladimir told me, with absolute sincerity, that he wished we could go on living like this together, forever. I was suffering from the usual hangover but had pushed him away the previous night and closed the bathroom door the next morning. I came out 30 minutes later in tears. "I think I'm pregnant." I looked up at Vladimir trying not to cry. "I'm so sorry. I should have gone on the pill. It's all my fault." I'd barely finished the sentence, folding into his arms and sobbing on his shoulder.

Vladimir hugged me tightly and kissed me gently. "We can do it."

I looked up at him again in deadly earnest. "I have money. You can stay at Stern and I'll care for our baby. We'll be happy, I know it."

But he wouldn't let me tell my parents. This was America. This was 1980. We could do what we wanted, he said. We didn't have to feel ashamed about having a child out of wedlock, and we would tell my parents in our own good time. He was persuasive and unyielding. Alone and vulnerable, I relented.

By the time I called him a little less than nine months later in the middle of an accounting class to tell him my water had broken, I was ready to become a mom. We rushed to NYU Medical Center, full of excitement and foreboding. I clutched his hand as I was pushed on a gurney from one room to another. He stood by my side to ensure there were no complications.

I remember that it hurt like hell and I called him a bastard more than once.

He didn't seem to worry. "You have never looked more beautiful," Vladimir told me.

The doctor, a gruff, monosyllabic woman, demanded one last push from me, I was now exhausted. The doctor ran from the room with one hand across our baby's crumpled face. I squeezed Vladimir's hand and wearily opened one eye with a weak smile. "We did it!"

Then I looked up to see a woman standing in the doorway, unsmiling. She looked so stern, something was wrong. I backed away in the bed as this woman walked slowly towards me.

"I'm so sorry."

I screamed, yanking my hand from Vladimir's. "No! My baby!"

"There was nothing to be done. He was already dead." The older lady didn't move from the bedside. I tried to get up but Vladimir had hold of my hand again and the woman blocked the door.

"I need to see my baby!" I was screaming. "Let me see him." Vladimir leaned over and hugged me tightly. "He doesn't even have a name," I cried.

"Don't worry," he answered. "You'll get through this."

I clutched him tighter, a shudder of fear piercing my heart. "As long as I have you?"

"I'm sorry, but that can't happen."

I stiffened against him. "What..what do you mean? I thought..."

I felt the pain as Vladimir pulled away, "I have to go."

The sour-faced doctor moved in with a male nurse holding me down on the bed. "You need something to help with the shock."

I reached out again for Vladimir just as the doctor plunged something into my arm, and everything went dark.

58 ON FIRMER GROUND

The two women sat in silence in the bustling airport, one locked in the past, the other fearful for the future. "So, what happened next?" Alina was still tightly clutching Emily's hand.

Emily was drained and closed her eyes for a moment. "I went back to the dorm. His things were gone. He just vanished. I couldn't stay after that happened. I boarded a flight three days later and went home to Holland." She swallowed hard. "This is my first time back." Her words tailed off.

Alina didn't know what to say and just kept tightly holding Emily's hand.

"You see, Alina," Emily took Alina's other hand. "I felt the same way as you. I couldn't stay here, not after what happened. I needed to be back home in a place where I felt safe and protected."

They sat in silence, each deep in thought, before Emily finally announced it was time.

They walked slowly to the departure gate. "Alina, when you want to come back - and I know you will - I will help you. I promise."

They were at the TSA departure security. Emily couldn't go any further. They hugged tightly. "This is just a hiccup," she said. "You will go on to do some great things, I know it."

"Thank you for everything you have done for me Ms. Emily. I will never forget your kindness."

Emily felt a strong maternal tug, but quickly composed herself and smiled at the young girl, her eyes shiny with tears. She walked away, her heart heavy, taking one last look at Alina as she turned the corner towards the exit.

The woman walking in front of Emily collided with a young man hurtling at breakneck speed towards the gates. Emily rushed to help the woman, who was now shouting at the man's back. "Why don't you watch where you're going?"

"Sorry…so sorry!" he called, behind him. He sprinted off and all Emily saw was the back of his head.

"Handsome, but STUPID! " grumbled the woman.

Emily picked up the lady's newspaper and helped her up. The man kept running.

Alina smiled thinly and showed her ticket and passport to security. She thought she heard someone shout her name. But nobody knew her name here. She heard it again and glanced over her shoulder. That's when she saw him.

"Wait, Alina!"

She stood confused for a minute, still clutching her documents, stuck between her old life and the new. She could put her head down and carry on back to Moscow - or she could risk everything and stay. Alina hesitated a second longer.

Then she took the first tentative step back to Roman.

59 REUNITED

Once Alina heard Roman's side of the story she had a few minutes to make up her mind: whether to give him and America another chance, or to turn away and make a final dash for her flight.

She chose Roman.

Neither knew quite what to do next, so they just continued to hold hands smiling at each other.

The relief on Roman's face was evident; a second more and she would have been lost to him. If he had any doubt about the depth of his feelings, the sheer panic he felt at the thought of losing her made things clear. To hold Alina's hand as they walked away from the departure gates was all Roman needed.

"I am so happy I got here in time," he said softly.

"Me too." Alina's eyes burned into his.

"I have my driver waiting outside. I will take you back to Harvard. You probably need to let them know?"

"Yes, thank you." Alina needed to talk to Emily. Roman signaled for his driver. He didn't try and hug Alina; a look was plenty.

So this was his destiny after a lifetime of assimilation; he'd fallen in love with a Russian girl. He couldn't wait to tell his father. Russia wasn't a concept of a better life any longer. He didn't have to rely on his father's stories. It was so real he could almost touch it.

Across the city, sitting in her car in the afternoon traffic, Emily was lost in her thoughts. She had been hesitant leaving her young charge, so sad and vulnerable. It reminded her how emotionally raw she still was herself, some 30 years later. But at least now Alina was going home to what she knew, to be with her family. She was too delicate for America, Emily realized, despite her intelligence and yearning for a better life.

Emily wondered who the caller was as her cell phone came to

life, and an unknown number appeared on her screen. "Emily, it's Alina," came the excited voice. "I want to stay! May I please come back to Harvard?"

Emily was stunned. "Are you sure, Alina?"

"Never more," she said quietly, looking up at Roman as she spoke softly into the phone.

"Okay. I'll turn around and come pick you up. It's going to take me about 30 minutes though."

"Oh no, Miss Emily! You don't need to trouble yourself coming back. I will meet you at the university later." The line went quiet and Emily heard Alina take a deep breath. "Roman is with me."

That's when Emily knew. The man who had rushed past her at the airport. That had to have been him. "Oh, I see." Emily paused as she tried to register what had just happened.

"I'll meet you in the quad. I'll make all the arrangements, it shouldn't be a problem." She hesitated. "But… are you sure, Alina? I mean really sure?"

Alina understood. "Miss Emily, you have helped me so much. Thank you. You've given me new courage."

"You must do this for you." Emily's voice was suddenly harder. "Never define yourself for someone else, especially a man."

"Miss Emily, I promise you, I will not let you down."

Emily already knew this was true. "Alright then. I will see you later and Alina…" she added quickly. "I am very happy you're staying."

60 FIGHT CLUB

There was a small restaurant on the way back from the studio the contestants stopped at a couple of times in the early stages of the competition for a quick cocktail. The owner would find them a quiet table overlooking the Pacific Ocean. It was harder now that the show was so popular, but tonight, Cameron was alone and asked the limo driver to wait outside. He hoped he could slip in for a drink unnoticed. He ordered a Mexican beer at the bar and took it across to the same table he'd sat at with the others.

There was a family out on the patio and a young couple sitting at a raised table by the bar. Otherwise, the place was empty. Closing his eyes, enjoying the slight breeze off the water and the chance to relax.

"Excuse me, aren't you Cameron?" The blonde from the bar was leaning over him, her soft perfume filling his senses. "I knew it was you. I bet my friend."

Cameron smiled. All this was still new to him. And she was pretty.

"Would you like to buy me a drink?" Clearly an autograph wasn't going to be enough. She sat down a little too close to him.

"Sure," Cameron mumbled. "What about your, er…friend?"

"Oh, we're not together and he knows how crazy I am for you. I've voted for you every round." She smiled at him seductively.and he thought to himself, why not?

He ordered her a drink and looked across at the guy, who was staring at his phone, apparently unconcerned. Cameron turned back to the girl and just had time to ask her name before he was grabbed from behind and dragged out of his chair by her 'friend.' In one motion he was pulled up and thumped in the face, knocking him to the floor. A foot slammed into his ribs as he tried to get up, but the guy stood over him, accusing him of trying to steal his wife.

On his knees, Cameron put a hand to his face and saw it was

covered in blood from a cut above his eye. He looked back up to see the girl filming the whole thing with her phone. The barman and the family were gone and there was little Cameron could do to stop the couple as they made a dash for the side door.

The girl paused just long enough to say: "Sorry about that Cameron. I really did vote for you. Good luck!"

And that's the last he saw of them until the video turned up later that night as an exclusive on TMZ. In 30 minutes it had more than two million views.

61 MIRROR MIRROR

Grace cherished the few precious moments of solitude. The Green Room was cozy, peaceful, and safe. In a few minutes, she would be walking out on the stage with Todd, Cameron and Tom for the next challenge in front of millions of people.

Staring at her face in the mirror, the cut still raw under the make-up, Grace finally felt fully alive. If anything, the attack only served to make her stronger, more determined to make a better life for herself and those around her. She could bring people together. She could make a difference. She searched the counter for her lipstick, and looking back into the mirror she practically jumped out of her skin.

Cameron's reflection had appeared behind hers. She spun around. He touched her arm, making her jump again. "Grace, I am so sorry. I didn't mean to scare you, I knocked but you didn't hear."

"That's okay. I'm just a bit on edge, that's all." Wearing a simple Caroline Herrera dress, she searched her dresser drawer to find the carnelian and silver spiral necklace with matching earrings she'd found at a street market last summer. She turned to face him. "Are you ready for the next challenge?"

"Sure. Whatever. You know that it's packed out there. Even Jen is here to support us. Who'd have thought?"

Grace smiled at him through the mirror, saying nothing.

"You look stunning by the way," he added.

"Thank you. I'm sure you say that to all the girls," she smiled.

"Actually I…." He caught sight of the deep bruise under the make-up. "Grace, what is that?"

"What?" Grace's hand instinctively flew up, pulling her bangs across her forehead. He gently moved her hand to reveal the dark welt.

"Oh, it's nothing. I fell in the bathroom, I…."

"Hit your head on the bath. Yeah, oldest one in the book and I'm not buying it. What really happened?"

Grace hesitated. "Since when was he so concerned? Hang on, you have a cut about your eye too." She frowned. "Were you bar brawling again?"

"Something like that. Tell you what, you share your story and I'll share mine?"

"I don't want to talk about it, so please don't ask me again."

He looked at her strangely. "You're a weird one Conwright. Always trying to be so strong and brave. You can trust me you know." There was silence, and he saw her jaw tighten, her eyes revealing nothing. "Okay," he sighed, heading for the door. "Good luck tonight."

"You too, Cameron," she murmured.

He shrugged and left.

Grace sat down to finish getting ready. She tried to concentrate on the challenge ahead, but all she could think about was Cameron.

62 LOVE HURTS

Roman waited patiently in his father's office. Nobody knew they were father and son; it was still becoming increasingly difficult for them to get time together the closer the mission came to completion. Vladimir was against the meeting but Roman argued that his office was the most sensible place to talk. Who would ever suspect anything there? He didn't want to wait any longer to tell his father about Alina. She was everything he could possibly want in a bride and Roman wanted to ask for his blessing before asking Alina to marry him.

When Vladimir finally arrived 15 minutes late he was irritable and stressed. Things were not going to plan. "We need to talk about contingencies," he told his son. They talked business for 30 minutes. Usually that was all they talked about, but this time Roman needed to steer the conversation in a different direction.

"It's my birthday tomorrow. Does that make you feel old?"

"Yes. Ancient." His father offered a rare smile.

Roman took that as a good sign and forged ahead. "It's also the anniversary of mom's death. Can you tell me a little about her again?"

He could see the pain in his father's face. Discussing Roman's mother was the one time he saw his father soften, if only a little. He had no photos, no relatives, only his father's memory to go by.

"You've heard all this before."

"I just like to hear it."

"She was beautiful." Vladimir was lost in thought. "She was bright and clever and crazy and wild. I don't really know what she saw in a boring guy like me." He looked across at Roman. "You are so much like her." His voice cracked a little. "She was studying political science, the same degree as you."

"Do you miss her?" Roman always asked the question.

"Every day," was always the answer. Vladimir had chosen a

lonely path a long time ago. It tortured him, wondering how his life could have been with his son AND a wife. But now, he was close to making all the sacrifices worthwhile. That's when Roman told him about Alina and he could see everything they'd planned falling apart.

"This is not the right time." It wasn't up for debate. "You must stop seeing her."

"I can't do that." Roman was defiant. "I thought you'd be pleased that she's from Russia."

Vladimir wasn't used to being challenged by his son. He stood up and crashed his hand down on his desk. "Why do you think we've spent all these years turning you into the perfect all American boy? Do you understand nothing?"

Roman was stunned and Vladimir continued. "We haven't worked this hard for you to wreck everything by marrying a Russian girl! That would be madness! If a whisper of this gets out we're finished. You must end it…NOW!"

Confused, frustrated, and hurt, Roman just shook his head at his father. "I come to you happier than I have ever been in my life, eager to share this news with you…and this is your reaction?" Turning on his heel, he was at the door. "You want me to be this perfect, confident, successful American - But I'm not just an American, and neither are you. Why can't we be proud of who we are? What are you so afraid of?"

Vladimir said nothing, just glared back at his son.

"I just don't understand you!" Slamming the door, Roman stormed off. He realized this was the first time he had ever done that.

Vladimir looked at the closed door for a moment, and sunk into the chair, exhausted. As he watched Roman's hurt face just now, the memories of his son's mother in the delivery room that day came flooding back. He could see her now, the same hurt expression etched on her face. They were so alike in so many ways.

63 FLASHBACK

Vladimir, Manhattan 1980

Emily's arm was draped across my chest in our closet apartment in the East Village. She reeked of vodka and cigarettes, a combination that worked the previous night but disgusted me now.

Her pretty mouth, lipstick dissolved in our kisses, was slightly open, her panda eyes scrunched shut against the morning light. I looked down at her concave stomach, a silver bar shining from her belly button, and wondered if my baby was somewhere inside. I leaned up on one elbow to check the alarm clock just as it exploded with Blondie's 'Call Me' and I squinted at the digital display, lost without my glasses. I couldn't believe it - the time was 11:30 a.m. The date blinked: October 24, 1980. I had a class at 8.

Jolted awake, Emily drifted into the bathroom holding her head. "I made the alarm for later," she said, leaving the door open. "You need to chill out."

I scrabbled around for my clothes and was dressed by the time she climbed back into bed, her mop of pink-streaked dirty blonde hair pulled up into a loose bun.

"You've missed class now. You might as well get back into bed." She was wearing the unbuttoned dress shirt I'd worn the previous night and pouted up at me like a naughty schoolgirl.

Not for the first time, I was tempted to stray from the plan. I knew it was risky to choose the hot girl. But I couldn't help myself. "I'm going to see the T.A.," I mumbled. "Try and get a make-up assignment."

We attended the same Stern Business School at NYU, but I knew she didn't care about missing classes. She missed more than she attended. Emily called after me, but she used my American name; the one all my friends used. "Pick me up some aspirin, would you? It must be something I ate last night. My head is killing me."

Barreling down the four sets of stairs from our tiny three-room walk-up, I knew exactly why my girlfriend was suffering. She'd been so busy downing cheap white wine there hadn't been time to eat. We'd made love in a sloppy, drunken frenzy after the cold air outside the bar had virtually poleaxed Emily; she certainly had no clue whether or not I'd used a condom. That much, at least, was going to plan.

She was a trust fund kid from the Netherlands and had only been in the city a few months. She had few ties there and just a few friends from our classes. That was how I justified selecting her. If only she wasn't so damn amazing. To my surprise, my mother didn't oppose my choice. Even if a bohemian, sexually promiscuous Dutch girl was hardly her ideal choice, as my mother, she recognized good genes when she saw them. As long as I didn't reveal my true feelings, I had no trouble justifying my decision to pursue Emily. I couldn't drop my grades at school though. That would never fly.

I rushed a handful of blocks to Stern and paused for a second outside T.A., Carol Becker's door to look suitably contrite. I'd considered Carol at one point; she was attractive in a sharp-faced, brainy kind of way, and she clearly liked me. But she came from Long Island and had too many friends.

The inevitable finally happened about five weeks later, the morning after I told Emily with absolute sincerity that I wished we could go on living like this together, forever. She was suffering from the usual hangover but had pushed me away the previous night and closed the bathroom door the next morning. She came out 30 minutes later in tears.

"I think I'm pregnant." Emily looked up at me but this time her eyes were full of tears. "I'm so sorry. I should have gone on the pill. It's all my fault." She barely finished the sentence, folding into my arms and sobbing on my shoulder.

I didn't have to pretend. I hugged her tightly and allowed myself to dream about running away and starting a family where nobody knew us, where nobody could reach us. "We can do it."

She looked up at me again in deadly earnest. "I have money. You can stay at Stern and I'll care for our baby. We'll be happy, I know it."

But I wouldn't let her tell her parents. This was America. This was 1980. We could do what we wanted. We didn't have to feel ashamed about having a child out of wedlock, but we would tell her parents in our own good time. I was pretty insistent.

By the time she called me, a little less than nine months later in the middle of an accounting class to tell me her waters had broken, everything was in place. We rushed to NYU Medical Center like any other expectant couple, full of excitement and foreboding. She clutched my hand as she was pushed on a gurney from one room to another. I had to be right there to ensure there were no last minute hiccups.

Strands of blond hair were pasted to her face with sweat, she grunted and groaned like an animal, her body was left torn and bloody and she called me a bastard more than once. To me, Emily never looked more beautiful.

I was so caught up in the birth and the joy at welcoming my baby boy that I forgot all about what would happen next. The doctor almost ran from the room with one hand across the child's crumpled face.

Emily scarcely seemed to notice but squeezed my hand and wearily opened one eye with a weak smile. "We did it."

Then with a feeling of utter dread, I looked up to see my own mother standing in the doorway, unsmiling and determined. Any fleeting thoughts of running away to live happily ever after evaporated.

The smile froze on Emily's face. She backed away in the bed as my mother walked slowly towards her. "I'm so sorry."

Emily screamed, yanking her hand from mine. "No! My baby!"

"There was nothing to be done. He was already dead." My mother didn't move from the bedside.

Emily tried to get up but I took hold of her hand again and my mother blocked the door. "I need to see my baby!" Emily was screaming. "Let me see him."

I steeled myself. Now was not a time to show weakness. I knew what I had to do. Emily understood very little about who I was, but it was enough. She could find me. She could ruin everything.

I leaned over and hugged Emily tightly, feeling the sobs wracking her frail body.

"He doesn't even have a name," she cried.

"Don't worry," I answered. "You'll get through this."

She clutched me tighter. "As long as I have you."

This was the moment. I could daydream but there would never be picket fences. "I'm sorry, but that can't happen."

I felt her stiffen against me.

"But I thought…"

"I have to go." I pulled away and the sour-faced doctor moved in with a male nurse holding Emily down on her bed. "You need something to help with the shock."

Emily reached out again for me just as the doctor plunged a syringe containing 5 grams of sodium thiopental into her arm, sedating her into unconsciousness almost immediately.

She slumped into my arms and I breathed in the familiar sweet scent of her skin, mingled with the faint aroma of sweat from giving birth to my son. It was the same smell I recognized after we made love. I didn't know what would happen to Emily. I didn't want to know.

My mother was standing in the doorway beckoning for me to leave. In her *arms, swaddled in white, was my son, Roman. With one last look at Emily, I turned and hurried out of the hospital room. Emily had played her part well. But I no longer had any need for her.*

64 HOME CHALLENGE

The opening credits ran straight into a shot of a large barn resting in the middle of a field. As the camera zoomed closer, the doors opened to reveal a concrete floor, high beamed ceilings and whitewashed walls. In the corner stood the remaining four contestants, waiting silently behind bench tables.

Tom removed a wad of notes from a briefcase. He ripped the paper seal and thumbed the $100 bills. He laid them back down, picking up another and then another; his fingers deftly removing the paper from the top layer until he had counted one hundred bundles of $10,000.

A cool one million dollars. He glanced at Grace who had been doing the same, but now was putting her money into piles, her face rapt in concentration.

Cameron to his left hadn't opened his briefcase yet. He had a bruise over his eye that had turned an ugly shade of purple. He looked worried.

Todd was scribbling notes and tucking them into each bank of bills. He took a deep breath.

Each iCandidate had a million dollar budget; all they had to do was decide how to spend it. A long line of people carrying signs and poster entered the warehouse, as an ear-splitting horn signaled for them to begin.

Grace started to run and was hit hard on her right side by one of the newcomers, her money scattering across the floor. She wanted to cry, but crying would only take up precious time. She turned and collided with Todd who looked as surprised as she, as they ended up in a heap on the floor. Collecting himself and standing quickly, he offered his hand, which she gratefully took.

He then sped off in the opposite direction. Grace managed to limp across the vast space and find her first objective. "Okay, okay, I can do this," she said to herself. She deposited $100,000 in a large black safe and immediately a neon light shot vertically above her head and onto a screen: HEALTH, $100,000.

There was a series of similar looking safes scattered all around the barn, each with a flashing neon side towering over it. The one for ECONOMY/JOBS showed $250,000.

Another for EDUCATION shot up from $50,000 to $150,000 moments after Tom and Todd sprinted forward to deposit their cash.

As each deposit was made, the various categories flashed to life, with a whooping sound and ribbons of color zipping across the screen. HOMELAND SECURITY/DEFENSE showed $40,000. HEALTH went up again to $180,000. INTEREST ON DEFICIT: $200,000. FOREIGN AID: $30,000.

The scene switched back to the studio where Kristoff walked to the judge's table to stand next to Jacqueline Toscane. "While the contestants are fighting to stay in this competition, would you like to explain to our voters at home, in your inimitable style, the purpose of this challenge and the insanity which beholds us, Jacqueline?"

"Of course. I'd be delighted." Jacqueline smiled into the camera. "This is our Home Challenge. The government spent $3.5 trillion this year of taxpayer money on the domestic programs it has to sustain. This challenge is not, I repeat NOT supposed to duplicate the amounts the government spent. Anyone of us can pull the actual figures from the Internet; the breakdown is on your screen as we speak.

We are instead challenging our contestants to a more instinctive test. We've given each of them a budget - a token sum of $1 million. A mini budget if you will. Their job is to disperse this money between the programs that mean the most to them, the causes that they would fight for if they were in office." She paused for effect, enjoying herself immensely. Wearing a tight sleeveless white dress which emphasized her toned arms and slim physique, she played to the studio crowd. "Equally important, at the end of this challenge, you, our lovely studio audience will be asked to cast your vote, only this time we're not asking you to vote for a contestant, but for the programs YOU want your money spent on." Jacqueline turned back to the camera. "You, too, viewers at home, we want to know what domestic issues are nearest and dearest to your life, your family, and your heart. So be ready to vote at the end of the show."

"Well done, Jacqueline. Is there anything else we need to know?"

"Yes, one thing the contestants mustn't forget, of course, is that we are charging them interest on this money, so they must not fail to budget for that. Our government spends more on debt interest than it does on any program within the Treasury and they have to account for that.

"Thank you, Jacqueline."

"My pleasure," she winked into the camera.

"Why couldn't they just do it here in the studio?" Walter Penske asked gruffly.

"Good question," Kristoff said. "We thought we would add a little spice to this challenge, and for that we needed lots of space! Our government should never forget that it's not their money they are spending; it's our money, YOUR money, America. For that reason, the contestants are being approached by representatives of you, the people, townsfolk with powerful voices, who are not afraid to share their opinions. They want to persuade our contestants to choose their interests, above all else."

65 ADDING UP

The camera switched back to the barn. Cameron watched his three colleagues racing around the hall like in a sped up cartoon. His head was banging like a jackhammer. Hundreds of men and women walked back and forth in the center of the hall, holding placards depicting their arguments on domestic policies.

They were not allowed to stop the contestants physically as they came through them, but could make their verbal appeals as loud and aggressive as they liked. Tom dodged around a woman whose placard read: HELP ME STAY IN MY HOME. STOP THE INSANE BANK CHARGES! Cameron wasn't so bothered by the protestors; he had to get over the fact that when it came to math, even on his best day, his mind would go completely blank. And this wasn't a good day.

Grace was caught in a back and forth dance as she tried to skirt around a man whose sign read: TAKE US OUT OF THE RED! NO MORE BORROWING FROM CHINA. Back at her station, her hands trembling, Grace couldn't make up her mind where to put her final deposit. Finally, she launched into action, heading to her left and being instantly surrounded by a group of college students protesting the rise in tuition.

"WE NEED MORE GRANTS!" they chanted. Grace ducked under their banner, depositing the last of her money in one of the safes.

"We are in the last seconds of this challenge," Kristoff raised his voice over the commotion. "Todd is finished, and he looks pretty happy with himself, Grace is making a last deposit, Cameron has completely lost it - I can't even begin to understand what happened there - and where for the love of God is Tom?"

The camera searched the hall, finding Tom in deep debate with a group demonstrating against cuts to Social Security benefits. He looked totally at home, shaking hands and smiling with the previously agitated protestors.

The horn sounded again and everything stopped. Three brief-cases sat empty on the tables, but the fourth still held at least $100,000.

"Ladies and gentlemen, that challenge was shot earlier today, just one hour out of town." Back in the studio, Kristoff stood alone on the stage. "They've made it back so please welcome fresh from their challenge in Ventura County, your iCandidate finalists!"

66 TAKING A BEATING

The American flag dissolved to reveal Tom and Grace hugging as they moved forward, flanked by Todd and Cameron. The entire audience stood to give them a standing ovation.

"Now this is where it all gets really interesting," Kristoff announced. "First, each of our friends should talk about the policies they spent the most money on and why. Up on the big screen, you will also see a breakdown showing exactly where their money went. As soon as they have had their say, it's America's turn to show what they think the country's priorities should be. The candidate most out of sync with the public is the one who will leave us. So Tom, you first. In a sentence please."

"I hope that America agrees with me when I say that the youth are our future; education comes first, followed closely by the economy and the deficit."

"Now Grace, what's your rationale?"

"My two biggest issues are cutting the deficit and creating jobs. That's why I allocated so much to cover the interest charges rather than fall deeper in debt to China and other foreign governments. I believe the best way to get new jobs is to spend more on key areas like education and health."

"Your turn, Todd. Keep it brief please."

"We don't need to pour taxpayer money into the health system or even into education. Both are unwieldy already and need to become more financially viable. The number one priority is the economy, next our boys in the military, and, of course, we must pay our debt!"

"Cameron?"

"I think we have to remember that our home isn't just the country we live in, we need to care for each other around the world, too. So, I allocated 30% of my budget to foreign aid and 25% to health. These are closest to my heart."

"Jacqueline, any last thoughts?" Kristoff paced the stage. "A brief summing up?

"Of course. Well, I'm a big fan of Grace. I admire her tenacity and her consistency and she keeps a cool head. That's critical in a leader. Tom isn't scared to show his individualism. He has strong convictions. But I have to say I'm noticing Todd more and more. He's gathering quite a big following." Spontaneous cheers and whistles erupted from the audience. "See what I mean?"

"Why is that do you think?" Kristoff asked.

"He has natural charm which is a plus, of course, and he really knows his stuff. He may be young but he knows his own mind. Most importantly his stand is always clear. There's no confusion." She paused, shaking her head. "Cameron, I'm sorry, you were all over the place, my darling."

Kristoff took over. "You didn't get to spend all of the money Cameron, let alone pay the deficit. Dare I suggest that your mind might have been elsewhere? Care to explain what happened?"

Everyone was still talking about Cameron's altercation – except Cameron.

"Just a little misunderstanding, I'm afraid." There was no point trying to explain. He suspected the whole thing was a setup, but he was never going to be able to prove it. It was bad enough getting beat up - now he'd totally blown the challenge. "My math skills are pretty bad." He figured he'd get out of it with as much dignity as he could manage and made a half-hearted attempt at flirting into the camera: "But I'm counting on having a few clever advisors when I get to the White House. Just as long as they're single of course…" But no-one seemed to be buying Cameron's cheerful facade, least of all him.

67 MILLION DOLLAR QUESTION

"So, studio audience, using your iVote device embedded in your arm rest, we're giving you each a cool $1 million to spend on the programs of your choice. You have the same challenge as the contestants. The difference is you can spend from the comfort of your seat," Kristoff explained. "Don't forget, you won't be voting for the iCandidates, you will be voting for the programs. On your screens are the categories, listed in no particular order. We want you to click on your top three choices, so if you want to contribute to Kristoff's pension fund, you would click Kristoff as one of your entries. Haha! Good try, eh? Good try!" The audience chuckled with him. "Don't forget about interest on the debt, too. Don't pull a Cameron now and get sidetracked! Sorry, Cameron."

Kristoff loved being in the spotlight. He waited for the camera to zoom in for a close-up. "Everyone at home, you know what to do. To finish off our show tonight, here's Rob and the Legacy with one of their biggest hits, 'Queen of the Road!' We'll be back tomorrow night with your results. Now America it's your turn.

"VOTE!"

68 SUSPICION

Ivan was waiting for Boris in the library. "Did you get them?" Ivan asked in Russian.

"Of course." Boris wasn't sure about his childhood friend's suitability for this mission. "It was no problem."

"But what if someone saw you?" Ivan always feared the worst. He was short and his hair was fastidiously combed. Boris was taller and scruffier, and always wore a "B" baseball cap. "Who's going to see me? Who's going to care about a couple of exchange students? You worry too much."

They were sitting in their usual place behind a bookshelf in the corner of the student library.

"I just like to be careful."

"Look, we've got simple instructions. We take it in turns, pick up everything we need on the list from different places. If we do get stopped – and we won't – but if we do, there is nothing suspicious about any of the individual components. The only danger is when we put it all together, and I'll be taking care of that. And by then, you'll probably be on the flight back to Moscow."

"But what about our studies?" Ivan was the brightest student at the seminary, but was only there to nurse Boris through his Harvard classes.

"What about our classes? That's not what we're here for."

"But it is Harvard. It would be good to get the diploma. You know, for the future."

"There won't be a future for Harvard if all goes well."

Alina was getting back the textbooks she'd handed in, her thoughts full of Roman. They had walked along the river and he had held her hand. She remembered the warmth of his touch and the way he had looked at her, the fresh hint of lemon when he leaned in close. They talked forever during dinner, and when he left later that evening Roman told her he already missed her. Now in the library, the phone he gave her buzzed quietly. She opened the text message from him.

I am counting the hours before I see you. A red heart closed the message and she smiled. Her heart felt full, she was so happy to be staying in America and studying at Harvard. She felt as if she were in a dream.

She was surprised to hear the familiar Russian from the other side of the bookshelf, and Alina felt a quick stab of homesickness. She would have been home by now, of course. Listening closer, she realized it was the boys sponsored by Roman's father's foundation. They had never been the least bit friendly to her. It didn't make a lot of sense what they were saying, but she didn't like the sound of it. She decided to tell Roman. He would know what to do.

69 THEN THERE WERE THREE

The results show wasn't the kind of cliffhanger Kristoff wanted. Everybody knew Cameron was going home. The results of the poll flashed up on the screen behind him.

Studio Audience/Audience At Home
30% - ECONOMY/JOBS
20% - DEFICIT/INTEREST ON DEBT
15% - HEALTH
15% - EDUCATION
13% - HOME SEC/DEFENSE
5% - FOREIGN AID
2% - OTHER PROGRAMS

"America has spoken and the economy and interest debt are the two areas where you spent the most money. Notice that although Todd allocated a whopping 30% to defense, he also matched both of the top areas, with 30% on the economy and 20% on the deficit. Grace was right up there, too, with 25% and 20% respectively. Grace and Todd, you are both safe.

"Now Tom, you were more conservative on America's top two, spending 12% on interest debt and 15% on the economy, but that's okay. You budgeted high for health at 30% and education at 20%, which were America's next two priorities. So you, too, are safe."

Cameron's head dropped. "That leaves Cameron. Unfortunately, Cameron didn't show the same kind of financial acumen as the other three surviving finalists. He spent a huge chunk of change, 30% in fact, on foreign aid, 25% on health, and 15% on the economy. His failure to invest any of his $1 million to pay off the national debt, for whatever reason, shows a definite lack of financial responsibility." Cameron was out. The viral video had sealed his fate.

70 MISS YOU

Leaving the stage, Cameron looked for Grace. There was something he wanted to get off his chest. He rounded the corridor and there she was. He dared to hope she was waiting for him. No-one else was around and they just stood in silence looking at each other.

"So that's it then. You're out." Grace's voice was flat. Did she sound disappointed? He couldn't help but hope.

"Yep. I blew it." He took a step closer. "Look Grace, when I was standing on the stage being told my fate, I wanted to tell the audience, and, well everyone actually, to vote for you in the finale."

"Why would you say that?" Her heart skipped a beat, but her defenses snapped shut around her. What was his ulterior motive, she wondered.

"Because I think you should win. Take the compliment Grace. Why is it so hard for you do that it?"

"Well, I'm just a little surprised. You might just be the most arrogant man I've ever met and you certainly lived up to everybody's expectations, didn't you?"

"You have such a way of making a man feel good about himself, Grace."

"Well, I'm sorry, you just bring it out of me."

Cameron was about to say something but Grace continued, her voice softened. "Something doesn't add up though. You may be a lot of things, but stupid isn't one of them. What really got you involved in that fight?"

"You wouldn't believe me if I told you," Cameron tried to sound casual, but Grace wasn't buying it.

"Try me." Grace answered. She thought she saw something raw cross his face, vulnerability maybe. It lasted just a second...

He was convinced he'd been framed and told her so.

Grace looked doubtful. "So, they just happened to be sitting in the very bar you walk into, plotting your downfall. That seems pretty far-fetched."

"You can believe what you like, but blondie was filming me while he stamped footprints on my face. They probably made a tidy sum for the footage," he shrugged.

"No-one tried to stop it?"

"The place was empty. Even the barman mysteriously disappeared."

Grace narrowed her eyes suspiciously and he knew she would never believe him, so what was the point in trying. "What can I say? Some things just don't add up...Now you, on the other hand, your figure is just perfect."

She rolled her eyes to the ceiling, but there was a different look there. She saw him, maybe it was just a glimmer of the real him, but he could tell that she had.

Grace crossed her arms. "You know, I think this whole arrogant-flirty-swagger thing you have going on might be a cover up. It's just too over-the-top to be real."

Cameron didn't know what to say so jumped back into jokey, safety zone. "Grace, here's your chance to tell me how much you'll miss me."

Grace drew back too. "Get over yourself, Cameron."

"Not quite what I was looking for. Some you win, some you lose, I guess." They reached the Green Room and Kristoff beckoned Cameron to join him in his office. "Good luck, Grace. I'll be thinking of you."

"Thank you. Good luck yourself." Grace watched Cameron walk away and, as unlikely as it seemed, she realized she didn't want him to go.

Tom found her standing in the same spot a few moments later. "Penny for your thoughts, my dear? Oh, and congratulations on a superb challenge!"

"Congratulations to you too, Tom! We did it! How completely insane is all this?"

"I think the crazy part is that this aging transgender is still in the race. I think they just like my fashion sense actually," he added, with a cheeky grin. He twirled around in a light blue dress, decorated with little american flags and matching shoes.

"That must be it!" Grace laughed. She adored this man. He didn't care in the least what people thought of him, always positive and probably the most genuine person she had ever met. "Listen,

I'm going to meet Gillian for a drink. Want to join us, Tom?"

"Thank you, Grace, that's very kind of you, but I'm taking my wife out for a real feast: steak, mashed potatoes, hot fudge sundae, the works. I thought it was going to be our exit dinner. Who knew?"

Over Grace's shoulder he saw his wife appear. She was beaming, and gave him a small wave.

"There's my angel now. She likes to stay out of the limelight - says I fill up the spotlight plenty for the both of us. I have no idea what she means!" A kiss on the cheek and he was gone.

Grace watched down the corridor as Tom and his wife shared a gentle embrace, how she threw back her head and laughed at something Tom said. Tom's wife was much more conservatively dressed in a beige sundress. Arm in arm, they left out of the back door.

Grace couldn't help but smile at how happy they looked. A pang of loneliness hit her, but she quickly buried it. Now was not the time. She had come too far to blow it now.

71 NO RETURN

It was several more days before Roman could get away, and when he spoke to Alina on the phone he was careful not to alert her that something was wrong. She was so different. Something had unlocked inside her and she was bubbling with excitement as she described walking the streets of Boston, feeling more and more at home in Cambridge. She couldn't wait to see him again. He kept up a forced jollity. The thought of letting her down again was so devastating he could barely concentrate at work. His father had been emphatic but unyielding – Roman must give up Alina or risk losing everything.

Roman walked the stairs to Alina's dorm room with a heavy heart. He hoped she'd understand, but he knew she wouldn't. He'd stopped her from going home only to break her heart again.

He knocked on the door and heard her apologize as she took her time to open it. Then she was there. The eyes looking up at him were the same, but the hesitation was gone. Her jet-black, silky hair flowed over her bare shoulders. She smiled shyly and his gaze was drawn to her lips. He longed to kiss her, and to touch her face. They recognized something deep within each other.

"Come," she said, pulling him into the kitchen. "Alma is out for the evening and I've cooked you something from home." And just like that, Roman knew that for the first time in his life, he would disobey his father.

72 HEART-TO-HEART CHALLENGE

In a black tuxedo, Kristoff described the final Heart-to-Heart challenge to TV viewers and the audience packed into Hollywood's Kodak Theater. He wasn't holding back the hyperbole.

"This is going to be the biggest Town Hall meeting in political history, right here in Hollywood! This is the future folks. If our estimates prove accurate, The iCandidate will be the single most watched TV show in history!" The front rows were crammed with celebrities; the entire theater was filled with signs and banners touting the finalists' names in bold colors. Kristoff held out his arms. "Welcome once more, America, to The iCandidate."

The theater erupted as the lights slowly dimmed. "Throughout this entire season, you've been writing in with your stories and your questions and we've picked some of you to be here tonight to present them to our three finalists face to face. There will be no hiding behind political jargon, just answers straight from the heart. The iCandidates each have just 30 seconds to deliver their best answer. What are we waiting for? Let's meet our first iVIP!"

Janet Wilson, a single mom from Mississippi, stood up and Kristoff went down into the audience to join her. In a halting, nervous voice, she explained how she discovered she had breast cancer shortly after her husband, Mark, died from a tumor two years earlier.

"I was terrified," the petite mother began. Her hair was beginning to grow back. "I lost my husband - the children's daddy - so having the disease back in our family was devastating. How could I look after my children, pay for the expenses, and survive?"

"So, on your darkest days, Janet, how did you cope? What kept you going?" Jacqueline asked.

"My children. It is as simple as that. They did the housework, helped with the shopping, the cooking." The young mother's voice started to break and Kristoff jumped in.

"Janet, I know you have a question you want to ask the finalists - and in consideration of allowing all our competition winners a turn, please pick the two you want to hear from most."

"Okay. My first choice is Todd. Do you think there is a cure for cancer out there, and if you were to become President of the United States what would you do to help fight the disease?"

"I want to believe we are very near to getting a cure for cancer," Todd started. "I dearly wish we had the answers and the cure already, so that your family could have been saved from so much suffering, Janet." He ran through a quick list of statistics and government bodies and comparative survival rates that seemed to confuse everybody, including the questioner.

Grace glanced at Janet, who looked blank.

"Janet, please choose either Tom or Grace for their response."

"Tom."

Tom cleared his throat. "Can I just ask you Janet, what treatments did you have?"

Janet smiled. "I had all the recommended courses of chemotherapy, and felt absolutely awful throughout, so I changed my strategy and went natural, juicing every day, blood cleansing tonics, herbs, homeopathy, you name it, we did it."

"We?" Tom asked.

"My children. And they prepared it all for me, and they had it too. I have no doubt in my mind, that's what saved me. Sunshine fixes they called them!"

Tom's eyes filled up with tears. "Janet, I believe you're right." As he looked around, it hit him. There were so many people here and they were all listening. There was a chance to make a real difference. Finding Gillian in the audience he winked at her. "One medicine doesn't cure all, how could it? We are all so different. Janet, do I believe there is a cure for cancer? I don't believe in a magic pill, no. But I wholeheartedly believe in an integrated approach. It is the only one that makes sense. If I become President I would fight to have more natural therapies approved, and money allocated to those areas."

"That's the answer I'm looking for. Thank you, Tom." Janet took her seat. But the audience reaction was muted. Were they still not ready for an integrated approach? Tom couldn't help wonder.

No one had really set the place on fire. So no home runs.

73 HERO

Returning from the commercial break, Kristoff tried to whip up a little enthusiasm. "Welcome back, folks, be ready to lose your heart to a military family."

Nicholas Byrnes stood up, brushing his hand through a straggly mop of graying hair. "Nicholas is a session musician from Rutherford, New Jersey. Ever worked with the Boss?" Kristoff asked.

"I've played a chord or two with him, yes." The audience burst into rapturous applause.

"You've certainly impressed this crowd, maybe we can have you play for us later?"

"It would be an honor," Nicholas was bursting with pride.

"So, I know you have two sons. They didn't follow you into the music business then?"

"John, our eldest, was a fine musician, but out of the blue he decided to join the military, and my youngest, David, who had just finished community college, had his AA degree and was transferring to a four year, signed right up with him. Both were deployed to Afghanistan." It was very quiet in the concert hall, and Kristoff knew this was going to be one of those memorable moments.

"That was four years ago. David is here with me but John, he...he never made it home."

Kristoff waited, allowing a few moments of silence out of respect for the father's loss, of course, but it had to be said, for it's dramatic effect. The audience was transfixed. "So, what is your question for the iCandidates, Nicholas?" Kristoff asked softly.

"Military officials told me that my son died a hero, protecting his country. Well, as it turns out, he was a victim of friendly fire. It was a terrible mistake. Even though I know the facts, the military chiefs will not admit it to me. They insist on telling me that he was a hero killed in action with the enemy." A ripple of discomfort ran through the crowd. "If you were leading this country, and you knew the real story, would you tell me what you think I want to hear, or would you just tell me what I need to hear, which is the truth? I'd like to hear from Grace first."

Kristof walked into the audience to Nicholas, putting a hand on his shoulder. "It doesn't get any more real than this. Grace, you're up."

Grace swallowed hard. "I am so very sorry for your loss, Mr. Byrnes." She didn't want to do this. She was aware of how quiet the room was. Finally Grace found the words. "My parents served the public, too, not in the military, but in politics. I was there when they were gunned down in cold blood. The killers were masked and to this day I do not know who murdered them, and probably never will. And although knowing this won't bring them back, the truth is a necessary component to heal." Grace's voice shook slightly. "We can wholeheartedly support our brave troops fighting to protect us, but at the same time have an opinion on whether a war is right or wrong." Grace looked at Nicholas, but his expression was impossible to read. "Nicholas Byrnes deserves our respect and that of the military. He deserves nothing but the truth."

The applause was again muted. Kristoff moved forward.

"Thank you, Grace," said Nicholas. "I'd like to hear from Todd, please."

Todd decided that there was only one way to play this. He moved away from his lectern, and towards the father. He was going for glory.

"I believe your son was awarded the Silver Star, is this correct Mr. Byrnes?" Nicholas nodded and Todd continued. "John Byrnes earned the Silver Star because of the example he set throughout his service to our great nation, not just on that fateful day that he fell." Todd paused and looked around the room. He had everyone's attention and he savored the moment.

"In my mind, John is a hero however he died. John made the ultimate sacrifice in the war on terror simply by choosing duty to his country over an easier life, and for that reason, and I think everyone in this room and at home will agree with me when I say this, John is, and will always be the people's hero! That is the truth here." Todd punctuated 'people's hero' with such emotion that the audience was on its feet giving him a standing ovation.

Nicholas had his head bowed, his shoulders shaking. Even the judges were standing and clapping.

Man, he's good, thought Grace. And he didn't even answer the question.

74 Q & A

The next iVIP was Sally Baker, a flight attendant for American Airlines who lost her best friend on 9/11. Kristoff had his arm around her when they returned from the commercial break.

"I don't understand why Muslims hate Christians so much?" she said. "What can you tell me that will make me believe you would do everything possible to stop another attack? I need to believe there is a future for my children. Todd, please?"

"Of course you do, Miss Baker," Todd said gently. "I am a believer in defending our great country with nothing left to chance. I would invest in the very best technology to beef up the security posts at the airports, in the air, and we would have more military patrols at all our borders. I want you to be able to sleep soundly in your bed at night, secure in the knowledge that I care. If anyone is going to stay up at night it will be me, protecting you and your family!"

Sally blew Todd a kiss.

"Tom, please." Again, Todd had avoided the question. But this time Tom didn't hesitate.

"Sally, I am so sorry that you lost your best friend because of 9/11, but let me be very clear when I say this: It was not a religion that attacked us on that awful day. It was al Qaeda; it was a despicable and evil act of mass murder and not the Muslim faith targeting Christianity. We cannot negotiate with terrorists and we cannot live in fear either. We are stronger than that, and Sally, you must believe and pass over that strength to your children."

Sally nodded thoughtfully, but she clearly wouldn't be voting for Tom.

Kristoff crossed over to the other side of the auditorium. "I'd like to introduce Eric Gonzalez, a Mexican construction worker from Santa Ana, California. Go ahead Eric."

"Good evening, Grace, Todd, Tom. I have always worked hard.

My employer laid me off a year ago because there were no houses to build. I have a wife and three kids to support, but there are no jobs. Tell me something I can tell my wife when she cries at night-time? Please can I hear from Grace first, and then Tom, please?"

"My answer has two parts. Firstly, we have to keep the jobs here and not watch them being outsourced to China and India. Secondly, we need to invest money in the country's highways, bridges, tunnels, and even government office buildings. Mr. Gonza-lez, you would be able to use your skills in construction in these areas and not just have to rely on a buoyant housing market for your line of work."

"Good stuff." Kristoff moved it on. "Ready, Tom? Thirty sec-onds to answer Eric's question."

"Job creation is vital and the only way to go is to increase our access to all reliable domestic energy, wind, solar, nuclear, and yes, oil and natural gas. Our nation has ample energy reserves that can contribute to our economy for decades to come. We need to tap into those resources. And for Mr. Gonzales in your line of work, there would always be a job for you in the construction side of things."

Kristoff was getting antsy. He wanted more drama. "Next is Madison Grey, a nurse from San Antonio, Texas who has a multiple choice question for you all. Go ahead, Madison."

"We all agree that many professions such as teachers and nurs-es do not receive incomes to match the important work they do. If you could play Robin Hood, which one of these would you take from to pay us more?
a) Professional athletes
b) Hedge fund/investment guys
c) Pharmaceutical giants

Todd jumped in. "I would make it my business to ensure nurs-es and teachers salaries would be raised significantly. My ideas for clean energy programs would boost our economy, resulting in our budget deficit being reduced. My energy bill will result in the growth of jobs, which, of course, will bring more money into our programs. That is how I will give you your raise, Madison."

She didn't look impressed. "Okay. Thank you, but you didn't actually answer the question. Tom, what would you do?"

"Well, I like to think myself as a bit of an athlete," he quipped, "and I'm not sure I would want to penalize all the investment guys; there are some good ones out there trying to help folks save for a rainy day. So I would have to go with c) Pharmaceutical giants."

"Grace?" Madison Gray looked disappointed with the answers she had heard so far.

"Hello, Madison. I agree with you that salaries paid aren't always reflective of the important work our teachers, nurses, and other healthcare professionals do. So I would have to say... a, b and c."

Madison jumped up, clapping wildly. The majority of the studio audience followed.

"Thank you, that was easy," Grace said shyly. Kristoff moved in quickly. Time was running out...

75 THE CLAWS ARE OUT

The clock was almost out and the debate remained deadlocked. "Ladies and gentlemen, we have time for just a couple of questions from the audience." Kristoff was still hoping for some last minute fireworks. Desmond had vetted the questioners and was in his earpiece urging him to choose a woman wearing a white hat in the front row.

"Yes, the lady in the front, what is your question ma'am?"

"Do you think that America really is ready for a woman President."

"This should be interesting," Gillian whispered to Jen and Dulce, who were sitting by the side of the stage.

"I'd like to hear from all three if we have time, starting with Tom."

"Well, this is an interesting question, and my answer will be unique. I was born a man, so I have plenty of testosterone running through my veins, and yet, I always felt more in touch with my feminine side, hence the outfit, ladies and gentlemen." The audience laughed as Tom gave a little curtsey in a red and white dress with oversized blue buttons. "I never knew if I was supposed to be a man or a woman. I felt stuck between two places, a man in a man's world, but knowing in my heart that it wasn't really me. Confused? Yes, I was, too. But all I can say, is when you choose your leader, gender shouldn't be an issue. Think about the essential qualities you want in a leader such as integrity, loyalty, focus, love for the American people, and a deep desire for a better world. There's no confusion about that."

The audience were on their feet.

"Thank you, Tom, well said. Now Todd?"

There was a pause as Todd looked around the room. "I love women!" The audience cheered. "I also have the absolute utmost respect for women as equals in the workplace. I would go so far as to say I have seen many women kick ass in the corporate world. I have so much admiration for my opponent, Grace Conwright, and it has been an absolute honor to compete against her in this competition." He paused, smiling at Grace.

"Likewise, Todd. But I think Britain's Dame Margaret Thatcher said it perfectly, 'In politics if you want anything said, ask a man. If you want anything done, ask a woman.' No offense," Grace added with a cheeky smile.

The audience laughed.

Todd's phone vibrated. He risked a look. 'Use the attack!!' Todd's heart sank. "Sorry, Grace, I hadn't quite finished."

"Go ahead, Todd."

"But I have to say this, ladies and gentlemen. I truly believe that America needs a leader who has the physical presence to stand up to countries across the world. There is a reason why our leaders have all been men." Todd walked purposefully over to Grace and put his arm around her shoulders. It was easy to see that he stood a foot taller and weighed 100 pounds heavier. "No offense meant to you, Grace," he squeezed her slim shoulders before walking back to his podium.

"Oh, none taken, Todd, but I disagree," Grace said, her ire up. "It takes the right man, or the right woman, to run anything, be it a country or a business, and to say otherwise is naïve and sexist. And there are a growing number of strong women leading their countries in Europe and South America, as well as other parts of the world. In fact, the UK just chose a woman for their Prime Minister for the second time."

Grace received a powerful round of applause and Todd felt his phone vibrate again.

'The attack!!!'

He'd gone too far to go soft now. "Strong? That's such an interesting word isn't it? We use it to describe so many things, don't we? Strong words, strong actions, the strength of our convictions, or morals. But what if we choose to concentrate on strength in the pure physical form. Who is stronger? I don't think anyone here would argue that a man is usually physically stronger than a woman. So, if an enemy were to attack us, and let's just say, for arguments sake, that enemy was a man, he is physically strong, aggressive and unyielding. Who do you think will offer the best defense? A man or a woman?"

Grace's eyes bored into Todd. "I think a woman would fight to the death," she said deliberately.

"Yes, but a man wouldn't have to. He is on equal footing, and has a better chance of overpowering the attacker. A woman starts at a disadvantage."

Grace's voice was like steel. "That depends on the tools she uses."

"But at the end of the day, that wasn't enough was it, Grace?"

Grace stopped. Flashes of her attacker's fist on her cheek and the memory of being slammed against the gravel filled her head.

The judges whispered to one another. Like the audience, they didn't understand what was going on.

"What are they talking about, do you know?" Jen asked Gillian.

"Todd's knifed Grace in the back," Gillian said so quietly the others didn't hear.

Grace and Todd continued to eye each other. Kristoff waited. Time was almost up. Too late to ask another question.

Grace finally found her voice. "A smart leader builds a team of trust and unity. Do the people ultimately want someone who acts alone and thinks they are better than everyone else?

No, I think the people want a leader who mirrors their thoughts, their wishes, and conveys those ideas with conviction. When strength is needed, strength lies in banding ideas and power together. The leader, be it a man or a woman, is never alone. In the immortal words of one of our own great Presidents, Franklin D. Roosevelt: 'Let us never forget that government is ourselves and not an alien power over us. The ultimate rulers of our democracy are not a President and senators and congressmen and government officials, but the voters of this country.'"

The audience went wild – particularly the women. Todd tried in vain to come up with a line that would floor her, but it was too late, Kristoff was running onto the stage.

It was over.

76 SHOWDOWN

In just 24 hours, Tom, Grace or Todd would be crowned The iCandidate. "This is it folks. We've reached the end of our competition. They've done all they can and now it's up to you, America. We'll have our studio vote in just a moment, and you at home, please be ready to start voting." Kristoff shouted over the credits. "Our special results show is tomorrow night, at Dodger Stadium, so, as usual, we're going to keep you in suspense for twenty-four hours. When you're ready studio audience, whose iVote are you sending?"

"MyiVote?" the audience shouted.

"That's right. So you all know what to do."

The screen flickered into life, and two bar graphs and a pie chart loomed in bright colors as the votes translated to the screen. Within one minute all the studio votes were in.

"This is amazing. Could it be any closer?" Kristoff gasped. "For the very first time in this competition, Grace has taken the lead, only by a hair, but with 44% to Todd's 42%. Tom trails with 14% of the vote." Everyone now knew this was just between Todd and Grace.

"Now it's up to you at home," Kristoff spun to face Camera One. He closed the show: "Vote for the iCandidate that echoes your own thoughts, your beliefs. Vote for the man or woman who you believe can achieve extraordinary things. And yes, vote for the iCandidate who you think could go on to become the President of the United States. To quote a certain Texan Republican senator who upset a few people over in Cleveland, 'Vote your conscience.' I can't see what's so bad about that. We'll see you tomorrow night. From myself, the judges, and our very impressive iCandidates here at the Kodak Theatre in Hollywood, goodnight and God bless!"

Grace left the stage. Gillian was waiting to congratulate her. Todd tried to squeeze past, obviously in a hurry, but Grace stopped him. "Well done, Todd, that was quite an adrenalin rush out there tonight and you did a fine job. Except for that cheap shot at the end, of course." She extended her hand and he looked embarrassed, hesitating before taking it.

He glanced at Gillian. "You too, Grace. You were a formidable opponent. I was just trying to make my point. You know it wasn't personal."

"Oh, but it was to me. Let's hope for your sake, women voters still love you."

He walked away wearing a tight smile as Gillian narrowed her eyes. "Typical man. But it's all karma. You're gonna win, Grace."

77 IN THE GAME

Todd's research on the movers and shakers in Washington was so thorough he immediately recognized three people sitting at a discreet table at a private club in downtown Los Angeles. Desmond was with the middle-aged trio in their blazers, slacks and twin set.

"I think you guys probably know plenty about our three finalists here," he said standing up. "Todd, Grace, Tom, I want you to meet Senators Timothy Sheff, Bill Foreman, and Congresswoman Denise Fury."

The other three iCandidate founders, Jacqueline, Kristoff, and Mason, joined them a few minutes later. The euphoria of the final show earlier that evening had quickly worn off and Grace felt physically and emotionally exhausted. Why they'd been dragged there she had no idea.

"I don't need to tell you guys that we are talking in absolute confidentiality," Kristoff said, squeezing in next to Tom. They were sitting in a dimly lit alcove in a quiet corner.

No, you don't, thought Grace, because I don't actually know why we're here.

The century-old club located inside a grand, renaissance style building was in the city's business district. "Our friends here," Desmond made a sweeping gesture towards the lawmakers, "kindly agreed to make the trip across country to meet the three of you."

"We're honored," Grace offered graciously.

"They'll be backstage with us at the results show tomorrow and I've assured them a big surprise. Bill, would you mind explaining what's going on?" The balding senator looked like he had never had to shave a day in his life, although he must have been at least 50. He had a habit of smiling after virtually every sentence.

"As you may know, I was closely involved in Bob Carson's re-election campaign and Timothy, my colleague from across the aisle, single-handedly got George W. Bush elected the second time around; he marshaled the evangelical Christian vote. Denise mobilized the current president's Internet donation network. Long story short, we know how to win presidential elections and we're prepared to help you."

"But we don't even know who the iCandidate will be until tomorrow," Grace said.

"That's not important," Desmond responded. "One of you will be the iCandidate, one of you will be the running mate. The third... well, we will get to that in a moment. The point is that our friends here are prepared to help make the iCampaign a reality."

"That's fantastic," Tom gushed.

"But why would you do that when you're already in Congress?" Grace asked, slightly confused. "Won't your parties go ballistic?"

"They will be unhappy, certainly," Senator Sheff said. He looked a little like Pee Wee Herman. "But you can leave them to us."

"We're not alone," Rep. Fury interjected. "Many of our colleagues are facing a lot of pressure from our constituents to make the kind of changes being talked about on The iCandidate. Quite simply, many are being told to join forces with you or risk taking a beating at the ballot box. There are at least 100 of us who are defending narrow majorities and are willing to try something new; but, we need to determine whether the show's popularity is just a flash in the pan."

Peering more closely at the three finalists above her bifocals, she added: "We need to know whether you're serious. That's why we asked to meet you tonight."

"We couldn't be more serious. We haven't come all this way to let up now. This is just the start." Todd had a habit of making everything he said sound like part of a speech.

"My thoughts exactly," Desmond added. "But I can see that our friends may still need some convincing. I think that after tomorrow night, you will see just how serious we are."

"I'm sure we're all looking forward to that," Senator Foreman took a sip of wine. "And if that turns out to be the case, I think I can speak for all three of us when I say we'll be prepared to work with you and develop the campaign."

"Our only proviso," Senator Sheff leaned forward, "is that our involvement remains confidential, at least in the early stages."

"There is something else." The congresswoman brushed her boyish bangs away from her face. "We each want cast iron guarantees that we'll be in the Cabinet if we pull this thing off. I want Education, Bill wants Defense and Tim has his eyes on the Treasury."

Kristoff glanced at Desmond before answering. "I'm afraid that's out of the question, our other iCandidate finalists will certainly want to be considered and we…"

"How about this?" interrupted Desmond. "Help the iCampaign to victory and you'll all be in the Cabinet, but we can't guarantee your exact roles. Is that reasonable?"

Rep. Fury looked at her two colleagues and they all nodded. "It looks like we have a deal."

78 SHOWTIME

Todd believed himself invincible; he'd visualized this moment so many times in his head. Although he felt bad about bringing up the attack on Grace, he really felt he had no choice.

Tom knew he wasn't going to win; he was astonished he'd survived so long. He never even thought he'd make it through the first round; the fact that he'd come so far gave him hope that America had also come much further than many gave it credit for. He was happy just to enjoy the moment.

Grace looked out across the sea of people and it literally took her breath away.

The finale was originally going to be held at the Staples Center, but there was so much demand it was switched to Dodger Stadium which is three times bigger. She never expected to win either, and was pleasantly surprised every time she passed through to the next stage. But she wanted this now, for a number of reasons. Her parents, of course. She wanted to win it for them, to make sure everyone in the country knew about their sacrifice. But most importantly, she wanted to win for the great majority of ordinary people who wanted the same things she did; a roof over their heads, food for their families; a little room to dream of better days, and for their opinions to matter.

"Ladies and Gentlemen, we're finally here." Kristoff's voice echoed across the vast floor of the stadium. "Allow me to introduce your judges one last time."

The judges walked out from the back of the stage, the men in tuxedos and Jacqueline in a flowing, white backless gown. "Please also welcome back Dulce Ramirez, Cameron Banks, Rich Francombe, Jennifer Flynt, and Gillian Lawfull!" The five walked out on stage together to deafening applause, waving and smiling at the crowd.

In turn, Kristoff asked them how The iCandidate had changed

their lives. A brief video depicting each contestant's journey was played on giant screens around the stadium.

"Tonight is just the beginning for our winner," Kristoff pointed out, moving back to center stage. "He or she will get to choose their dream team from a pool of campaign experts recruited from across the political spectrum. The first ever iCandidate will lead the new iCan Party in the iCampaign in this year's presidential election. This is history in the making, America, and here are the three finalists at the vanguard of the new political frontier - Tom Jodes, Grace Conwright, and Todd Greenacre."

They walked out together with Tom, more formal than usual in a cherry red suit, Todd, looking a million dollars in a black Armani tux, and Grace stunning in a midnight blue, Badgley Mischka, one-shoulder, ruffled organza gown.

The nation was kept in suspense while Rob Balfour and Sir Paul McCartney performed solo versions of their greatest hits. Nicholas Byrnes, the father of the Marine killed by friendly fire, was invited to join them both on stage for an encore.

Next, the judges preened about how they had chosen such wonderful candidates.

Tom, Todd, and Grace were watching the show in silence from the wings with Tom cracking jokes despite their nerves frayed ragged by the wait through a succession of commercial breaks. Then it was time.

"Everyone at home please read through the shortlist of finalists on your iCandidate app and pick the one you want to lead your country," said Kristoff. "Please start our final iVote NOW."

He paused. Even the unflappable presenter was caught up in the moment. "The next President of the United States does not need to be Dennis Saxon or Harriet Carson. You have seen the alternatives for yourself. You judge them every week. You know what they can do. Ladies and gentleman, it's time for us to step up for what's right. Let's make this iVote count."

The lights went down. This was it.

79 AND THEN THERE WAS ONE

The ratings had gone through the roof. "Tonight, I can tell you that a record number of people voted for our three iCandidates, and there are but a handful of votes dividing them!" Kristoff announced. "Now that is democracy in action. Let's get right to it!"

He waited for the crowd to quieten.

"In third place...Tom Jodes."

Tom stepped forward looking unusually bashful. "Forgive me America," he smiled, his voice wavering. "What kind of goon starts to cry at a moment like this? A big soppy girl, that's all. Wait, that's me! You know how I feel about being here, I've said it all before. You know, too, how touched I am that you accepted me, I mean look at me! But you carried me throughout this amazing journey to the final three." He paused and looked around the room, his eyes glistening. "You looked through the bad wig and polyester dress and you saw me, you got me. You are testaments to my faith in the American people. For those who say Americans are blinkered or narrow-minded, I say, look at me! You gave me a chance to shine. I'll always love you for that."

Tom looked out into the audience. "My home town of Rayville is not perfect by any means. We went through a rough time in the recession, and people worried about their jobs. Some of the sidewalks are the devil to walk down in heels and the entertainment doesn't match up to the big city lights. But the one thing I hope for is that none of the people in our town feel alone. We don't just love our guns and our religion. We care for one another."

This was a different Tom compared to the wisecracking Mayor the public was used to. "If I was President, that would be one of my main platforms. It's not a question of small towns versus big cities. Either can be as embracing or as lonely as we make it. In my opinion as an ex-iCandidate contestant there is nothing more important than being with your friends and family through the good times and the bad."

The studio erupted with cheering and clapping as Tom embraced Grace and Todd before turning back to the audience. "On that final note, it has been an immense honor to share this stage with the remaining contestants. I know with absolute certainty that you will find the iCandidate who will lead this country to greatness - and that, I'd bet my pantyhose on!"

As he left the stage, Desmond beckoned Tom into his office. Perhaps the journey isn't over after all, Tom thought.

"Thank you for being a part of this incredible process to revolutionize the way politics occurs in America. You, the people, watched, you listened, and you voted!" Kristoff paused, and everyone waited. Not a whisper could be heard, just the slight crackle of the sound system, as Kristoff raised the microphone to his lips.

"Ladies and Gentlemen, our first winner and The iCandidate is....

GRACE CONWRIGHT!"

When Kristoff read out the final results, Todd was so convinced he'd won that he stepped forward to shake the host's hand before it struck home that it wasn't his name he'd heard. Equally dumbstruck, Grace started applauding Todd, as her iCandidate colleagues mobbed her in a flurry of red, white, and blue confetti.

Jacqueline walked out in the middle of the chaos and fought to be heard above the noise. "As everybody now knows, our iCandidate winner, Grace Conwright, will be representing the new iCan Party as its presidential nominee in the forthcoming election, with Todd as her running mate." Todd waved at the crowd, trying desperately not to show his disappointment. "Tonight," Jacqueline continued, "I'm excited to share with you an announcement that we have been keeping secret the entire show. It is my absolute pleasure to inform you that Grace Conwright, the people's choice for The iCandidate, will have an election fund of $100 million at her campaign's disposal to put her on an equal footing with her opponents."

For two or three seconds there was a stunned silence as the words sunk in.

Mason smiled out from the control room. That'll grab Washington's attention!

80 WOODSTOCK

The cars crept in throughout the night in a long, slow crawl into a perfect Great Plains summer. Every hotel within 100 miles was full; a vast campsite in a farmer's field was already heaving with Gore-Tex, and it was still a full 24 hours before the first iCan Party Convention was scheduled to begin just outside the small, north-central town of Lebanon, Kansas. Campers took turns getting photographed by a stone marker with an American Flag that told anyone who was interested that they were in the exact geographic center of the lower 48 states at 39.50 Latitude and 98.35 Longitude.

"This is so sick. It must be what it felt like to be at Woodstock." Mason looked out across the mass of people. It was his idea to hold the iCampaign's launch party in the center of the heartland, and he'd been losing sleep ever since worrying whether people would come. Desmond and Jacqueline pushed hard for Washington, insisting it was the only location if they wanted to be taken seriously. Kristoff wanted to stay put in Los Angeles, to cement the idea in the public's mind that the iCandidate was born from this unique meeting point between politics and entertainment.

But Mason prevailed this time, as the four friends stood together in the large bay window of the hill-top hotel suite Kristoff had booked, providing a great view of the scene below them. "It's so easy to fall back now and start copying what the other campaigns are doing," he had told them as the scale of the incredible political pilgrimage unfolded in front of them. "People want something different. They want to be excited about politics again. They don't want all the ugliness they're seeing from the conventional parties."

"I'm a believer Mace," Kristoff agreed. "Except I'm having trouble believing that this many people are already here and we have another day before we get under way. It's awesome."

"Calls for a celebration don't you think?" Desmond said, and walked across to the bar, to open a bottle of champagne. "You were right Mace. This venue is perfect! Good job!" Desmond couldn't contain his excitement.

"Well, we still have a long way to go," Jacqueline took the glass and stared out of the window. "But I have to admit, this turnout is amazing. I'm actually stunned."

Kristoff raised his glass. "A toast to Grace. It's not going to be easy to beat the two party system, but let's show the the non-believers what we are made of. Let's take it all the way to the White House!"

The four clinked their glasses: "To the White House...and President Conwright!"

Grace, Todd and the other iCandidates were staying in the large house belonging to the farmer who'd given them his land to use for the convention.

In his new role as iCampaign Manager, Kristoff's initial inclination was to keep the team holed up before introducing them in a blaze of lights and sound on stage. But with Mason's 'change' philosophy ringing in his ears, he decided to do the exact opposite: all eight of the iCandidates had been happily wandering amongst the growing crowds ever since they arrived the day before. Kristoff could see Rich and Tom laughing with people lining up for the portable toilets on one side of the field. By the house, Gillian was holding a baby and talking with the parents. Over by the food tent, Dulce was happily chatting with a group of teenagers.

Cameron, dressed in designer jeans and a white button down shirt that emphasized his lean, muscular physique, leaned against the stage, surrounded by a group of panting women desperate for his autograph, or just a word with their idol. At times, he tried to disengage himself, eager to mingle with the rest of the crowd, but he never managed to move more than a few feet without being mobbed again.

"It's going to be an incredible day tomorrow," Kristoff said. "Can I persuade you to stick around, Des?"

"No, I'm heading home to work on the technical aspects of the campaign funding. There's going to be an almighty shit storm once the Democrats and Republicans realize we're not going away. I'm amazed we haven't had more crap to deal with already."

By mid-afternoon the following day, when Rob Balfour's band, Legacy, launched into its second encore, a rainstorm gave it an authentic Woodstock feel as it soaked the audience singing familiar anthems. The clouds parted just in time for the real stars to take their turn on the convention stage.

One by one, the iCandidates addressed the cheering crowd, delighting them as each explained their role in the iCampaign and spelled out the iCan Party message: how the people who voted for them on the show had given them a voice. Speaking in the order in which they departed The iCandidate, Dulce (Outreach Director) was first up to say that she intended to ensure Latinos were represented at the very highest levels of government. Grace stood in the wings, congratulating each of them as they finished. Rich (National Field Director), Jennifer (Communications Director), Tom (National Press Secretary), Cameron (Battleground States Director), and Gillian (Senior Adviser) each told the story of how they came to try out for the show, and how it had changed their lives.

Jennifer revealed an emotional side towards the end of her speech. She had her hair in soft curls, and some people in the crowd didn't even recognize her at first. "So we will drag the antiquated political system, kicking and screaming if we have to, into a better world, an enlightened world and we will do it in the very capable hands of Grace Conwright. She is brilliant, innovative, compassionate, and in this race for each and every one of you. I am honored to work as Communications Director for the iCan Party and I am proud of you all for being apart of our vision."

Grace hugged her as she walked off stage. "I don't know what you did with the old Jennifer, but I'm loving the new one." Grace was visibly moved.

"Don't get carried away, and for goodness sake, don't get mushy on me." Jennifer smoothed her black linen suit that Grace had crushed in the embrace. "Ugh, I'm going to have to get this suit pressed again."

Grace was unperturbed. "Thank you, Jennifer, for what you said."

A faint glimmer of a smile crossed Jennifer's lips. "You're welcome."

Cameron finished his speech and swaggered off stage carrying a teddy bear and flowers thrown on the stage. Grace looked disapprovingly at him. "Perhaps you could remember that this is a political convention not a rock festival, Cameron."

"Ah, I see you missed me, Conwright. Come on admit it, you're happy to see me."

Grace was happy to see him, but she was never going to tell

him that. "Just do your job, and I'll be happy."

Enjoying the banter, he replied: "I love it when you're bossy."

Todd appeared at Grace's shoulder. He kept insisting he wasn't going to spend the entire campaign trying to steal her thunder. Now she was going to find out. "Okay, it's my turn. Ready to be amazed, Grace?"

"I don't know, am I?"

He was like a puppy, determined to win Grace over. "I'll get them warmed up and you can finish them off." Todd went off script and got the biggest welcome of the day with a savage attack on the Washington gridlock. "The people's right to change what doesn't work is one of the greatest principles of our system of government. It was Richard Nixon who said that," Todd shouted over the more exuberant fans. "But it sums up why we in the iCan Party feel so empowered by you, the people, to change the way our government works."

And then it was Grace's turn.

81 GRACE

It was nearly 9:00 p.m. before Grace walked out into a single bright spotlight to the sound of Jimi Hendrix's Star Spangled Banner. Kristoff knew Mason would enjoy the Woodstock tribute. At first, Grace appeared dumbstruck at the staggering size of her support and she seemed to have lost her nerve when she walked quickly back into the wings, only to emerge leading the rest of the iCandidates behind her.

They all stood clapping in the middle of the stage along with the crowd as Grace stepped forward to the microphone, simply elegant in a cream Ralph Lauren dress. Quietly at first, Grace talked about how her parents were gunned down in cold blood on a stage such as this; murdered for their beliefs by an unseen menace that thought power was too dangerous in the hands of the people.

Gathering force and volume, Grace vowed that she, too, would give her life to protect America's freedoms if she was required to. "Thinking for yourself doesn't mean you're not thinking about each other, " she explained. "The very foundations of this country grew from our forefathers traveling across the ocean, in great peril, for the opportunity to live in freedom, in a land where everybody has a voice, not just the rich or the privileged. We have created a nation of different cultures and different races and I pledge to you all tonight that I will do everything in my power to ensure those voices are heard again."

It was quiet out in the crowd. Grace said that after the death of her parents, she thought she could survive by looking after herself, creating a smaller world and making sure she was okay in her little piece of it. "But I was wrong. As Tom told you earlier, it is our families, our friends, and our communities that make us who we are. This is a new America. It's about breaking down the barriers and abandoning all the prejudices of the past. This is not Dennis Saxon's Republican Party; it's not Harriet Carson's Democrats. In the iCan Party you can be anti-guns and pro-life, against same-sex marriage and for gays in the military. It's all about individual views, coming together. So America, we've been waiting for change to come for too long now. But we're not here to seek blame, we're here to claim ownership of our destinies. We are all responsible for our own dreams, our own happiness, and our own future. So who can do this?"

"iCan," came back the resounding chorus.

"That's right – and I can, too. The New World has finally come of age. Washington just hasn't realized it yet. But they will. I promise you that!" Grace told the roaring, jubilant crowd, as night fell on middle America.

PART TWO

82 CAPITOL HILL

From the picture windows in his Capitol Hill office, the second-ranking member of the Senate looked west across from the white mansion on Pennsylvania Avenue to the National Mall. The Washington Memorial dominated the afternoon sky and Abraham Lincoln, enduring and implacable in white marble, stared back from his throne in the distance. To Patrick Cahill, the majestic view captured everything that was strong and permanent about the nation's past. But for the first time in his 49 years in office, he could feel the pillars of power begin to crumble.

He'd worked long and hard to ensure that nothing moved in Washington without his say-so; Politico last year put him ahead of the President in its top ten list of the nation's most powerful politicians. Now, it was all in peril because of a stupid game show.

He turned back to the room, sparsely decorated with a few family photographs, to meet the glare of the Republican nemesis he'd battled his entire career. "Something has got to be done," he said.

After decades of bitter political rivalry, Cahill and his opposite number, Senator Randall Ainsworth, called a temporary truce after finally agreeing on one thing – The iCandidate had put the future of the republic in jeopardy. Through four wars, Watergate, the collapse of the Soviet Union, and the 2008 economic meltdown, Washington's two elder statesmen had resolutely refused to acknowledge one another, let alone engage in a debate.

Leaning on his cane as he creaked into a chair by the unlit fire, Ainsworth, the Senate's oldest serving member at 91, said the words he never dreamed he'd ever utter to Cahill:

"You're damned right."

What had started out as a water cooler joke among lawmakers from both houses, had become, in the minds of senior Democrats and Republicans, the biggest threat to America's two-party political system in the nation's history. Right up to the finale the previous night, The iCandidate spectacle was regarded in Washington as a Hollywood gimmick. The leaderships from both parties had their concerns about Saxon, but at least he was a monster they understood and had, in their way, helped create. The iCandidate was wading into untested waters that threatened in a very real way to wash away everything in its wake.

Even the show's most ardent admirers said that while it was a brilliant concept, the idea of using a reality series to select a challenger in the next presidential election without the involvement of the two major parties was naïve and unrealistic. But when the number of votes cast for the three finalists was revealed at the end of the show, the Beltway took notice. And these weren't teenage girls and couch potato moms who voted over and over again for their talent show favorites; it was one person, one vote, just like the real thing. The Washington Post argued in an Op-Ed that The iCandidate's online voting system was even better than the real thing. With a thumbprint needed to access the voting card there was no room for cheating, stealing identities, or stuffed ballot boxes. "It was clean. It was simple. It was genius," said the Post.

Still, even that didn't get Cahill and Ainsworth's full attention. Rather, what really did it was the announcement made during the confetti hailstorm at the end of the show: that the winner was to get $100 million to fund the iCampaign run for the White House.

They knew all too well that hard cash, the real currency of electoral success, was the price any candidate had to pay to have a hope in hell of winning. The moment the campaign war chest was revealed, Cahill knew he had to bury his obstinate Irish pride and make the call. All senators, and most congressmen and women, with the exception of the rawest rookies, were allocated a hideaway office somewhere in the U.S. Capitol. Freshmen members could expect to be cloistered away somewhere in the bowels of the four-story building -- not that an outsider would have any clue who was where.

None of the so-called hideaways had numbers, and an unwritten law handed down through the decades meant that even the most voluble senators suddenly went quiet when asked about the location of the sanctuaries. But one of the rare partisan measures agreed by everybody through the years was that the most senior of lawmakers got first dibs on the best quarters, regardless of party. Any veteran politician with green eyes on Senator Ainsworth's sprawling office had long given up waiting.

Built as part of the new Senate wing in the 1850s and complete with its own Constantino Brumidi fresco, Ainsworth called his suite of prime Capitol real estate Elba, because it was where he spent his time in exile during his out-of-favor years in the minority.

Ainsworth wasn't surprised that Cahill had his private line, nor was he taken aback by the call. He'd been thinking about doing the exact same thing. The current President may have talked a lot about change and shaking up the system, but he, like others before him, quickly learned the only way to get anything through Congress was to toe the party line once the cameras were off.

This show was quite another matter. The thought of trying to deal with a President with absolutely no party affiliations or loyalty was unthinkable. Cahill's candidate Harriet Carson was feeling the heat from these TV upstarts, but so was Ainsworth's chosen Republican candidate, Dennis Saxon. The old man had pulled the strings so deftly to get the billlionaire in pole position he wasn't going to lose control now.

With all the key figures in the nation's political boiler room now present in the clubby, green-carpeted, third-floor hideaway office divided by a heavy door and a narrow corridor from the Senate Chamber, Cahill was keen to get going. The meeting was called to order. His aristocratic features silhouetted in the picture window, the Democrat scion banged his cane on the wooden floor. "We have to stop this dangerous and humiliating farce that has somehow tricked millions of Americans into drooling like demented sheep in a tidal wave of opportunism and false hope."

A murmur of approval rumbled around the table. Few congressional colleagues – and certainly no Republicans – had been invited inside the Bear of the Senate's inner sanctum before. "Too much is at stake to allow this cancer to destroy the very foundations this city is built upon," he continued. He poured an ample measure of neat Bushmills into a glass and gestured to his audience to do the same. There was no ice and certainly no mixers, and although the sun was setting over the Capitol, Cahill made no move to turn on any lights.

To the left of Cahill at the secret meeting were fellow Democrat heavyweights Jed Rawlston and Peter Fulbright from the Senate and Cahill's son-in-law Daniel Grey, who, at 47, was by far the youngest in the room. Ainsworth was accompanied by his Senate protégé, Tom Beattie, and two congressmen, Gerald Sumpter and

Ed Masonic. Ainsworth sat stock still in his chair with his eyes closed, looking like he was dead until the whiskey bottle was handed around and he reached out his glass. Leaning against an intricately carved antique bookcase at the back of the room was White House Chief-of-Staff, David Platt.

"I'm afraid we've been relatively slow off the mark in this situation, a fair amount of damage to the system has already been caused. So this is no longer a time for talking, that opportunity has passed us by. It is a time for action. To that end," Cahill added with a flourish, "I have asked one of my oldest colleagues in Washington to come and speak with us."

83 THE SPY

Cahill paused for effect. "Walter, please come on out."

The familiar figure of Walter Penske shambled in, still wearing his tux from the previous night. He shook hands with Cahill and Ainsworth and pointedly ignored the others, barely concealing the disdain in his red-rimmed eyes. He sat down next to Ainsworth as Cahill continued. "Walter believes, as I do, that this whole iCandidate thing has gone too far and he has agreed to help in every way possible to eliminate this cancer before it can do any more damage. Isn't that right, Walter?"

"It is Paddy," he said, pouring a glass of whiskey. "When I signed on as a judge I never, not for one moment, believed they would seriously attempt to put these people on a par with real politicians. It's an absolute travesty that they're wasting so much money on this. It's the reason this country's in such a mess."

"With all due respect, Mr. Vice President, why did you agree to be a part of the show in the first place?" Grey was the only one bold enough to ask what the others were thinking. "It seemed a strange decision for a statesman of your stature."

"Believe me, I was going to turn them down. I had no desire to deal with amateurs at this stage in my career." Penske nodded at Cahill. "But my friend Paddy here asked if I wouldn't mind keeping a closer eye on things for him."

"Walter's agreed to stay on with the so-called iCampaign as a senior advisor and strategist and will consequently be closely involved with their candidates," Cahill said. "I will, of course, be speaking to him on a regular basis."

"Can I ask a question?" Platt spoke up from the back of the room.

"Of course, David."

"Do you know where all this money is coming from? We're talking about $100 million and there are very definite rules about campaign funds."

"I don't know," Walter said, begrudgingly. "The candidates didn't even know about the $100 million until last night. I thought they were going to get some tin pot campaign team and that was that."

"Without the money the iCandidate would have gradually just faded away," Platt said. "But that's not going to happen now. That's why I think we need to challenge the source of this money. They lose the money and they lose any kind of hope of being a factor in the election.

"Can I ask the President's position on this?" Ainsworth had opened his eyes, but didn't turn around to look at Platt.

"He still isn't taking it seriously. He actually seems to like the Conwright woman. I had to virtually hold him down to prevent him accepting an invitation to make a surprise appearance in the finale."

"That would have been madness," Cahill said.

"So, he doesn't know you are here, then," Ainsworth interjected.

"No, and neither does Harriet, but I think it's important for us to work together on this."

"Thank you, David," Cahill said. It was almost dark now and long shadows stretched across the office. "Nothing can be left to chance this time. I don't need to remind you," Cahill stood up to indicate the meeting was over, "that this gathering didn't happen. From now on, everyone should speak directly to either Randall or myself, either by phone or in person. No emails," he added, ushering them out of the darkness into the harshly lit Capitol corridor.

"And keep Harriet and Dennis out of this."

84 $100 MILLION CHALLENGE

To get to the U.S. District Court downtown in Los Angeles by 10:00 a.m., Mason was up at four to make the 68-mile drive into Nebraska to catch the first flight out of Kearney Regional Airport on his way to Los Angeles. In spite of the hullabaloo the night before, there was a very real chance that Grace Conwright's iCampaign could be over before it began. A judge agreed on extremely short notice to hear a case brought by attorneys hired by Cahill, which challenged the legality of The iCandidate's $100 million election fund. With Federal Election Commission rules only allowing for individuals to donate $2,500, they wanted to know where all this money was coming from - particularly as there was no iCan Party structure until after the show's finale.

No one connected to the iCampaign was taking advantage of the 2010 Supreme Court ruling, which allowed corporations, unions, and individuals to make unlimited donations to Super Political Action Committees – outside groups set up to campaign for their favored candidates. While Grace had no backing from any Super PAC, several were set up by Cahill's supporters specifically to knock her down.

Kristoff had left Kansas immediately after Grace's speech to be back in L.A. with Desmond in time to prepare, but Mason had to handle the media before making the trek. Desmond had known there would be questions. He just wasn't expecting to explain the new party's financial structure to a judge.

After navigating the L.A. rush hour and security checks inside the North Hill Street building, Mason arrived sweaty and breathless just before 10:00 a.m. to find the others already in the courtroom. Once again, the place was overrun with media, and Tom, in his new capacity as iCampaign Press Secretary had flown back with Kristoff and was fending off questions from all sides.

"All will become clear, ladies and gentlemen," he shouted over the questions. "But first we have to let the attorneys do their thing."

"Could this be the end of the line?" called out a reporter from the Los Angeles Times. "What do you say to reports this morning claiming there could even be arrests if that $100 million turns out to have been raised illegally?"

"I would say that's ridiculous," Tom replied, straightening his skirt. "You have to give the iCampaign a little credit. It's not as if nobody had thought about this. Who would have thought that the President would manage to raise most of his donations for the last election in $5 amounts over the Internet? These are changing times, my friends. Interesting times." With that, Tom ducked into a side room to confer with Mason, leaving the media to stew outside.

The hearing had begun.

85 LOVE, LIES & SUSPICION

Roman saw his father's name on his phone and knew it was the call he was dreading.

"So, you've finished it then?" Vladimir was daring him to deny it.

"Of course father." He couldn't tell the truth. Not now. Not with so much happening.

"Good. For you to be seen with a Russian woman would be madness. You understand that don't you, son?"

"I do, father." Roman wouldn't have time to see Alina until it was all over. He would deal with his father then. There was another more pressing issue he had to bring to his attention. "You know the two boys you brought over to Harvard from Russia?"

"Of course."

"Alina heard them speaking in Russian. She said it sounded suspicious."

The other end of the line went silent. "I thought you weren't seeing that girl."

"This was before."

"So, what did she say about Boris and Ivan?"

"Only that they were talking about following orders and it sounded like they were involved in something bad. That's not true, right? You've always said this is about bringing peace to the world and making things right."

"Of course they're not involved in anything bad. They're kids." Vladimir was indignant.

"See what I mean about this girl turning your head. I've brought dozens of students over from Russia and now you're questioning me?"

Roman wanted to be convinced. "Just as long as I know we're doing this for the right reasons. I was born in America but I still love Russia and America equally. You were born in Russia, so do you love both countries equally, too?"

Vladimir just laughed. "Your blood is Russian, no matter your birth country."

"But do you love America?" Roman persisted.

"Of course." He paused. "How many times do I have to tell you? Just be sure to do your job Roman, and I'll take care of everything else."

86 PRESS CONFERENCE

David Mason was standing at a shabby lectern outside the Downtown court building with Desmond, and Tom next to him. Standing just behind them with a couple of burly bodyguards were Kristoff and Jacqueline.

Mason read out a brief statement explaining that the judge had dismissed the complaint brought by the Democrat and Republican presidential campaigns. "The iCampaign would like to thank Judge Peter Wilson for agreeing to consider this application so quickly, and for his prompt adjudication. I can confirm that he found there was no evidence of electoral malpractice. The iCampaign is very much still on track, and we hope you will all vote for The iCandidate, Grace Conwright."

Mason introduced Desmond to answer any questions.

"What do you say to claims that you weren't transparent about your fundraising methods?" The CNN reporter jumped in first.

"There was no secret. We were going to put all the details on the website. We just didn't know that Mr. Saxon and Harriet Carson were going to take legal action. That just meant we had to get moving."

"So, tell us how it came about?"

"It was the simplest idea in the world," Desmond said. "We sent out millions of emails to everyone who voted during the season of The iCandidate and asked them to contribute to the iCan Party. They could donate up to the $2,500 limit for individuals. We also posted a request on The iCandidate website. There really was never any mystery to it."

"So, how much did you raise and how long did it take?" The elderly ABC Political Editor veteran was a known pal of Paddy Cahill.

"The donations totaled more than $120 million. We closed the fund after 24 hours."

"Why did you do that?" The ABC man seemed irritated.

Kristoff leaned in to answer. "We didn't want to appear greedy. To compete with the big boys, Grace needs all $100 million at her disposal. That's not really so much if you have the right strategy.

87 VP DEBATES

As much as it still secretly riled Todd that he was forced to play second fiddle to Grace, the Vice Presidential Debate was his chance to shine. With the first Presidential Debate still two weeks away, he finally had the stage to himself. And he was loving it. Without a party line to defend, he was allowed free rein by Kristoff, confusing and frustrating his rivals as the debate wore on.

While Harriet's running mate Senator Tom Klein was a comparative newcomer, he was still firmly socialist in his outlook. Republican Governor Matt Petty came from the evangelical Christian right of his party. Neither could work out where Todd was coming from.

He was for free trade and raising taxes on the rich. He wanted more offshore oil rigs to help lower the cost of gas, and more green energy projects to cut carbon emissions and help save the planet. He wanted to get rid of earmarks allowing lawmakers to pin their vanity projects to bills, but didn't see why lobbyists couldn't work effectively in Washington.

"This is plain madness," an exasperated Klein exploded. "Your views are a mass of contradictions and they don't even match those of your party's presidential candidate. It's virtually impossible to have a meaningful debate when there is no correlation in the issues you are discussing."

"That's the whole point," Todd argued. "You just don't get it, do you? Issues aren't black and white like you try to make them in Washington, and especially on the campaign trail. Everyone's an individual and they have their own unique take on life. These are the people we represent."

"But it's not realistic." Petty couldn't get a handle on Todd's strategy either.

"Answer me this, then," said Todd. "How many times have you seen a President make all sorts of ideological promises on the campaign trail and then backtrack when they get into office? They have to wheel and deal and compromise to get anything done."

"But that's what governing is all about. What you are talking about is creating constitutional chaos," Klein insisted.

"What is chaotic about the iCan Party's plan to cut the deficit?" Todd replied. "I'm saying that we can cut $4 trillion by raising taxes and by cutting benefit programs like Medicare and Medicaid. It's a tough pill to swallow for both parties and it obviously would involve sacrifice by the public, but it would stop this country spinning out of control and falling further and further into debt to China. Okay, we would raise taxes for the wealthy, but there would be cuts in the corporate rates and for the poor and middle class."

Jacqueline stood in the wings watching with a keen eye. She'd been rehearsing with both iCandidates and Todd was sticking exactly to the game plan.

"Klein will talk the whole debate without taking a breath if you let him. So don't," she had told Todd in the final moments before he went on stage. "Be sharp and to the point and hold your own. Don't underestimate Petty either. Some of his views may be a little out there, but he's bland compared to Saxon, and he's there to balance out the ticket. He's no fool, no matter what they say."

She'd nodded approvingly at Todd's appearance. "Nice suit." It had all been going so well when the adjudicator, Paul Field from PBS, asked Todd the one question he dreaded most. Petty stumbled through a long-winded monologue about the importance of family values, ignoring attempts to keep within his allotted five minutes, when he turned to face Todd. "So, everybody knows you well from your TV reality show, but how can you expect to understand American families when you're single?"

This was the one bone of contention between Todd and his handlers. He didn't believe his personal life was relevant. Now it seemed he had to explain his thinking to the American public. "I'm not ruling out marriage, when the time is right, but I've been a little busy lately…"

There was a twitter of laughter from the audience.

Plowing on, Petty asked bluntly: "Do you really think people will vote for a bachelor Vice President?"

"I don't see why not. President James Buchanan never married and Grover Cleveland waited until he was in the White House to get hitched, so, it's not like it would be a big deal to have a single VP." Todd had stuck to his guns right from his first appearance on

The iCandidate. "I don't feel it is necessary for everybody to know all of my private business."

"But Todd, surely you understand that the public has a right to know about who you might be dating." Klein finally had something to work with.

Todd wasn't backing down. "I truly believe the celebrity culture is everything that is wrong with public life today. I am not asking for privacy for myself, I am asking it for every American. That is our right. And, by the way, this campaign is not a reality show – it's the real thing."

The applause from the audience was surprisingly warm. Enough so that Petty and Klein backed off. The post debate opinion polls showed The iCandidates were closing in on the leaders. A "Meet the Viewers" tour of battleground states Florida, Nevada, Pennsylvania, and Ohio had been huge. The iCampaign movement was growing.

88 DOUBLE TROUBLE

Alina had spotted Boris and Ivan that morning on The T train she took from Cambridge to Boston, although they hadn't seen her. They were walking ahead on the platform and she got onto the busy carriage behind them. Rush hour would soon leave much more room, but she liked to get into the city early for her walks around Boston Common-- it was still less crowded than the buses in Moscow, where she never got to sit down.

Boris looked daggers at her whenever their paths crossed in school, but she would smile at Ivan, who always looked so nervous he made her feel better about her shyness. As Alina grew in confidence, she ventured further afield from the Harvard campus, and had taken to heading for Boston Common or walking along the Charles River Esplanade, marveling at the row boats, and the girls in tight Lycra shorts and skimpy vests running along the waterside - she could still never imagine being that daring.

Alina hadn't paid the two Russian boys a second thought until she went in search of a soda off Boylston Street. Walking past a narrow alleyway she almost bumped into Ivan, who looked like he'd seen a ghost.

"Alina, what are you doing here?"

"Just walking. How about you? Are your studies going well?" Alina felt like she should make some effort at conversation.

Ivan looked terrified. "Yes, yes. Well, have a good day." He spoke in excellent English but looked down, clearly not wanting to talk.

Over his shoulder, Alina could see Boris with another, much older man, who was putting what looked like two thin metal tubes into a big linen sack. It was hard to see the man's face in the shadows, but he had a graying beard. Ivan moved over to block her view.

"See you at Harvard," he said, his face damp with sweat.

Roman had told her not to worry about the boys.

She assumed they were probably collecting something to do with a study project and carried on past. She'd walked about five yards when a hand grabbed her shoulder and pulled her back.

"What are you doing here?" It was Boris and he was yelling in her face. "Why are you following me?"

Knocking his hand away, Alina told him to leave her alone. "I didn't know you were here. I just bumped into Ivan – and anyway, the last I heard - Boston is a public city, everyone is welcome!"

She glowered at him and he stared back, his expression stony, his eyes darkened in anger. He was carrying the linen sack in one hand. He didn't move. Ivan was cowering behind him. Boris was his usual scruffy self, in a pair of ill-fitting jeans, a t-shirt and a baseball cap. He seemed, to Alina, tenser than she'd seen him before. It was like he was running through options as he stood silent in front of her. Finally, he stepped aside. "Stay away from us. You have been tainted by American ways."

The threat sent a chill down Alina's spine. She hurried on and didn't look back.

89 THE ULTIMATUM

The internal phone buzzed in Alina's dorm room at 8:00 p.m. The only person she knew who could be visiting so late was Roman. Her heart quickened as she picked up the receiver and pressed the button to answer. The voice at the other end sounded like Roman. But it wasn't him.

"Hello, Alina. I'm so sorry to trouble you so late in the evening but I was just passing and wondered if we could have a quick chat. I should probably introduce myself, I…"

Alina recognized the voice as Roman's father. "I know who you are, sir," she interrupted. "If you could just give me a couple of minutes I can come down and meet you in reception."

"That's quite alright. I'll come up. Privacy would be better."

She'd been jumpy since the strange confrontation with Boris, but it's not like Roman's father was going to attack her or anything. He probably wanted to get to know her a little better, if she was going to date his son.

"Of course." Alina pulled on a sweatshirt and did her best to straighten her hair while throwing the clothes strewn on the bed and around the room into her closet. This wasn't how she'd planned to meet Roman's father. Five minutes later there was a tap on the door and Alina showed Vladimir into the tiny kitchen area she shared with Alma. His black hair was swept back, and he was meticulously dressed in a pinstriped suit.

She felt embarrassed offering him one of their two plain wooden chairs.

"Oh, don't feel bad at all. I had a room exactly like this when I was a Masters student here. Had a wonderful time!"

The only time Alina had met him was at the Harvard alumni reception when she first met Roman. He was much more casual and friendly this time, settling into the chair and accepting her offer of something to drink.

"So, Alina, how are your studies going?"

"Really good, thank you, sir. I'm very grateful for the opportunity." She was still standing, unsure what was expected of her.

He smiled, loosening his tie. "That's wonderful. I know Moscow, and I know about the district where you are from. You have come a very long way. Your parents must be very proud."

Alina nodded. She didn't know what to say.

"Are your studies keeping you very busy? I'm sure they must be. Education is so important." He looked at her for confirmation. He could see what his son saw in her. She was, indeed, very beautiful. "I'm sure you must understand that my son is also very busy. It wouldn't be good for him to have any diversions right now."

"Yes, sir, but…"

Vladimir put up a hand to silence her. "I understand that this must be a very attractive situation for you. You go from the ghetto to Harvard, meet your American prince and live happily ever after. What an incredible fairy story, eh?"

"It's not really like that." Alina felt the shift.

Vladimir's smile was gone. "My son told me about you and we agreed that he would no longer see you. We both feel it's for the best."

"But that can't be…"

"Oh but it is, Miss Alina. I felt it was necessary to see you on my son's behalf and to offer you an added incentive to do the right thing just in case you have mistaken his intentions. He can be impulsive when it comes to women."

Alina hadn't heard from Roman for a couple of days but he'd told her he'd be buried with work. Now she didn't know what to think.

Vladimir carried on. "I will arrange for your family to move out of the district you are in and into a house in one of Moscow's nicer suburbs. You don't have to thank me." He got up to leave and the smile was back. "It will be my pleasure."

"But I thought you would approve. Because I am from Russia." Alina couldn't believe it. "He told me you were in favor of our courtship."

"It's because you ARE from Russia that I don't approve," he said without attempting to explain any further. "But you are from our country. You understand these things. Sometimes families just don't…work together. We have, how do I say this, different expectations."

A cold fury seized Alina. "If I'm not good enough for you, or your precious son, that's one thing – that's your choice." Her lips were quivering so hard she could barely get the words out. "But I am not for sale, and neither is my family. Now would you please leave!"

He was already at the door. It didn't matter if she accepted his offer; in fact, he was impressed she hadn't. Under different circumstances she might have made a good bride for his son. But right now, that didn't matter. "I'd prefer it if you didn't contact my son again," he said, closing the door behind him. "Believe me, it's for the best."

90 OUT OF THE ROUGH

As the iCan Party gained momentum so, too, did the attack ads attempting to shut the campaign down before it did any more damage.

"We're getting killed." Desmond was standing with the rest of the gang on the 5th green of the Pelican Bay Golf Course in Newport Coast, California. "We need to fight back and hit the other candidates as hard as they're hitting us. Politics is a cutthroat business – we need to get a little dirty."

The four decided to keep the game on their calendars as an opportunity to discuss the latest iCandidate crisis, and the impasse they'd reached with Grace over the handling of the iCampaign.

"It's no use, Grace won't go for it. Any negativity and she refuses to get involved." Jacqueline took another look at the hole and stroked her ball right in the center. "What with her insisting everything must be positive, and Todd doing his privacy thing, they're making it very difficult for us."

Mason had already lost count of his shots. He was holding the flag for the others. "We just need to do something about the attack ads. You've got to talk to her Jaq, or we're going to blow this."

The TV and radio was awash with anti-iCampaign messages. Many of them were paid for by Super PACs, and they questioned everything from Todd's bachelor status, and his choice to drive a BMW rather than a car made in Detroit, to Grace's citizenship, even though they had to go back to her Antiguan great-grandmother to find a relative not born in Illinois or Indiana.

Desmond was monitoring the polls. "Not so long ago, we had all those people, all potential voters, send their cash to help finance this campaign, but we're losing them. People aren't taking us seriously enough and they believe the lies they are being fed by the Carson and Saxon people. We've got to stop them somehow."

"How are we going to do that if Grace won't let us go for the other parties?" Kristoff couldn't believe the position they found themselves in. "Aren't we supposed to be telling her what to do?"

They walked together in silence to the next tee. Jacqueline refused to play off the women's tees, and still won most times. She was about to take her drive when she stopped. "We have to combat them with the truth. Grace will go for that. We hit back with the facts. We'll just tell the people the truth and let them decide. But we have to be out there, day after day, and we must confront their lies and smear tactics so voters know the truth."

Even Mason seemed mollified. "I don't see how Grace can say no to that. When we get back to the office I'll work on some Internet ads. I feel so much better now. I've even got a good feeling about this drive."

Then he crushed the ball into the deep rough about 20 yards away.

91 OUT OF FOCUS

The President was getting increasingly irritable with his team because of long separations from his wife and daughters while he campaigned for the very woman he'd battled eight years earlier. The party hierarchy talked relentlessly about preparations for the presidential debate that was now just days away.

They were worried; he could sense the unease. He'd heard that Paddy Cahill was pulling the strings for Harriet's campaign and he wasn't comfortable with it. The attack ads they'd been running were mean and cynical, yet he had to concede they appeared to have fatally wounded Grace Conwright's chances.

Cahill was confidently predicting the iCan Party would be a non-factor come Election Day. But the President wasn't so sure. He genuinely wanted Harriet to succeed, but he liked Grace, too. He understood her journey better than most, even if she took a different path than his own.

He'd told Harriet she shouldn't dismiss the number of people it took to raise all that iCampaign money. Some of them would now be harboring doubts; but they hadn't gone away, he thought. They were invested in the iCandidate - and investors always prefer a pay out.

Cahill didn't bother to look up when Harriet questioned him on the president's concerns.

"You can't run a country with eight people and the public realizes that. They had their fun with their little reality show. Now it's time to let the professionals handle it. We need to focus on Saxon because he could hurt us."

Cahill, his glasses propped on the end of his nose, got up carrying an armful of papers, gesturing haughtily for Harriet to leave. "I can't talk now, but I've told you already that you don't need to worry. It's all here. Three tracking polls have you in the lead by some distance, two put Saxon out in front and there is absolutely no sane pollster giving the iCandidate people a hope in hell's chance."

"I don't agree, Paddy," said Harriet. "Conwright could beat us. I've seen a whole different set of polls that suggest they're turning things around. I'm being told that all they need to do is keep their base happy – all those folks who voted in the show – and they could conceivably catch us, even beat us, right on the line."

Cahill put down the papers and opened the door for Harriet to leave. "Horseshit," he said. "I want to keep the focus on Saxon. The iCampaign is dead. I guarantee it. Just remember: when you win in November, you owe me."

92 OLE MISS

The set up at Ole Miss, two days later, was different from the VP debate; three chairs set around a semicircular table, and the host, former NBC anchor Tim Bogart, sat nearly in the audience. It was to have a more town hall format, with questions asked by selected students in the crowd. All three participants received warm applause, but it was obvious that Grace Conwright received the biggest welcome.

Jacqueline had warned Grace that Harriet would try and use her experience to make her look naïve and stupid. "But it's going to be more difficult for Harriet to attack you now. She might risk losing the female vote and that would be disastrous for her," said Jacqueline. "She may take a different approach and be sympathetic, even a little condescending towards you, and save all the vitriol for Saxon."

Jacqueline was concerned about Grace's skinny political resume becoming the dominant talking point. But it didn't seem to worry Grace. "Saxon has less political experience than I do, so he can't take me on for my lack of experience, and Harriet has been around so long she risks being seen as too much of a Washington insider. I don't think it's going to be an issue," she insisted.

The more time she spent with Grace, the more Jacqueline was impressed. The iCandidate hardly needed coaching.

It was Dennis Saxon who jumped straight off the blocks to dominate the debate's early parries. He scored strongly with his attacks on the administration's failure to sustain the economic recovery, and maintained a vehement criticism of the President's overhaul of the nation's health system.

Cahill's strategy and advice to Harriet was clearly to ignore Grace while being deferential to Saxon; the opposite advice the President offered and, initially at least, disconcerting to both women. Towards the end of the debate, with the honors roughly even, the expected question came up as to how Grace could possibly expect to govern on her own without any support in Congress.

"What makes you think we don't have any support on Capitol Hill?" she shot back.

Saxon twisted the knife. "Because there are no iCan Party representatives. It's as simple as that."

"I think you will find that we have more support than you might expect from such a new organization. We're not the only people who are sick and tired of the political dogfights...Ladies and gentlemen, would you please stand up so we can see who you are?"

With that, two rows of senators stood up along the back of the Gertrude C. Ford Center, about 15 in all.

The gang of four had spent four days on the phone laying down the line to all of the iCampaign's potential supporters in Congress. It was time to stand up or get out, and they convinced the lawmakers to go public. Mason was more direct. "Piss or get off the pot," he told one cautious congressman.

"These fine representatives, ladies and gentlemen, have pledged their support to the iCan Party," said Grace. "They will remain Democrats and Republicans, but they will join with me in getting this country to work when I win on November 8th. Others will join them, of that I am absolutely certain. We're not talking small change here, we're going all the way."

Harriet half-heartedly congratulated Grace at the end of the debate – the first time she'd actually looked at her - as the audience surged forward holding out their programs for autographs. "That was an interesting little stunt you pulled off there."

"Yeah, I'm sorry. That's the problem with having TV people run your campaign. They get carried away with the dramatic impact thing."

Grace caught Jacqueline's eye across the room, and got an enthusiastic thumb's up.

93 CAHILL'S FURY

On the eve of the election, an army of minions in pinafores were tidying tables, chairs, and a mountain of food left over from the $10,000-a-plate campaign fundraising dinner. Guests were still talking in clusters sprinkled around the giant marquee set up in Patrick Cahill's front yard. There was the usual mix of politicians, Hollywood types, and wealthy donors happy to buy the opportunity to take their photos with Harriet Carson and her husband.

It was a Democratic Party pre-election tradition to hold the event at Cahill's Connecticut mansion, and although the President had agreed to attend he was in-and-out in minutes, on his way back to Washington.

"The man's an idiot," Cahill told his son-in-law as they walked back to the main house to escape the evening chill. Cahill was in no hurry, leaning on his stick and picking his way carefully down the stone path. "The way he talks about his days as a community organizer in the bowels of Chicago, you'd think he'd rather be back there."

"What do you mean?" Daniel Grey asked. "He seemed on top form to me."

"Is that what you'd call it? If he said one more complimentary thing about that damned Conwright woman I was going to throw up. If I were his wife, I'd be getting a little worried. He's got a major crush on her and her party of half-wits."

Grey spent his entire courtship of Cahill's daughter, and the first few years of their marriage, as much in awe of the old man as everybody else. But lately his father-in-law seemed like he was losing the plot. "That reminds me, how is your plotting with Ainsworth going? An unlikely meeting of minds if ever there was one."

"You and Ed did a good job getting the attack dogs riled up. Those ads are putting pressure on all the main players, but it's not enough. We're going to have to step it up."

The two men climbed the steps to the front door, with Grey supporting the old man up, one at a time. They walked through into the parlor where Patricia Grey had already set down a tray of tea and shortbread on a table in front of the fire.

A copy of the New York Times was also on the table, its front page almost entirely taken up by a photograph of Grace. "I know she's on the other side, dad, but don't you think she's just wonderful?" Patricia picked up the paper. "I do love Harriet, of course, but when Grace talks, it's like she's giving voice to my thoughts."

"Not you, as well. This is getting ridiculous," Cahill grumbled, settling down into a battered brown leather armchair. "Can't you see how you're all being played? These people are patsies for the business interests in this country who want to take power away from the elected institutions that have protected the American people for generations...First the President, then my own daughter. Next you'll be standing up for them, Daniel."

"No, but I think they should be given a fair crack." Grey grimaced as he waited for the inevitable explosion. "I think we should go after them, yes, but we should keep it above board."

"What do you know? You're barely out of diapers and you want to tell me how to deal with this threat to everything I've worked for my whole life?" Cahill's face turned puce and he spat out a shower of shortbread crumbs in his finger-jabbing fury. "How dare you support those TV losers? I've shown you nothing but kindness, you married my daughter, took my patronage and this is how you repay me – with betrayal?"

"I'm not betraying you, sir. I'm only urging a measure of caution." Grey had never seen Cahill like this.

"This iCampaign business could destroy America. It is not a time for the weak and the cautious. Your generation has grown soft. It's all been so easy for you. Now's the time for action before it is too late."

"Daddy!" Shocked at the tirade, Patricia burst into tears.

"Stay out of it, Patricia. Go and help your mother."

"But, daddy!"

"Go!"

Patricia looked from her father to Grey and backed out of the room. She was used to her father's temper, but he'd never shouted at her. She was his only daughter, and he'd always been so good to Daniel. But lately, her husband had become increasingly worried over her father's obsession with destroying the iCan Party.

"I don't get it," she told him. 'They are just saying a lot of things we've always believed in as Democrats." Patricia was raised to speak her opinions and she simmered in the kitchen for a few minutes as her mother barked orders to the staff. First, she had to stop crying. Then she decided to vote for Grace Conwright – but she was never going to tell her father.

94 TAKING SIDES

It was just after 9:00 p.m. when Alina's intercom buzzer went off, just as she was about to get in the bath. She'd turned off the phone Roman gave her days ago and the only person she could imagine who would call at this hour was his father, trying to blackmail her again. Perhaps he thought her refusal was simply an attempt to push up her price.

He WOULD think something like that.

She ignored the buzzer and climbed into the piping hot water. She wasn't going to fall into the same trap this time. She was leaving for New York with Emily the next day. She would try to forget she'd ever met Roman. Forty-five minutes later the buzzer was still going off every couple of minutes. Sitting in the bath she could hear it through the door; there was no way she could go to bed like this.

Eventually she cracked and picked up the phone. "Leave me alone or I'll call security. I don't want your son or your money."

The voice on the other end sounded like Roman, but it couldn't be him. "Alina, please listen to me. Why aren't you answering my calls? What has happened?"

She wanted to put the receiver down but she didn't. She just held it there. "Alina, are you there? Please speak to me."

"Your father has made it clear what you both want, so what's left to discuss?"

"I don't know what he... oh, hello, Alma. Let me help you with your books..."

"NO! Alma! Don't let him in!" But it was too late. They were on their way up. Alina was furious. She was waiting for him, hands on her hips, when he came to the door. She refused to let him in, closing the door behind her. They stood in the drafty corridor. "You have ten seconds."

"I had no clue my father had come to see you. He had no

right." Roman pressed his two hands together to his chest.

"Well, he was very clear that neither of you wanted me in your life, and that you have no time for romance right now, certainly not with a Russian girl." Alina paused a moment. "But he did offer to move my family out of the slums if we stopped seeing each other. How very generous of him." Her voice shook.

"Alina, my father doesn't know what I need. He could never understand what we have together." Roman's voice softened. "If I could only see you for two seconds on any given day, those two seconds are the best part of my day." He could see Alina's resolve weaken just a little. "So, what if we don't have too much time for romance right this minute, we will. Things will calm down. Then I can show you just how much I love you."

Alina's hands dropped from her waist. She longed to believe him, but Vladimir had been so definite. She couldn't face any more hurt.

"Alina, my father was wrong and I'm so sorry he put you through this. I promise you I had nothing to do with him coming here." Her eyes held him at bay. He wanted her to know everything. "I did tell him we were over because I had so much to deal with; I couldn't handle his meddling as well. I was just waiting for the right time to explain it to him. I'm so sorry. I was weak. Please, can you forgive me?"

A group of students shuffled past, paying little attention at first, but then turning around and whispering to each other, watching Roman drop to one knee. He pulled out a tiny box from his pocket and Alina gasped. "Alina, I love you, with my heart and soul. Marry me? Let me spend my life proving that to you, each and every day?"

Suddenly it was like every bone in her body gave out. Leaning back against the wall for support she slowly slid to the floor beside Roman. "Of course," she said, stunned. "Of course I'll marry you...but you might want to tell your father this time!"

They had at first ignored the gallery of students who burst into noisy applause down the corridor, but now Alma smiled shyly at them and bobbed a curtsey which made them cheer even more. They kissed again and Roman knew beyond doubt that whatever plans his father had for him, they would have to include Alina.

95 NEW YORK

For all their differences, Alina still felt some similarities between the busy hustle of Boston and Moscow; but New York was something else. She'd never seen anything like it, and as she toured the sights with Emily, she was alternately terrified and enthralled. America was no longer an alien culture to her. Sewing for endless hours in a bleak, damp Moscow factory never seemed so far away.

The past few days had been the hardest for Emily...

Returning to New York University was not something she ever thought she would have to do, but luckily her charges there were settled and happy and everything was going smoothly, much to her relief. Emily was flying back to the Netherlands the following afternoon. But first, she wanted to keep her promise to Alina and show her the city.

At the end of the day Alina and Emily were exhausted. They wandered back downtown through the coffee bars and record shops of Emily's youth in Greenwich Village.

Sitting at an outside café table in the evening twilight, Emily was glad she'd come, happy she'd confronted the past she'd run away from all those years ago, but never really escaped.

"Are you okay?" Alina reached a hand across the table.

"I am. I really am." Emily took a deep breath, pulling in the past, and then letting go. "So Alina," she smiled brightly at her young companion, still marveling at the transformation from terrified, alienated student to this confident and beautiful woman sitting in front to her, "tell me how your grand love affair is going?"

Alina blushed but made no attempt to disguise her feelings for Roman. "He makes me happier than I have ever felt in my life. I didn't even know you could feel like this about someone."

She couldn't help smiling. "That's wonderful, Alina. I'm so happy for you." And she was. Emily secretly hoped that it wasn't too late for her to feel that way again, too. Perhaps now after facing her demons here in New York, she'd finally feel more open to the possibilities. Her eyes wandered across the street to a row of more elegant brownstones and a middle-aged man in a suit hurrying down the steps. Something about the way he moved made her look again, and at just that moment he looked back across the street at her before disappearing around the corner.

"Emily! Emily what's happened?" Alina saw her friend's face turn deathly pale.

"I actually don't feel so well," stammered Emily, pushing back her chair. "I need to get some air."

"I'll come with you." Alina went to stand up as well.

"No, no, I'll be fine. I just need to walk it off. I'll see you back at the hotel in an hour."

Emily didn't know where she was going. She just knew she couldn't stay there.

96 CUPID

Grace was exhausted. She'd been on the road non-stop for what seemed like forever and it was nearly the end. After yet another speech in yet another city, she headed back to the refuge of her Miami Beach hotel room, making her excuses to avoid a booster cocktail party, complaining she felt a migraine coming on. The closer she got to election day, the heavier the burden of leadership weighed on her. Everything was happening so quickly and standing alone in the middle of her hotel room, she wished desperately she could speak to her father; it was something she'd thought more about in recent weeks. Tears pricked the backs of her eyes, and she felt overwhelmed with doubts.

Her cell phone rang. It was Cameron. She needed a friend to talk to, but she wasn't in the mood for his games. "Cameron, what's up?"

"You are. I saw you on TV the other night whipping their butts and I thought I'd call to congratulate you."

"I wouldn't go that far. But I think it went okay. How's it going in… where are you anyway?"

"Georgia. It's supposedly known for its peaches, but I'm not seeing any."

"Are you talking about the fruit?"

"Maybe." Cameron's voice was light and playful.

Grace groaned. "Well, thanks anyway, Cameron. It was nice of you to call." Grace was too tired for his inane banter.

"Wait. Look, I know you're busy. I just wanted to say you did us proud. My mom thinks you rock." Cameron sat in his hotel room, also alone. He'd been on the road non-stop as well, ever since the show's finale and, although he rarely dropped his guard, he just wanted to talk to someone. He wanted to talk to Grace.

"I beg your pardon."

"My mom. She's liked you from the start. She said you were

her second favorite in the competition after me, but I have a sneaky suspicion you were her top choice all along."

Grace had trouble answering. She was thinking about her own mom. "Don't be weird," she managed.

"Grace, are you okay?"

A small voice replied yes. Cameron tuned in to her mood. "It's true. My mom adores you, and I'm okay with that. Now, if it had been Todd…"

Grace tried to laugh but all Cameron caught was a sob and some sniffing. "What is it Grace? Did something happen?"

"No." She paused, trying to decide whether or not to confide in him. "It's just that days ago I was debating with Saxon and Harriet for heaven's sake! I was on this crazy high, and now I'm standing here on my own in a strange hotel room, God knows where, feeling…I don't know…"

"Lonely?"

"Yes, I guess I am." She couldn't believe she was telling him this.

"It's tough at the top. I heard the President cries when he loses at golf."

Grace smiled in spite of herself. "What makes you cry then, Cameron? Apart from math."

"Ouch, that was below the belt."

"It was wasn't it…sorry. Has anyone ever broken your heart? There was a pause as Cameron struggled for a comeback. "Cameron?"

"Something like that." Now Cameron's voice sounded distant.

"What happened?"

"We don't need to talk about this. You don't want to hear about it."

"Actually, I do, if that's okay? It would make me feel better to know the playboy has a heart. Even if it was broken."

He let out a sigh. "I was 26, it was a long time ago. We were engaged."

"What was her name?"

"Emma. She was 23 and, well…she was perfect."

Grace sat down on her bed and kicked off her shoes. "What happened?"

"She died."

"Oh, Cameron, I'm so sorry." Grace was stuck for words now. Do you mind me asking?"

"No, it's okay. We lived in L.A. at the time, she was a nurse and she went off to work one day with a slight headache and came home two hours later having been diagnosed with inoperable brain cancer. We were supposed to get married that summer but she never made it that far."

The line went silent. "Oh, God, that's awful."

"Yeah, well, who said life was a bowl of cherries. Or, was it roses? Gotta take the bad with the good, I guess." He sounded even further away now. They were both quiet for a moment.

"I need a drink." Grace poured herself a vodka tonic from the mini bar. "Care to join me?"

"Way ahead of you. I'm already on my second beer." It was then that Cameron asked the question that had bugged him ever since Grace turned up with that cut on her forehead. "You didn't fall in the bathroom, did you?"

"No." It felt good to talk about it with Cameron. She told him about the attack. "He was so vile and I still can't get his voice out of my head," she said of her attacker. "If it hadn't been for Todd, I don't know what would have happened."

"Wait! Todd?"

"He saved me, Cameron. This guy was about to rape me, but suddenly Todd was there, beating the hell out of him. He saved my life."

Cameron didn't know what to say.

"I know you and Todd have this testosterone thing going on, and I know he's a little conceited, but he saved me. He's my hero."

"Well I guess he's mine too now. Did you report the attack?"

"No, maybe I should have. I didn't want to deal it. But he knew who I was, Cameron. It wasn't random. He said they didn't want any more blacks in the White House."

"He warned you to leave the show then?"

"Yes…" Just the thought of it made Grace's flesh crawl. She went over to the door to make sure it was bolted.

"Grace, obviously I'm not much help to you in Georgia, but when we're in DC tomorrow, well, if you need anything, you know who to call."

"Yes, I'll call Gillian," she joked. "Thanks, Cameron. It's nice to know." They talked a little more. She wasn't sure if it was the vodka or talking with Cameron, but when she got off the phone, Grace felt much better.

97 ALONE AGAIN

Jennifer unlocked the front door of her Manhattan apartment for the first time in four months and moved from room to room opening the blinds. It had been her home for the last five years, but it felt cold and stark without Chrissie's comforting touches. She realized now she had no pictures of her own, no plants, no curtains. She shivered. Everything was perfectly nondescript. Her housekeeper had recently been in and freshened up the place and her mail was stacked on the breakfast counter along with Chrissie's. She left it untouched and walked across the thick carpet, sat on her perfect cream couch, and stared at the blank flat screen TV.

She had no recollection of her life here before Chrissie. Work had been everything and her wife had been her delicious secret. They had never invited friends over for dinner or drinks because she didn't want anybody to know. She opened the empty fridge and closed it again. Glancing at her dining table she realized she had never sat around it with family or friends.

How that must have hurt Chrissie. And how she missed her now.

Why had she thrown away the best thing that had ever happened to her for a fling with someone she now believed to be evil?

She'd just met with all the others for a breakfast meeting in the Marriott at Los Angeles Airport before they all flew off in different directions around the country to vote. Then they would head back to Washington to be with Grace and Todd as the final results were calculated.

Jen sat down on the cold couch and tried Chrissie's number again. Perhaps this time she'd answer.

98 (UN) SERENDIPITY

Vladimir knew who she was the moment he saw her sitting in the cafe. The way she pushed a stray blonde hair from her eyes was all he needed. He'd seen her doing the same thing over and over in his dreams.

All those years ago, he'd argued against giving Emily a second syringe that would have killed her in the maternity ward. Everything was in place for her death to be covered up to look like natural causes; when he insisted she remain alive, his only weakness in 35 years. Bribes were spread around to ensure Emily would never know the truth about her infant child, and to ensure her passage back to the Netherlands.

Ever since then it had been his dream, and his nightmare, that Emily would return one day.

What was she doing back in America? And why right here, in the place they had fallen in love? He had to know. Vladimir couldn't take any risks at this stage, there was far too much at stake. He'd never heard from Emily and a private investigator reported she rarely left Holland.

He peered around the corner and could still see her sitting in the cafe with a dark haired young woman, who had her back to him. They stood and hugged their goodbyes, and Emily headed his way.

Vladimir had no choice. He had to know. She rounded the corner and walked straight into him. Feigning surprise, he apologized. She was wearing jeans and a long, white raincoat, her body still lean and strong.

"I knew it was you…"

Emily took a step back. "I wish I could lie and say this is a nice surprise." Her voice trailed off.

"You look fabulous." Vladimir said softly. He meant it. Closer up he could see the slight worry lines around her eyes but they only made her look more beautiful. She wasn't wearing any make-up. "It's so good to see you."

Vladimir was trying to decide what to do. For now he settled on telling her the truth. "I have thought of you so many times, wondered how you were."

"Really?" Her voice was cold and unnaturally thin. She shook with anger, not trusting herself to say anything else.

"Do you live here now?" he asked, nervously looking around.

"No, I'm just here for a few days. Do you still live here then?"

He nodded, looking back to the brownstone he'd just come from and fidgeting with the keys in his hand. "Look, Emily, I have my car right here. Can we perhaps go somewhere more private, just to talk."

Emily was shocked. "Why would I go anywhere with you?"

"Please? There are things that need to be said."

Neither moved.

"I think it's a little late for that, don't you?" She looked at the man she had once loved with her whole heart, who she thought had loved her; a fresh wave of pain coursed through her body, as strong as the day he had abandoned her in that hospital room. She wanted to strike him, to hurt him the way he had hurt her.

"You deserve an explanation for what I did. Please, Em? Let me explain."

She hesitated. As unbearable as it was to be near to him, part of her desperately needed to hear what he had to say. "Okay, but I need to be back here in an hour. Can you do that?"

"Yes, yes, of course. Good." He opened the door of the silver Mercedes parked outside his house. Walking around to the driver's side, he quickly checked all around to see whether anyone had spotted them. The street was deserted. Starting the engine he turned to her. "We'll grab a quick coffee and I'll explain everything."

99 FALLING

The sky darkened and it started to rain as Vladimir drove across town towards the Hudson. Emily looked at her watch. Alina would worry if she were late. "I don't have long," she said.

"I know a place we can talk in private." Vladimir pulled into a deserted parking lot off the West Side Highway. The clatter of rain and the rhythmic clicking of the windscreen wipers were the only sounds. Emily turned her head away from Vladimir, staring out of the window.

"I'm sorry, Em. For everything..." Vladimir had played this scene in his mind over and over, but now he didn't know what to do or say.

Emily glanced back at him. Her eyes were wet and he put a hand out to brush the hair from her face just as she reached up to do it herself. "Don't do that." She knocked his hand away. "Do you know that after all this time, I have never even wanted to try to have another child?" Vladimir dropped his hand and just listened. "And it's because I never said goodbye to my baby... to our baby." She was shaking... "It was a boy wasn't it?" Her words hung heavy in the car; the windows steamed up from the heater, the rain still beating down on the windows.

"Yes." Vladimir said quietly.

Emily nodded, barely able to keep it together. "There was no closure." Her voice cracked. "You just left me there alone. How cruel." Emily was in tears and Vladimir tried to pull her close to him. He could see the faint lights of the boats on the river.

"Don't!" She pushed him away. "You wanted to explain, so start explaining."

"You couldn't possibly understand the pressure I was under back then. I didn't have a choice." He knew there was nothing he could say to make it right.

"Pressure?" Emily was frantic. "What kind of pressure could

possibly make you abandon me after everything we'd gone through?"

Vladimir opened the door and climbed out into the rain. A couple of cars shot by on the road behind them, but otherwise it was quiet and the parking lot was empty. The passenger door slammed and Emily walked around the front of the car to face him by the pier. "Pressure from who? To do what? None of this makes any sense."

The years fell away and all he saw was the young girl with the soft blonde hair he loved and lost a lifetime ago. He needed to see something in her eyes that he could live with, some empathy for what he'd gone through, too. "What if our baby hadn't died that day?"

He saw Emily's eyes widen and again he reached for her, pulling her close, pushing his lips onto hers.

In that moment, he was 23 again, kissing the girl he loved in his box room apartment.

Pushed up against a wood piling, Emily was unable to move before kneeing him in the groin, doubling him over. He slumped on the gravel holding himself.

She looked down at him, wiping at her mouth. "Why would you say something like that?

Vladimir stood up and grabbed her again, even more roughly this time, his fingers digging into the soft flesh of her arms. She tried to squirm away, but he held her in a vice grip. Their eyes locked and she saw the truth…and he realized there was no going back. With all his might he pushed out hard with both hands.

Emily's panic-stricken face as she reached out for him was the same as it had been when her baby was taken from her. Then she tumbled back over the edge of the dock and vanished from sight.

100 PSYCHO

Emily saw the silhouette of Vladimir's face peering over the edge of the pier as she clung onto a cable five feet below. It was strung across the concrete and she grabbed it as she fell to stop herself from plunging into the freezing river below. Although she could see Vladimir's outline against the moonlit sky, she was hidden in the shadows; the sound of the rain and the rough water crashing against the pier camouflaged her heavy breathing.

Even after waiting what seemed like an eternity, Emily didn't dare cry for help. By inching along the slippery cord, she managed to swing her legs onto a ledge. She battled to steady herself. There was a set of iron rungs overhead, but they were just out of reach from the narrow ledge where she crouched, shivering against the cold.

When she thought Vladimir had gone, Emily unfolded herself and reached out to see if she could touch the closest rung. It was agonizingly close but not close enough. As far as she extended her left arm it fell short every time. The concrete was black and smooth in the darkness. There were no cracks or handholds. Her only option was to stand facing the wall and jump sideways, enough to grab the rusty metal.

She waited five more minutes, not just because she was worried about Vladimir, but also because she was trying to summon her courage. If she missed she'd drop into the icy water; she wasn't a good swimmer.

A deep breath. Then another. She wriggled 180-degrees around until she was facing the rock, her lips pressed tight against it, her legs bent but not so much her knees would push her off balance. One more deep breath. Then she jumped, trusting her right hand to save her.

Her fingers closed around the metal, but the swinging motion of her body wrenched them away. She was falling down now, the sideways trajectory lost. She was dropping straight with both hands brushing down the wall. Her right hand felt metal too late and missed, but the left hand closed around it just enough to arrest her fall and give her the moment she needed to get both hands on the rung. She swung there screaming in terror and relief, eventually finding the lower rung to rest her feet and take the weight from her arms. Then, very gradually, rung by rung, she climbed back to the surface, finally crawling over the lip and lying exhausted by a bench, trying to catch her breath.

There was nobody in the parking lot. Emily was filthy and her arms and legs were cut to pieces. Much worse was the trembling that rocked her entire body with the realization that the man who fathered her child was some kind of a pyscho monster.

101 BACK FROM THE DEAD

Covered in scratches and bruises, Emily managed to stagger down the road to a dingy, dim-lit diner. The rain had started up again and she was soaked. Her long blonde hair was matted with blood from a nasty gash on her cheek, and her white raincoat was now torn and splattered with mud. She'd lost one boot scrabbling for her footing. Her cell phone was in her bag she had left in Vladimir's car. With no other sign of life anywhere, she banged on the door of the closed restaurant and cried out for help.

As the shock began to wear off, the pain in her leg and side hurt more and she slumped down on the steps under a canopy shielding her from the downpour. It was there that Jilly Calabrio, the diner owner, found her a few minutes later.

"I was involved in an accident," Emily told her. "If I could just use your phone?"

She wasn't keen. The diner was in a tough neighborhood and Jilly had seen it all. "Just one phone call." She threw her an old, moth-eaten blanket. "Then you'd better get out of here before I call the police."

Emily took the cellphone and was going to call 911 but something held her back. Before he pushed her Vladimir had hinted that their son might be alive. She needed to find out the truth.

Emily called Alina and asked her new friend to come and pick her up in a cab. As long as Vladimir thought she was dead, she wasn't in any danger.

Emily knew what she had to do next. She had been running away from the truth for too long. She knew where he lived, and his home was more likely to yield the clues she needed.

Her heart quickened. Perhaps their son was there.

102 DIXVILLE NOTCH

It was Tom's idea to be in Dixville Notch, New Hampshire for the start of one of the most nerve-wracking days of his life. For pure emotional drama, it promised to surpass even his first uncertain steps teetering down Rayville's Main Street in a pair of heels.

Tom's appointment as the iCan Party's Press Director proved to be a masterstroke.

He stuck strictly to the new party line of telling the truth. Grace had wholeheartedly approved Jacqueline's honesty policy. If the criticism was justified or true, they said as such. If it was a lie, they were equally forthright. Neither Dennis Saxon or Harriet Carson had come up with an effective way of combatting it.

Standing in the ballroom of Dixville Notch's rambling Balsams Hotel just before midnight, Tom was about to witness a voting process with its roots back in the 18th century. Of the town's 75 residents, only 26 of them were eligible to vote and they were all crowded around Tom chatting about Grace's chances. Camera crews and journalists outnumbered the locals two-to-one.

Tom had done his research thoroughly. He wanted a publicity coup for the iCampaign to come out of the blocks running on Election Day.

"Where's Grace? Why isn't she here?" a teenager asked, explaining she had celebrated her 18th birthday just three days earlier. "I made sure I was registered so I could vote for her... I've been behind her right from the start, so have all my friends. She's awesome!" Even the local Democrat organizer seemed a little star struck. "That's a lovely dress, Tom. Isn't this one of those dusty halls your iCampaign is always going on about?"

"I don't know what you mean," Tom replied. "It's spotless. If we were all voting online I'd still bring my computer in here to do it. I love this place. It reminds me of Rayville, my hometown back in Colorado…the only trouble is we'd be waiting all day for the town clerk to turn up for the count! Between you and me, he couldn't organize a drink up in a brewery, but he's so earnest you can't get mad with the guy." The small crowd loved him, they couldn't get enough.

"Shouldn't you be back there voting?" someone called out.

"Absentee ballot, darling. It's going to be a busy day."

"Not for us," the Dem Organizer smiled. "We're nearly done, but I'll be watching the TV with great interest to see how you get along."

Then at the stroke of midnight, each of the 26 took turns in the booth inside the Ballot Room to cast their votes. The whole process took just a few minutes and when it was over the first result of the presidential election would be declared. It would be a while before the great majority of the results started flooding in from the rest of the state and across the country. All the polls were predicting a close finish. But for now, in one small corner of New Hampshire at least, it was first blood to The iCandidate.

103 THE BREAK-IN

Emily checked her reflection in a compact, pulling the baseball hat tighter over her head. Alina had begged her to go to the police, but Emily was adamant. She needed answers and she didn't trust the authorities to get them. In the end the two had struck a compromise. Alina would call Roman. "He'll know what to do." She was distraught. "Perhaps he can find out something about the person who did this to you."

The young Russian had washed and treated Emily's wounds and they agreed Alina would call Roman in the morning. But before Alina woke the next day, Emily quietly dressed in the dark and slipped out. Now she was standing in a bookstore across the street from Vladimir's brownstone.

While there was no lasting physical damage, everything hurt from her escape the previous night. She'd sat in a café for a couple of hours and moved on to the bookstore. There was no sign of life from the house, but his car was parked outside and there was a light coming through one of the upstairs windows.

Alina was calling. Emily bent over the phone in the gloomy store and texted that she wouldn't be long. There was something she needed to do. While clicking the send button, Emily finally saw movement across the street. The door opened and Vladimir came out with an older, dark-skinned woman. He was laughing at something -- like nothing had happened. Emily's blood went cold. They got into his Mercedes and pulled into traffic right outside the bookstore. The elegantly dressed, elderly woman turned her face - and Emily was back in the maternity ward on the worst day of her life. It was the woman who had taken Emily's baby.

Ten minutes later, Emily pulled her cap down even further and walked slowly over to Vladimir's house, which sat behind a low wrought iron fence and up a short block of stairs.

She recognized the name on a bunch of letters stuffed into the mailbox. The door was locked, but Emily had a theory that most people lived in mortal fear of losing their keys. She rifled into the mailbox and was on her third terracotta plant pot when she found the key buried in the soil.

With trembling fingers she unlocked the door and placed the key back in the exact spot she had retrieved it from. The rooms were dark and exquisitely furnished, but there were no pictures on the walls and no ornaments of any kind. Emily stood staring around the reception room unsure what to do next. It all made sense when she was keeping the place under surveillance. Now that she was inside Vladimir's home she didn't know what to do. There was a light on behind a closed door. The room faced the front, so it must have been the light she saw from the street.

Cautiously, she turned the handle and creaked open the door to find a small office dominated by a large desk in the window. She crossed the room and was about to open the single desk drawer when she saw it.

There were no pictures on the walls of the office, but in the middle of the rosewood desk was a single, gilt-edged frame. In it was a photograph of Vladimir – his face was half turned away from the camera but Emily knew that profile, would recognize him anywhere, the man she had loved with her whole heart and was laughing as he watched a child about to blow out the candles on a cake.

One, two, three, four, five… they were celebrating the little boy's fifth birthday. He had dark hair, big, beautiful eyes, and was smiling up adoringly at his father.

Emily picked up the frame and slowly traced her fingers over the features of the boy's face - her son's face. Her dreams had been filled with such scenes for as long as she could remember. She had imagined every one of her baby's birthdays.

Yet, this man, who she had loved and now hated, had actually been there. For all of them. Every birthday, Christmas, his first day at school, every memory that he had selfishly enjoyed, he had stolen from her.

A deep pain radiated in her chest and she gulped for air. Why would he deny her this, her right to know her son, and why, too, would he deny their son his mother?

He would rather kill her than let her know that she was a mother?

She continued to stare at the picture of her little boy, transfixed.

Then a click broke her out of the reverie. There was a turn of the key in the lock and Emily froze by the desk, paralyzed with fear. She could hear talking from the hallway and in a panic quickly stepped into a giant closet filled with packing boxes, closing the door behind her and trying to breathe as lightly as possible as she heard someone come into the room and a chair scrape as they sat down.

She still had the gilt frame in her hand. She heard numbers being punched into a phone and Vladimir's voice, right next to her, arranging for a car to pick him up and take him to the airport. Drawers were opened and shut and she could sense him standing there.

"Mother, did you move that picture on my desk? You know I like to keep it in my office."

A woman's voice replied impatiently: "The cleaner's been. It's around somewhere. Come on, you'll miss your flight."

"Can you please look for it?"

"Yes. I have to go vote around the corner first and then I'll find it. Don't worry. I'll come out with you."

Moments later, both walked out of the front door, locking it behind them, and Emily carefully emerged from her hiding place, waiting a little longer before slipping out, still clutching the frame to her chest, into the anonymity of a Manhattan afternoon.

The world was suddenly a very different place for Emily than it had been just 24 hours ago. She was a different person now. She was a mother!

Now she must find her son.

104 ELECTION DAY

Just after 8:00 a.m. that morning, a smiling Todd went through the paces at his polling station photo-op in Rutherford, New Jersey. He signed autographs as he chatted with iCandidate fans while waiting in line to vote in an elementary school classroom.

Much was at stake in the next few hours. "Yes, I'm very confident," Todd told a New York Times reporter. "Certainly, we are prepared to govern; and no, it is not a handicap never having held office in Washington before. I think most voters would think it an advantage."

"Thanks for all your support and encouragement," he said into the CNN camera as he left the polling station where record numbers had already arrived to vote. "I'm going home to catch my breath before heading back to Washington to wait for the results to come in... No, as I said, I am not nervous. I am confident the people of this country feel exactly the same way as I do. It is time for some real change and Grace Conwright is the person to make it happen."

105 LAST MINUTE DOUBTS

Grace, already on a flight from Chicago to D.C., was a jumble of nerves. She had her ever-present entourage of aides and security staff with her, but no real friends. Gillian and the others were all back in their own hometowns to vote and Grace felt alone in spite of all the attention.

Her thoughts flitted to Cameron, but she quickly pushed them aside. The phone conversation they had from her hotel room the previous day had been comforting. But to think there could be anything else in it was ridiculous. He'd lost the love of his life a long time ago. She at least understood why he acted the way he did with women. She just wasn't going to be one of his conquests.

Going back to Chicago fueled her homesickness. As much as she tried to push the assassination of her parents to the back of her mind, she couldn't help but dwell. She couldn't tell anybody, not even Gillian, but she was consumed with doubts. She had no experience in government, let alone running it. What on earth was she doing? Who did she think she was, conning all these people into thinking she was somehow their voice? It was madness.

Everything in her being was telling her to throw in the towel. Before it was too late. What if she turned to one of the dozens of journalists bombarding her with questions and told them it was over, that she had changed her mind?

At that moment, flying to her destiny, she would gladly have swapped places with Todd. He wanted her job so badly and Grace remained baffled over why the public had chosen her. Tortured by her scattered thoughts she tried to get some sleep for the first time in nearly two days. Her system was so wired, the previous night she hadn't even gone to bed, preferring to sit through endless cable TV discussions about her worthiness as a candidate.

For months the polls had her a distant third behind Harriet Carson and Dennis Saxon. The pundits wrote off the huge success of the show as an aberration, saying that when it really came down to it the public wanted an experienced political campaigner, not the rookie winner of a Hollywood reality series. Saxon seemed immune to the criticism and for that, at least, Grace admired him.

But in the past few days she had pulled up to within a couple of points of the Republican firebrand, with the analysts changing their tune and suggesting undecided voters were shifting in favor of Grace. The iCan Party's independent spirit had struck a deep chord among many conservative voters uncomfortable with Saxon. Her rallying poll numbers ignited what Grace feared was a full-blown panic attack. She was having trouble breathing and didn't dare get up in case another passenger tried to talk to her. Try as she might, she couldn't get the thought out of her head. She could win.

106 DOWN TO THE WIRE

Paddy Cahill nursed a fuller than usual tumbler of Bushmills and stretched his arms above his head as he leaned back in a battered, brown leather armchair. He'd decided to spend the afternoon in his Capitol Hill office. A Cuban cigar sat next to the ashtray; he considered lighting it.

He called strategist Jean Harris in to congratulate her... The iCampaign was doomed after a string of early results were divided pretty evenly down conventional party lines. Harriet had taken Connecticut, Delaware, Massachusetts, Illinois, Maine, Maryland, D.C., and Vermont. After the initial excitement in Dixville Notch, the rest of New Hampshire – a state that often predicted the winner – also remained loyal to the Democrat nominee.

Saxon was the projected winner in South Carolina, Kentucky, Tennessee, New Jersey, and Oklahoma. The score so far for the iCan Party? Zilch.

"They're done. It's over," Cahill said to Harriet as they looked over her victory speech one more time.

"Let's give it another 30 minutes, just to be sure." Harris was checking through all the exit polls. "Remember back in 2004, when the early results all pointed to John Kerry winning. How did that end up? With four more years of Bush, that's how."

Cahill was unmoved. "The Times and the Post are already calling it. Call David Mason and see if they are capitulating yet. If not yet, see if he'll give you a time. This is not a day for the faint hearted."

He turned around to see if Harris heard him but she'd gone. There was something in the latest exit poll that worried her, and she wanted to test the water with the President's Chief-of-Staff David Platt, a more experienced election campaigner.

"This new batch of exit polls being released show that voters overwhelmingly support Grace Conwright," she said, speaking quietly so Cahill and Harriet didn't hear. "That makes no sense with the early results; maybe people were just messing with the pollsters when they said they voted for Conwright? I'm not sure if I believe this, but 67 percent said they're voting for the iCandidate. We're also getting word that it's turning into a massive turn out. It could end up as high as 82 percent. You've got to believe a lot of that is because of the whole reality show factor."

"It's not like we haven't been warning you, Jean." Platt was unsympathetic. "The President has told Paddy a number of times to be more mindful of this but he ignored him."

"So do you think it's right?" There was a flicker of fear in her voice.

"Could be nothing, Jean. But the Carsons shouldn't be claiming victory just yet."

107 MISTAKEN IDENTITY

With his usual resourcefulness, Kristoff had managed to get a permit to hold a massive results party at the National Mall. Win or lose, Grace and Todd were going to throw the biggest political bash in history, right in the shadow of Congress and the White House.

Mason was the last of the gang to reach the makeshift iCan Party offices set up behind the Lincoln Memorial, where they planned to watch the final results come in together. When he'd left the hotel, they were all but counting Grace out, saying what a breath of fresh air she'd been, but lamenting how much longer it would take to really crack the two-party system. Mason turned on the giant TV in front of the office conference table to see the next wave of results.

Tom put his head around the door to say he was in another small conference room watching CNN with the others. "We'd actually like a quick word with you about something, David. Do you have a minute?"

"Sure. Come on in." There wasn't much else he could do right now other than wait for the results...and hope.

"It's a little delicate," started Tom, as Rich and Dulce traipsed in, "but some of the team believe that one of ours, Cameron, to be precise, may have been up to no good."

Mason was aware Cameron wasn't especially popular with the others, but assumed it was a personality clash and no more.

"Well he got himself kicked off the show because of that bar brawl which wasn't smart, but we think he may have been trying to jeopardize the chances of the other iCandidates all along." Rich obviously wasn't a fan.

"I have to tell you guys, there was nothing Cameron could do to affect the outcome of the show," said Mason. "It was all carefully and tightly controlled by Desmond. He made sure there was no interference from the outside." Mason's attention was drawn back to the TV screen where a breathless anchor was announcing breaking news coming after the break.

He wasn't in the mood for listening to gossip or playing detective right now. "Look I don't know where this is all coming from but guys any minute now it sounds like we're going to be told that the iCan Party has lost, so shall we just try to go out with a little dignity?"

Rich ignored him. "And then, of course, there was the affair." He looked embarrassed at bringing it up.

"What affair?"

"We believe he seduced Jen and then blackmailed her into quitting the show."

Jennifer and Gillian came bursting through the door at that moment, carrying a tray of coffees and cupcakes. "Thanks for telling us you'd switched rooms, these trays are heavy!" Jen grumbled.

"Anyway, food for the troops." Gillian put her tray down on the table. Everyone looked at Jen who froze, and the room went silent.

"What's wrong? What have we missed?"

Tom looked uncomfortable so Rich cut in. "We're just telling Mase here that there's a feeling that Cameron's not been a straight arrow. A few of us think he's been trying to sabotage us all along, from the first day of the show until now. Especially you, Jen."

Jennifer carefully put the tray down and looked at Mason. "I don't understand."

"Jen, we're talking about your breakdown on the results show. We know he must have messed with your head after the affair ended...." Tom tailed off.

"How do you know I had an affair?"

"Are you saying you didn't?"

"Look. I did have an affair, and when it ended it, he tried to blackmail me, and yes, I lost it..."

"There! See, I knew it!" Rich was beginning to think they'd been imagining it.

"But I honestly don't know what you're talking about." Jennifer continued. "I didn't have an affair with Cameron."

There was a stunned silence. "Well if not Cameron then who?" Rich asked, perplexed.

"Oh my God!" Mason cried. "Look at this everyone!"

They all turned their attention to the TV screen; The breaking news was in. Grace had picked up Ohio, Florida, Pennsylvania and Virginia, all key swing states with thin majorities in the last election.

Gillian screamed.

Tom jumped up from his seat, quickly adjusting his slip. "It's happening, it's actually happening!"

Rich whooped for joy and picked Jen up like a doll, swinging her around. "Put me down you big goon," she laughed.

Soon they were all hugging and congratulating each other, with Jen's affair completely forgotten.

108 THE KISS

Steadily but irrevocably, a trend grew with Grace first catching up with and then pulling away from her two stunned rivals as the cold, crisp Washington afternoon turned to evening. With the darkness came the stunning realization that the curtain was falling on the legislative centerpiece of the defining democracy of the past 100 years.

If the votes kept rolling in at the same pace, the iCampaign tally would be such a landslide that by the time the west coast results were counted, they would hardly matter. Grace didn't know whether to scream out in triumph or cover her head and hide. She settled for closing her eyes and her ears from the unrelenting statistics pouring out from the TV screen.

She was uncomfortable with all the fuss at headquarters and sought the peace and quiet in the studio village erected behind the Lincoln Memorial in readiness for the party later. She was trying to gather herself enough to scribble a rough draft of a victory speech and jumped up startled when she heard a gentle knock on the door. It was Cameron.

Things had been so hectic that the two of them hadn't been alone together since the phone call. "I just came to wish you luck Grace. How are you feeling? Ready?"

"The truth?"

"No. Of course not."

"In that case, yes, I am totally ready and I've never felt better."

"You're going to be great."

"How do you know?"

"Because I have faith in you. You're the smartest woman I've ever met." His voice was soft, and for a moment she felt herself transfixed. Quickly shaking herself out of it, she responded with a curt nod. "Well I must get on."

He stepped towards her smiling. "Strange behavior at times

though. Why is that, by the way?"

Was he trying to play her? Grace put her defenses back up. "Honestly? I find your playboy act a little nauseating."

Cameron spluttered. "Seriously!"

"I know I'm quick to judge, but you're such a flirt. That's your reputation isn't it, the playboy?" Cameron feigned shock. "Perhaps you shouldn't listen to rumors."

Grace realized she'd never actually seen Cameron with a girlfriend, but then remembered a more persistent rumor from their time on the show. "You can't deny you were running around with Jennifer?"

"Can't I?" Cameron looked genuinely shocked now.

"I thought you weren't taking the competition seriously, and I guess it bothered me."

Cameron stared back in amazement. "What are you talking about? I wasn't running around with Jen, or anyone else for that matter."

"Come on, Cameron. You were always texting with her, and disappearing...." She trailed off, feeling foolish. This wasn't the reaction she was expecting at all.

"I'm always texting with my sister and my nieces and nephews. We Skype a lot, too. You thought I was having an affair with Jennifer Flynt? That's hysterical! You really don't know me at all!"

"Well, I thought I did."

Cameron's head was bowed and Grace was horrified she'd offended him, but when he looked up, the glint was back in his eye. "Were you a tiny bit jealous, Conwright?"

"No, of course not. She seems far too bright." They both laughed.

"Well, now that you have finished insulting me, can I say something?"

"Of course."

"Why are you deflecting from this huge moment Conwright. It's your moment and you are about to make history. I'd say there's a lot there to get excited about!"

She didn't want to tell him that she was still consumed with doubts, that she wanted her father, she needed her mother, that she just wanted to curl up in a corner and close her eyes. "It's hardly surprising when there appears to be a very good chance I am about to become the first woman President of the United States. Not a lot to be calm about there."

Cameron put his hands on her shoulders. "Listen to me Grace. You deserve this. There's a reason you made it here today. The American public relates to you, they see your strength and they know they can trust you. Although I might have to have a word with them when it comes to your lousy judgment on the male character. Or specifically, mine.

Grace finally let her guard down and sobbed. "I don't feel strong at all. I can't stop thinking about my parents and how they must have felt in their last moments. I'm living their dream but I can't escape from the nightmare. I don't think I can do it, Cameron. I really don't."   Her attacker's masked face flashed into her head again, and Cameron pulled her close.

"I can't imagine how tough it's been for you," he whispered. "It's really hard to understand why such terrible things happen, but rather than see your parents' deaths purely as a tragedy, you could look at it as a legacy they left you – a legacy to carry on what they started...

If you can truly feel that then you'll be able to walk out on that stage tonight and claim what's rightfully yours. You won't be scared; you won't feel alone, because it will no longer be a burden to carry around. It'll lift you up and drive you on to achieve your dreams."

Without her family, or special someone, something had always been missing from Grace's life, and in just these last few moments, Cameron had made her feel that everything was going to be okay. Maybe even more than okay. "Thank you, Cameron," she lifted her head from his shoulder and looked deeply into his eyes.

If he gave himself time to think about the next move, he would never have dared place his hand gently under her chin and tilt her face to his as he slowly leaned forward. Grace closed her eyes…and a loud knocking on the door made them both jump.

"Miss Conwright, Mr. Kristoff would like to see you." Grace pulled away, embarrassed and flustered. "More results. I have to go. Do I look alright?"

"Beautiful. You're beautiful."

She was torn, wishing she didn't have to leave just yet. She paused at the door. "Cameron, I…" He reached her in two strides and pulled her into his arms, kissing her with such passion she couldn't breathe.

They pulled apart as the door opened and Grace - all thoughts of the election momentarily shoved aside by a jumble of new emotions – followed after Kristoff's assistant.

"Good luck, Grace, and remember what I said about being strong."

"What did you say again, I forgot?" She stopped in the doorway, smiling back at him.

"Feeling a little better, I see! Glad I could be of assistance."

"Will you be out there with me?" she asked, serious again.

Standing in the middle of the room, Cameron saw much further ahead. "Always," he said.

109 SNAPSHOT

Roman would do anything for Alina; but he really didn't want to get caught up in some domestic scandal that his girlfriend's mentor was involved in. Plus, the timing couldn't have been worse. But Alina was unusually insistent and sounded frightened.

Alina had never struck him as the dramatic type, but she was talking about Emily's life being in danger, involving an ex-boyfriend from many years ago.

The best he could do was bring Alina and Emily to him. He simply couldn't get away.

"She'll be safe at the hotel," he told Alina, "and it will give me the chance to see you again. I just won't be able to spend as much time with you as I'd like to."

Roman was still in a meeting when he got the call that they had just checked into the hotel. He made his excuses and jumped in a cab across town. Knocking softly on the hotel room door, Alina opened it just a crack before quickly pulling him in.

The curtains were tightly drawn, and at first he didn't see Emily sitting on the couch, her blonde head bowed to cover her face. She looked up at him, embarrassed by her tears.

He chose a seat across from where Alina sat holding Emily's hand. "I'm not sure I can do anything to help, at least not today," Roman said. "But I'll do what I can."

Emily was aware she was leaving so much out as she tried to explain how she'd met her old college boyfriend in the Village, and how he'd tried to kill her years later.

Roman's eyes were glazing over. Emily knew she sounded crazy, and she was struggling to hold her emotions together. He stood up, and paced the room, trying not to sound as agitated as he felt. "Look, I'm sorry but this seems to be a matter for the police. I can make the call if you want but…"

"What about the photograph?" Alina knew there was something Emily wasn't telling him.

Emily picked the frame from her bag and started to pass it to Roman but stopped. She knew it was hopeless. "It's nothing. I'm really sorry to involve you guys in this. Please, you mustn't worry."

"Wait, can I see the photograph?" Something in Roman's expression had changed.

"No, it's okay."

"I'd really like to see it." He reached out a hand. "Please, Emily."

She didn't want to let the only link she had with her son out of her hand, but she slowly passed it over. He recognized the frame before he saw the familiar photo it contained and slowly sat back in the chair, still looking at it.

"Where did you get this?"

"I went back to his house this morning while he was out...the man who tried to kill me. I...I believe this is my son..."

"What's wrong?" Alina saw the look on Roman's face.

He sat there, not moving, staring at the picture. His head was spinning. Nothing could have prepared him for this moment. "My grandmother took this photograph," he said finally.

"What do you mean?" Alina's eyed widened. "How does your grandmother know them?"

Roman was looking at Emily as the impact hit her; her hand flew to her mouth. "This man is my father, and the child blowing out the candles, that's me."

110 VICTORY

The huge flat screen covering one wall was the only light in their office.

Kristoff sat with Mason and Jacqueline staring at CNN. All the iCandidates, except Todd, were sitting around the room, too. It was just after 11:00 p.m. and Grace, flushed from the cold and emotionally overwrought, walked in and sat down. Gillian crossed the room, sat next to her, then took her hand.

Grace gave her a grateful smile. "I have something to tell you," she said in a low voice.

"Is it more interesting than becoming President?" Gillian joked.

"No, but close," Grace whispered with a smile. "I kissed Cameron."

"I knew you two were meant to be! How will Cameron feel about being the First Lady, I wonder," she laughed.

"Oh my God, Gillian, I can't believe this is actually happening. The Presidency, I mean."

Grace was squeezing her hand so hard, it was going numb.

"It's going to be fine," Gillian reassured her. "We're all here for you."

Moments later a sheepish-looking Cameron walked in. Locking eyes with Grace, they shared a smile that Gillian caught.

"Oh my - look at you love birds!" she whispered, the obvious delight spread across her face.

"Where in God's name is Desmond? Why isn't he here?" Kristoff shouted.

"Don't panic," Mason said. "He went to fetch something, he'll be here soon."

"Grace," Kristoff said, "If you win California's 55 electoral votes that will take you over the 270 total you need to win. The polls have closed over there now…how do you feel?"

"Numb. I can't believe it. It's like it's happening to someone else."

"Well you'd better believe it's happening to you" Kristoff laughed. Although he was a little in shock himself. They all were. "The real job begins once you are in the White House." He was interrupted by a call and picked up the phone.

"It's for you, Grace."

"Oh, okay."

"Hello Grace, this is Harriet."

"Mrs. Carson, nice to hear from you. How can I help?" The reason for the call hadn't yet dawned on Grace.

"I would like to think we could be friends at some point, but for now I'm calling to congratulate you."

"Oh, that's nice, thank you... very much." Grace was taken aback by her friendliness.

"I suspect you'll be getting a similar call from Saxon soon, if you haven't already. It looks like the night, and the next four years, belong to you. I'm still scratching my head trying to understand how you all pulled it off, but you did; and for now, that has to be enough."

"You were a very worthy opponent," Grace told her.

"Maybe so, but it obviously wasn't enough." Harriet dropped her voice, as if she was speaking in confidence. "I've been hard on you at times, but you've always been very gracious. If it's not my fate to be our first woman President, I have to say that I'm glad it's you. I know your parents are looking down on you tonight, and they must be very proud."

Grace choked up and she struggled to keep her voice steady enough to thank her.

"I must go," Harriet said. "I have a party to attend back home in Chapaqua and it would be a shame to waste all that champagne. Enjoy your celebration."

Getting off the phone, Grace finally grasped the enormity of what was happening.

"That's it," Kristoff said, jumping up. "We took California. God bless the Golden State! Congratulations, Grace, or should I say, President Elect Conwright!"

Everyone jumped up to hug Grace. Dulce and Gillian were both crying, even Jen wiped back a tear. Tom and Rich both pulled her in for a bear hug. "No-one is more deserving," Tom managed, his bottom lip quivering with emotion. Tom let her go and Grace spun around, dizzy with the emotion of what was happening. Cameron was waiting.

"You did it," he said simply.

She stared at him and suddenly didn't care what anyone thought. Moving towards him, she rested her hands on his chest and gently kissed him. The room fell silent until Rich let out a cat call whistle.

"About time!" said Gillian and suddenly everyone joined in, laughing and hugging the two of them.

"Where's Todd? He should be here, too." Kristoff looked around the room in disbelief. "What the hell are they doing that is more important than this?"

"They'll want to be here when Saxon calls, and, of course, the President." Jacqueline said. "Knowing Greenacre he'll try and take the call," she smiled, hugging Grace.

111 THE CONFRONTATION

Roman didn't know what to believe. To accept Emily's story would be to question everything his father had ever told him. It would make everything he'd worked so hard for a complete lie.

He wanted so much to believe he had a mother; but to do that he'd have to also believe his father tried to kill her.

He'd fled the hotel room after seeing the photo of his 5th birthday. He could still see Emily's pleading, tear-filled eyes following him as he backed out of the door.

Alina cried after him to stay but Roman had to speak to his father. He had meetings all day but headed straight to his father's office.

Vladimir had three colleagues with him when Roman barged in. Roman then asked the others to leave. He just needed five minutes with his father. Just for once, Vladimir wasn't arguing. He'd never seen Roman like this.

"I can't go through with this. It's too much. I can't do it."

"Everything's going to be okay, my son." Vladimir had never seen his son cry. "Don't worry, I'll take care of everything."

"You always promised to tell me the truth." Roman walked around the desk.

"Of course."

"Then how come a woman has just told me she's my mother?"

Vladimir's expression didn't change. "That can't be," he replied calmly.

"She has a picture of me...and she said you tried to kill her." Roman's face was deathly pale.

Vladimir put both hands on his son's shoulders. "This is a crucial time for you, son. People are going to claim all kinds of things but this is not true." He held Roman's shoulders tighter. "Look at me, it's not true!"

"But why would she say these things?" Roman looked even

more confused.

"Money, power, who knows? A European woman has been stalking me for sometime and I obtained restraining orders to keep her away from me. I didn't realize she would go after you."

Roman felt deflated...and relieved. "But where did she get my birthday photo? It was the one from your office."

"There was a burglary at the apartment this morning. I didn't want to bother you with it, today of all days. Where is she now, this woman? I'm afraid she could be a danger. If not to us then certainly to herself."

"She's at The Jefferson..."

"Is she alone?" Roman paused.

"Yes." Roman wasn't going to change his mind about Alina but his father and grandmother were all the real family he had. He had to believe him. "I need your word that this woman is not my mother."

"You have my word. You must trust me. You are my family."

"And father, everything we've worked towards is to build a more peaceful world, isn't it?"

Roman wanted so much to trust his father. He had to.

"Yes my son. As I said, you have my word." They hugged, something they rarely did. "You are a brave man. Let's talk again a little later today. I know you have much to do."

Roman left and Vladimir closed his office door, telling his secretary he didn't want to be disturbed for ten minutes. Sitting back at his desk Vladimir opened the drawer, took out a "burner" phone he had in a plastic zip bag and dialed a local number. "Boris," he said. "I have something else that must be taken care of today. It's at the Jefferson Hotel..."

112 STARS AND STRIPES

Moments later, Todd arrived followed soon after by Desmond carrying two bottles of champagne. "The Mall is bursting at the seams. Have you seen it out there?" Desmond said. "They're chanting your name, Grace. They want you to come out."

"I need to hear from Saxon first." Grace looked for confirmation from Jacqueline.

"It would be rude not to wait."

"He'll call any moment." Mason checked through the channels on the TV. "I'm surprised he didn't call earlier. Now he doesn't have a choice."

Desmond stood up. "I think it's an appropriate time to have a little champagne to celebrate before the madness starts." He popped a champagne cork; and as he started to pour, Desmond looked to Jen. "It's the perfect temperature -- 7 degrees celsius, just how you like it."

Gillian saw Jen's face darken. Moments before she'd been laughing and chatting with Tom and the others. Now she looked crestfallen. That's when it hit Gillian...Jennifer's affair had been with Desmond!

"Thank you, first of all, to Andy Kristoff, Jacqueline, and David Mason for being the dream team, for believing in this idea with me." Desmond was making his toast, oblivious to Jen's discomfort.

"Congratulations to all of the iCandidates, and especially to you, Grace. It's been an honor and a pleasure to work with you all!" He raised his glass. "So, let's make history."

"I think you're going to have to go out there Grace," Mason urged. "You and Todd should at least acknowledge the crowd. They're going wild. It seems like half of America's out there."

"Just a few minutes more," Grace pleaded. "I know there must be a good reason for the delay."

"It's your time now," Jacqueline reasoned. "You don't have to wait for anybody. I have a feeling that Saxon might be having trouble coming to terms with the defeat."

Todd hugged Grace. "I can't believe we actually did it," he smiled at her. "Ready?"

"Wait!" Fumbling in his pocket, Desmond brought out a small Stars and Stripes lapel pin. "I would like you to have this as a memento. It's very presidential." He fastened it to Grace's dress. "It's titanium. It will last forever."

"Thank you so much, Des. I'll wear it all the time, I promise." Grace took a deep breath and touched the pin. She was about to become the first iPresident elect of the United States.

113 THE IPRESIDENT ELECT

Todd marched out alone to the middle of the stage at the Lincoln Memorial. "They all said it was impossible," he shouted over a roar from the crowd. "They told us we were dreamers. They said we had no right to take on the big two. What do you think they are saying now?"

With the rest of the iCampaigners following him, lining up against the show's familiar American flag backdrop, Todd enjoyed his moment. This was his triumph just as much as it was Grace's. He worked as hard, if not harder, and he had won his share of the votes. "The iCan Party doesn't just talk about change. We are making changes right now and we will keep making changes until America's government is back where it should be – in the hands of the people. Today, we have been given a mandate to forge a new way of running this great country. We will not let you down. Now it is my great pleasure … to introduce you to … the next President of the United States…Grace Conwright!"

The crowd stretched all the way from the stage in front of the Lincoln Memorial to the steps of the Capitol nearly two miles away. The people had crowned their queen and now they rejoiced in her coronation.

114 THE BATON

Grace hugged Rich, Dulce, Jennifer, Tom, Cameron, and Gillian one-by-one, then Todd led her to the microphone before leaving her alone in the middle of the stage; a single spotlight shining down on her..

For a moment, she appeared too overwhelmed to speak. Dressed in a simple white gown, she looked tiny in the grandeur of her surroundings. Then she looked up with a huge smile on her face that filled the National Mall.

"We did it," she said. "We did it!"

And the entire country went wild.

"This is not the same America as it was yesterday or last year. This day marks the start of something new, a reappraisal of what we think is important. The nation has come together in the very best tradition of our great democracy to send a message. The message is that we have to work together for the common good, not against each other.

Party politics is dead. Now, we must all take responsibility for our beliefs." Spelling out her vision for the future, Grace didn't touch on the fact that she was voted America's first woman President until she neared the end of the speech.

"I am proud to be a woman and I am proud of what I have achieved, but I do not think this is about me being a woman. I believe this is simply my time. It is the iCandidate's time...

Ten years ago, my parents were killed on a stage such as this, if not quite so grand. They had a lot of dreams for our country, and for me that they were never able to see fulfilled.

But I hope, as a very dear friend said to me just now, that they are looking down on us and saying, 'You go, girl!' I know this isn't about me, it's much bigger than that. But for my part, I would like to dedicate this day to my parents and to everyone's parents, the people whose sacrifices make all of this possible."

Fighting back tears, Grace acknowledged Harriet Carson and Dennis Saxon. "I do feel for my opponents, who are both worthy adversaries. But, with all due respect, this is a new day. Change really has come to the new America."

Grace turned to the welcoming cluster of her jubilant iCampaign team when she saw the President heading from the side of the stage towards her. She still hadn't heard anything from Saxon.

At first Grace didn't know what to do, but the President made it easy for her, putting his arms out for a hug. The night sky filled with a fireworks display of flashbulbs as the moment was captured for websites and the morning news.

"Who could have thought so much change would come so fast?" he said to the crowd with a big grin on his face. "I was just hanging out at the White House, checking out the jobs wanted classifieds, so I thought I'd pop over and join the party.

I don't mean that literally of course, they look like they've got a pretty good leader as it is!

But seriously, what The iCan Party has done is truly remarkable. What Grace Conwright has achieved is awe-inspiring. Our first woman President, ladies and gentlemen," he added to deafening applause.

"On August 28, 1963, Martin Luther King changed the world with his 'I Have a Dream' speech from this very stage. In the years to come, I believe this moment may be spoken about in the same breath. If only Dr. King could have known that his brave, powerful words would lead to this: a black woman in the White House. His dreams, I am sure, have now come true and I, for one, will be offering all my support to make sure Grace achieves her dreams of change, just as I achieved some of mine.

My commiserations of course to my old colleague and adversary Harriet Carson and to Dennis Saxon too; but the truth is, America is digging politics right now – and that's a huge feather in the cap of The iCan Party and the iCampaign. Congratulations, Grace. I'm proud of you; and I wish you the very best of luck. God bless and God Bless America."

The President leaned over to kiss Grace on the cheek.

115 SAY GRACE

One mile across the Mall, Boris Kuznetsov watched the celebrations through a pair of binoculars from a prized viewpoint in the observatory on top of the Washington Monument.

He wore a 'Say Grace' t-shirt and appeared as swept up in the moment as everyone around him in the scenes being relayed on giant screens.

He'd camped out all day to be sure of his view. He was friendly and polite to other people in the line, telling them he'd traveled from Oklahoma to be there; but he spent most of the wait reading a paperback. Making sure to get a prime spot looking down from the west side rectangular window, 555 feet above the Mall, he appeared unmoved by the mayhem that greeted Grace's appearance; and if he was surprised by the President's sudden arrival, nobody would have known. In fact, he didn't even take out his earphones.

Just before the President leaned in to kiss Grace, Boris pressed two buttons on a small mechanical device and fled his spot to beat the rest of the crowd back down to the obelisk base.

Down on the stage a moment later, the President was confused as Grace went limp in his arms. He thought at first she'd fainted from the excitement, and then saw the blood on his white shirt and dropped to the ground with his arms still around her.

Bewildered and covered with blood he realized it came from Grace, now lying on the ground, lifeless, with a tiny bullet hole in her chest.

In that instant, the President was literally hurled off the back of the stage by a scrum of Secret Service agents.

With the spotlight still trained on Grace's body, Cameron reacted, running across the stage to cover her. As he reached Grace, a second bullet hit him; his shoulder erupting in pain.

The second shot broke the spell. Mayhem broke out on stage with everyone ducking for cover, fearing more shots from the unseen gunman. Ignoring the danger, Gillian ran over and cradled Grace's head, trying desperately with her bare hands to stem the flow of blood from her chest. Cameron, too, was losing blood, but he cried out for Grace to stay with him.

Unsure whether to move back or move in, armed police ringed the stage without a clue where to look for the assailant. The crowds had no such qualms, falling back in the Mall, many being trampled in the process.

Joining the throng rushing away from the Mall, Boris slipped down a side street. He no longer had any interest in the events unfolding on the iCampaign stage.

He still had work to do.

116 ROOM SERVICE

Alina and Emily were sitting on the edge of the sofa in their hotel room, watching the never-ending TV re-runs of the moment Grace slumped into the President's arms. Suddenly there was a knock on the door.

Roman had called a couple of hours earlier and asked them to stay put; he would speak to them later. But Alina was worried. He sounded different.

Emily was a mess. She was trembling uncontrollably and kept staring at the birthday photo. Only the election drama had shocked her out of her meltdown. Alina thought food might help and had ordered some soup and sandwiches. She was just about to open the door when she had a thought. "Emily, why don't you go in the bathroom for a moment. We don't want anyone to know you're here."

"It's only room service." Emily got up wearily anyway.

"Better to be safe."

Alina waited for a minute to let Emily lock the bathroom and opened the door to a female server waiting with a food trolley. Gesturing towards the table, the girl moved through the doorway. Before Alina could close it, a young man in a t-shirt pushed through behind her. He looked surprised to see her.

"Alina?"

"Boris?"

They stood stock still for a second as the server hurried out. "What are you doing here?" Alina's mind was racing and coming up blank.

"I have some business to do." He was speaking in Russian. "It has nothing to do with you."

"Then why are you here?" It still made no sense to Alina.

"I need to speak to your friend." Boris pulled a pistol with a long silencer out of a sports bag he was carrying. "You shouldn't be involved with these Americans. We saw you with your big shot boyfriend. You're nothing but a whore.!"

Boris grabbed Alina and held the gun to her head. "Come out, lady, wherever you are." He was talking in English now. "If you don't I'll kill Miss Alina and we don't want that do we? Are you going to leave her to die while you hide like a coward?"

The TV was still re-running the assassination attempt,   but Emily heard the accented voice over the commentary. She really had no choice. She unlocked the door and slowly walked out into the suite's living room. "Let her go," she said softly. "It's me you want. Please, just let her go."

"No!" Alina cried out as she was pushed roughly onto the floor.

"Stay there, both of you. Boris spoke in English, adding in Russian: "If you move, bitch, I'll shoot you."

He turned to Emily and told her to sit quietly and watch the television. "Don't look around," he barked. "Look straight ahead."

As he said it he raised the gun and pointed it at Emily. There was a moment's hesitation as he tightened the silencer barrel and Alina screamed and jumped on the gunman's back, scratching at his eyes. She hugged his neck, making it impossible to aim the gun at her, all the time digging at his face.

Caught by surprise, Boris fought to stay on his feet but lost his balance and fell backwards; the gun clattered onto the wood floor towards Emily, who dived to pick it up.

Alina couldn't keep hold of the wiry shooter as he ran over to where Emily was holding the gun. She pulled the trigger and a bullet ricocheted harmlessly off the food trolley. Boris was on her in an instant, wrestling the pistol from her grasp.

"Such stupidity! Now I'll have to kill you both. Don't move!"

The re-runs were still playing on TV, the grave voices of the commentator discussing the assassination attempt in hushed tones, and Boris gestured for the two women to sit back on the sofa.

"Where is your boyfriend now?" he said to Alina. "Too busy for you," he laughed, aiming his gun at her head. Sitting side-by-side on the couch, Emily reached out and held Alina's hand. They closed their eyes.

117 PANIC STATIONS

"For Christ sake, do something," Kristoff yelled at his security chief. Grace still lay on the floor, a red circle was spreading across the white dress.

Desmond crossed the stage, pushing the guards out of the way, and kneeled beside Grace. "We need help now!" he shouted, scanning the area for any sign of the paramedics. His eyes found Todd.

Todd froze when the first bullet was fired and remained glued to the spot as everyone rushed around him. But after the second shot he dashed to where Gillian and Desmond were helping Grace, to see how badly she was hurt. He clutched his head in disbelief, fighting to keep his composure. This couldn't be happening.

He knelt down beside Grace and took her hand. "Stay strong, you're going to be fine. You're going to get through this." Taking one last look across at Desmond, Todd scrambled back to his feet and ran off the stage.

After checking to see if Grace still had a pulse, Desmond ordered everybody to stand back so the emergency services could reach her. He gently removed the flag pin from her bloodstained dress so the paramedics could get to the wound.

The platform quickly filled with police and paramedics. Grace, unconscious but still breathing, was stretchered into a waiting ambulance with Gillian by her side.

Cameron, weak from loss of blood, was taken in another ambulance with Tom. The other iCampaigners followed in a police car.

The shooter was never found. It was only later that police discovered two futuristic-looking gun barrels attached to an electronic timer with titanium sensor triggers disguised in the rigging at the side of the stage.

118 HOSTAGES

Roman exited The Jefferson Hotel elevator on the eleventh floor and sprinted down the corridor to the suite he'd arranged for Emily and Alina fearing the worst. The door was ajar; he recognized the two heads of the women turned towards the flickering television. Standing over them was one of his father's Russian students; a gun in one hand and a phone to his ear in the other.

"I've been trying to get hold of you. What should I do with the girl? You didn't say anything about her."

Roman recognized Boris speaking Russian but didn't understand what he was saying.

"That wasn't part of the deal," the young man continued in English. "Okay, okay," he said and then hung up the phone.

Roman didn't have the time to reach Boris before he opened fire. He had no choice. "Put the gun down!"

Boris's gun swiveled around to point at him and Alina screamed out.

"Put it down, Boris. There's been a mistake. This isn't part of the plan." Roman could read the confusion on Boris's face; the gun now cocked and pointed at him.

"I spoke to your father. He said to kill both of them." The teen waved the pistol back towards his captives.

"Are you going to kill me as well? Do you really think you could do that?" Roman walked slowly towards Boris, his hand out for the gun. "My father would hunt you down and kill you himself"

The gun was pointed back at Roman who kept walking forward. Boris put both hands on the trigger trying to steady himself.

"Do you really want to tell my father you shot me? Is that your plan? Perhaps you should call and ask him about that, too." Roman was almost close enough to touch the silencer and stopped. "Just give me the gun and leave."

Alina stood up behind the gunman but was powerless to act. For a second it seemed like Boris was going to do as he was asked, but when his phone began to ring he raised the gun up again and took aim at Roman's forehead.

"Alina, NO! " Roman watched in horror as Boris was bowled onto the ground as a loud crack reverberated around the hotel room. Alina staggered into Roman's arms, her green kameez covered in blood. Her eyes were wide with terror; her hands clutched at her stomach.

"Put her on the sofa."

Emily helped Roman lay her wounded friend down and tried to stem the blood. She felt around the cloth at Alina's stomach. She looked up at Roman, tears rolling down her cheeks. "There's nothing here," Emily said. "She wasn't hit."

They looked down to see Boris's lifeless body, his t-shirt and jeans stained with blood. Roman slumped onto the sofa next to Alina and Emily. CNN was still playing the presidential assassination attempt over and over on the TV.

He knew now that Emily was his mother. He also knew just how far his father was prepared to go to get what he wanted. Hugging Alina and Emily close, as close as he possibly could, Roman felt a chill go down his spine.

Everything was spinning out of control.

119 ER

The beep of the monitors pricked the silence inside the hospital room; a faint rustle of fabric tapped the air as nurses moved swiftly through the corridor outside. Muffled voices could occasionally be heard somewhere in the distance, but here, cocooned away from the world, Grace was finally safe.

Gillian stood to stretch and walk to the window. It was snowing with soft steady flakes settling on the darkened streets below and in the branches of the trees sprinkled sparsely across the hospital grounds. She hadn't slept and only left Grace's side to go the bathroom.

Grace hadn't woken up. The bullet punctured her lung, and although the surgery was successful, she had lost enough blood to induce a coma. Gillian returned to her seat, holding Grace's hand, and started to tell her about the snow and about Cameron, who was down the hall recovering from surgery to his shoulder injury.

Grace had shrunk under a web of tubes. Gillian had no idea if she could hear her voice. But for now, talking to Grace was all she could do; that, and pray that at some point she would move just one muscle, one eyelash, anything to let Gillian and the others know that she hadn't left them.

"The others will be coming back to visit you soon, Grace. I wish you could see the room. It looks like a beautiful flower shop in here. At least maybe you can smell the flowers." She stared at her friend's face. There was no reaction. Gillian closed her eyes for a second, but quickly opened them again. She couldn't get the image out of her head; Grace lying in the middle of the Lincoln Memorial.

A nurse came in the room to change the IV. Gillian walked back out into the hospital corridor to find Rich and Jennifer helping Cameron towards Grace's room. "It's a miracle she's still alive. The bullet just missed her heart," Tom was telling Dulce.

Seeing Gillian come towards them, they all stopped in the narrow passageway thinking the same thing: it had been a long road, but they never dreamed it would come to this. Dulce moved first, arms open, and one-by-one, they all did the same. They made a peculiar sight - the hulking physique of Rich's football frame, his arm cradling petite Dulce, who in turn held onto Tom's ample waist. Wearing an emerald green chiffon dress, Tom's pudgy arm wrapped around Cameron, who linked arms with Gillian as she embraced Jen, who leaned on Rich's shoulder, thus completing the circle.

They stood together for a minute or two, finding a brief comfort in each other. "Let's get some tea," Tom said, leading the way to the hospital cafeteria.

"The doctor told me earlier that they can't predict if Grace will come out of the coma or when. It's too early to tell if she has brain damage, and to what extent. It could be days, weeks, even months." Gillian glanced at Cameron. "That's if she comes out of it at all."

Cameron's jaw stiffened.

"She'll be fine," Tom said, trying to sound upbeat. "She has to be."

"Has Todd been in?" Jen asked.

"Not yet," Tom answered. " He's been hounded by the media. They want to know if he's taking over as President. Nothing like this has ever happened before. Kristoff has him lying low for now."

"So you've talked to Kristoff?" Rich wiped his eyes with the front of his t-shirt.

"Yes, he was here," Tom explained. "I've told the media that we'll be arranging a press conference later today to explain Grace's progress. I spoke to them earlier, as well. As things stand, I believe Todd will take over as interim President if Grace doesn't..." He trailed off.

"Let's pray for Grace everybody,' Dulce beckoned, and six heads bowed as they joined hands around the white plastic cafeteria table.

120 AMAZING GRACE

After all the planning and all the work making the iCandidate dream come true, the Gang of Four sat in shocked silence inside Jacqueline's Watergate apartment. Mason was the last to arrive. He'd been updating the media every 30 minutes on Grace's condition. But the doctors had told him there wasn't likely to be much change in the near future, if at all.

Kristoff and Jacqueline had been to the hospital with the President. Desmond had been working with the White House to decide what was going to happen next. "It's pretty straightforward really," he told the others. "As the duly voted VP, Todd will be sworn in as President in January, unless Grace makes a miraculous recovery, which at the moment, I'm afraid, looks highly unlikely. I've had Cahill on claiming a constitutional crisis and talking about emergency powers and a bunch of other BS, but the reality is that we will still have the iCandidate as President, just not the one we expected."

"So much for changing the world. It's still the same cruel, nasty place." Jacqueline's eyes were red from crying and Kristoff put an arm around her shoulders to comfort her. "It's just not fair," she sobbed.

"I know this is tough," Kristoff said quietly. "But we owe it to everybody – we owe it to Grace – to make this work. We've got to focus and make sure the iCan Party can rule properly."

Desmond stood up from the kitchen table. It was 6:00 a.m. "You guys try and get some sleep. The President has organized a meeting with Carson, Saxon and myself in the West Wing in about an hour. I want to check on Grace and then I'll head over to the White House." He called for his driver to come and take him back to see Grace. He also desperately needed to speak to Todd, but he had to get his own head straight first.

On the way he asked to go back to the National Mall to get his glasses he'd left behind in the studio.

Morning rush hour hadn't yet begun, and the trip from his hotel to the Mall should have only taken a few minutes, but there was still heavy traffic all around the area. Impatient to get to the hospital, he got out of the limo and asked his driver to wait for him just up the street.

He came in from behind the Lincoln Memorial and walked around to where the massive stage had been constructed. Grabbing his glasses from the empty control room that was already being dismantled by the night crew, he walked around to the back, wanting one last look at the spot where Grace's dream had died. His security chief was still there and helped him past the lines of yellow tape and the scores of police officers and agents working the crime scene.

Desmond expected it to be dark; it was hard to see as he made his way around the scaffolding at the rear of the stage, where the noisy generators were still running. But as he came out onto the side of the platform it was bathed in soft light. At first he thought there must be a full moon, but he looked up to see the Mall still full of people. Some had candles and others held their cell phones high in the air. As Desmond moved to the front of the stage, away from the hum of the generators, a sea of faces, young and old, looked back at him.

They were all singing 'Amazing Grace.'

121 THE SWITCH

The beauty of the moment overwhelmed Desmond as he stood there alone, staring out at the real heart of the most powerful city on earth. Then a movement from the other side of the stage caught his eye and Todd came striding out purposefully towards him.

Desmond stood his ground and waited until Todd was close. Then he pulled the younger man closer so nobody else would hear.

"We did it, Roman. We really did it. Just you and I, my son." He made no attempt to hide his excitement. "It's everything we always dreamed of."

Todd stiffened and pulled back from the embrace, staring at his father. This was the man he had looked up to his whole life and wanted so much to believe in. But in the last hours the truth had turned to dust.

"You were always going to be President, Roman. Nothing was going to stop us." Desmond's eyes were shining with victory. "Look at these people. They're all here for you."

Todd didn't trust himself to speak. Not yet. He had to hold it together.

The singing gradually died away as Todd turned to face the huge crowd and the applause slowly swelled to a crescendo as the people hailed the next President of the United States.

He waved and tried to smile before stepping unsteadily back into the shadows. His overriding emotion wasn't one of excitement or anticipation: it was a paralyzing dread.

With a chilling certainty, Todd now realized that his father had manipulated The iCandidate to get his way. And now, he, Roman, was complicit in the plot.

Had his entire life been decided and mapped out by this man standing next to him? This crushing truth bore into his brain, his senses, and gripped his chest as he searched for breath...for the strength to pretend.

And for this moment, pretend he must.

His own father had been secretly scheming and plotting for years - for Roman's entire life - unashamedly using those who knew him and trusted him, all leading to this exact moment.

"Roman, get back out there," Desmond said through gritted teeth, reveling in the adoration of the unwitting crowd. Little did the cheering thousands know they were enthusiastically welcoming Moscow's Trojan Horse behind the walls of the White House.

Perhaps this wasn't the beginning at all, Todd thought, as tears streamed down his face.

Perhaps it was the beginning of the end...

THE END

ABOUT THE AUTHORS

Michelle Gardner is a British writer, a clinical nutritionist and QRA practitioner.

David Gardner is a British writer and investigative journalist. This is his fifth book.

They are the parents of three children, Mickey, Jazmin and Savannah and currently live in Laguna Beach, California.

IMMEDIATE BOOKS is an independent publisher. For more information contact admin@immediatebooks.com or call +1 310 433 2392